BAND OF
SISTERS

OTHER BOOKS AND AUDIO BOOKS
BY ANNETTE LYON:

Lost without You

At the Water's Edge

House on the Hill

At the Journey's End

Spires of Stone

Tower of Strength

BAND OF
SISTERS

a novel

ANNETTE LYON

Covenant Communications, Inc.

Cover image: *Hands* © LisaValder, courtesy of iStockphoto.
Vector Script Style Frame Border 03 © Robot, courtesy of Vectorstock

Cover design © 2010 by Covenant Communications, Inc.

Published by Covenant Communications, Inc.
American Fork, Utah

This is a work of fiction. The characters, names, incidents, places, and dialogue are either products of the
author's imagination, and are not to be construed as real, or are used fictitiously.

Printed in the United States of America
First Printing: March 2010

17 16 15 14 13 12 11 10   10 9 8 7 6 5 4 3 2 1

ISBN-13: 978-1-59811-852-0

For Sarah, Bethany, Meredith, Liz, and Sharissa.
And for their husbands, who were deployed to Afghanistan
May 2006–August 2007.

The Wives

Kim Howett (20)
Husband: Justin, Private First Class

Brenda McKewan (29)
Husband: Rick, First Lieutenant
Children: Bradley (7), twins Josh and Tyler (3)

Jessie Ryder (33)
Husband: Tim, Captain
Children: Alexandra (4), Rebecca (2), Joey (6 months)

Marianne Gardner (42)
Husband: Brian, Major
Children: McKayla (15), Bailey (12), Kevin (9)

Nora Lambert (55)
Husband: Russell, Colonel
Children: Dan (30), Missy (27), Nicole (24), Steven (20), Scott (18)

Chapter 1: Kim
Secret

Wednesday, August 25, 2009

Kim stared at the Chili's restaurant windows, trying to get up the guts to go inside. She'd already cut the ignition and held the keys in her hand. Based on Justin's e-mails describing the guys in his group, she knew that their wives, the four women she'd come here to meet, had to be older than she was. She also knew that they had over a dozen children among them and a combined experience of several decades of marriage.

They'd see her as a young thing with nothing to contribute, nothing in common. That is, nothing in common besides a husband deployed to Afghanistan.

But I am *young in comparison,* she thought, knowing that Nora had a master's degree and the other three held bachelor's degrees. *I barely squeaked through high school.* And she hadn't attended college, either—doubted she could get in even if she tried. She had recently finished training to become a dental assistant. So glamorous. So educated.

She put the key back into the ignition and turned it, making the motor hum to life, not wanting to go out to lunch with four perfect strangers where she'd feel like an alien. Maybe she'd go another time. Justin had left only three weeks ago. He'd be gone for a year. That was nearly fifty lunches she could still attend. Maybe. But then, if she didn't go in today, she probably wouldn't go to any of them.

She moved her hand to shift the car into gear but then paused and looked back up at the restaurant, wondering if she was making the right decision. Justin was already good friends with the four men whose wives were meeting here. When he came back, they'd almost certainly be as close as brothers. Soldiers didn't serve together and face dangers and death without bonding. Or so she'd been told. She'd need to know these women, if only so she wouldn't be totally in the dark when the five couples inevitably went out to dinner together after this whole deployment mess was over.

A woman lugging an infant carrier struggled along the sidewalk. She held onto a little girl with one hand and called out to a second, slightly older girl. Kim could hear her through the crack in the open car window. "Alexandra Marie, you get back here! A car's going to smoosh you if you don't. Good. Now hold onto my pocket as we walk. Mommy doesn't have an extra hand right now." The woman blew some hair out of her face, hefted the carrier higher with one hand—the other holding the littlest toddler in a death grip—and kept walking slowly toward the doors.

That's got to be Jessie. In their preplanning e-mail exchange, Jessie had said she might not be able to get a sitter and apologized in advance for bringing her three kids along.

I can't ignore her, Kim thought reluctantly, killing the engine. She got out of the car, swinging her purse strap over her shoulder as she locked the door and slammed it shut. She sprinted a few steps toward the woman and called out, "Jessie?"

The woman paused, holding the carrier on her hip as she looked around then yelled, "Alex! Get back here—hold *on*!" before laying eyes on Kim.

"Hi," Kim said with a little wave. "I'm Kim Howett."

"Oh, hi," Jessie said with a frazzled smile. She breathed heavily from her load. "Good to meet you."

"Can I help?" Kim asked, reaching first for Alex's hand and then her little sister's.

"Thank you," Jessie said, pushing some hair behind her ear. "It's such a circus going anywhere with all three of them." She held onto the baby seat with two hands now, which allowed her to carry it lower, bumping against her leg. While still awkward, her walk no longer looked so difficult or tiring. The baby began fussing, his bottom lip jutting in a pout as if someone had offended him. "Oh, goodness, now what?" Jessie said, pausing to search the blankets for the baby's pacifier. "I just fed him, and it's not time for his nap. Ah. Found it."

The Binky apparently solved the problem, as the chubby little boy sucked contentedly on it, making the plastic bear on the front bob up and down. Watching these children, Kim felt a touch of nausea; she couldn't imagine her life turning into such a "circus," as Jessie had put it.

Justin wanted a "big" family—at least half a dozen children by his definition. Kim wasn't sure she even *wanted* to be a mother, let alone consider multiple child*ren*. Of course, she never said as much. Not to anyone—least of all Justin. All he knew was that she wanted to negotiate the number. He never suspected her true feelings because she was a good Mormon girl, and didn't all good Mormon girls *want* to be mothers? They wanted to single-handedly multiply and replenish the earth and be happy every moment doing it. Right?

When they married last spring, Kim had known that eventually she'd be a mom—there was really no way to completely avoid the expectation she'd been brought up with—but she'd try to limit the number of kids to something more sane than half a dozen. Two sounded mighty good to her—spaced five years apart—but she knew she'd almost certainly cave and have more. Only two wouldn't look like a righteous Mormon family—unless she developed a legitimate medical reason that prevented her from having more. One could hope.

The entire concept of a gaggle of babies made her stomach turn. She nodded toward the door and put on a smile. "Should we go inside?"

Jessie led the way, and when they reached the door, Kim held it open for her. They found the corner booth where the other wives were already waiting, sipping ice water.

The woman on her left introduced herself as Brenda and was probably in her late twenties. She had long, brownish blonde hair pulled back into a clip and a pleasant, round face. When they shook hands, her fingers were a little cold. Next to her sat Nora, a brunette with short, uber-styled hair, dark eyeliner, and gold earrings. She wore a pale pink turtleneck and an off-white linen suit that was obviously tailored. Judging by the wrinkles around her eyes and mouth, Nora looked to be somewhere in her fifties.

She could be my mother, Kim thought with dismay. She hadn't considered that any of the wives would be *that* old. Except that Nora's husband was *Colonel* Lambert—a rank you didn't reach in your thirties.

Last was Marianne, who had dark red hair and a smattering of freckles. Brenda and Jessie looked like they were within about five years of one another, and Marianne was a little older, somewhere around forty, give or take a year. *Technically, she could probably be my mother too,* Kim thought with increasing discomfort.

"Nice to meet you," Kim said, sliding into the booth. She wouldn't tell them that only two years ago she was still attending Laurels. She fumbled with the menu on the other side of the table, nearly spilling someone's glass of water.

Jessie marshaled her kids onto the padded bench first so they couldn't escape, and the other women scooted in tighter to make more room. She found a high chair to prop the carrier on before landing with a slight huff on the plastic seat. "Sorry my babysitter fell through," she said with an apologetic shrug. "My neighbor's kids are getting over strep throat. They've already been on antibiotics for a day, but the nurse in me still worries. I didn't dare leave them, and my mom wasn't available. Hopefully next time it'll be just us grown-ups."

"No problem," Nora said with an easy smile. Her mouth was outlined with burgundy liner and filled with a slightly lighter shade of wine. She eyed the menu. "We've all been there."

Except me, Kim thought as Jessie searched the car seat—again—for the Binky. Kim wondered offhand if she counted as a grown-up. Legally, she could vote but not drink. She was an adult minor, sort of in no-man's land.

"So you're a nurse?" Nora asked, twisting her glass on the coaster.

"Was," Jessie said. Then she tilted her head in consideration. "Okay, *am.* But I haven't worked much since having kids. I was doing a few evening shifts here and there to keep my license current, but I quit a month ago. No way can I work while Tim's away. Maybe when he comes back, I can pick up a shift or two again."

The server came a minute later and took their orders. Alex and her little sister Becca argued over what they were going to get, since their mother insisted they had to share a meal—chicken nuggets or macaroni and cheese. Chicken nuggets won out as Alex declared she had to go potty.

Jessie excused herself. "We'll be right back. Do you guys mind watching Becca and Joey while I take her?" They all agreed. Joey began wailing the minute his mother was out of view. Marianne scooted close and unbuckled the baby then, picking him up and soothing him by bouncing and rocking side to side.

Kim looked away and swallowed, the feeling of not belonging practically screaming inside her. Marianne looked perfectly natural with the baby. Brenda and Nora cooed, taking the whole baby thing in stride. But just a few minutes before, Jessie had looked to be on the verge of a nervous breakdown as she juggled her kids.

I'd be a wreck, Kim thought. But she didn't want to think about that right now. She suddenly wished she still had the menu to bury her face in. Anything to keep her from thinking about what she suspected after having missed her last period. Becoming a mother would be hard enough when it wasn't something she wanted, but doing it alone during a deployment? *It's like whoever's in charge of Murphy's Law is laughing their head off.*

"I need brown!" Becca piped up suddenly. She had been busy coloring on a paper place mat with the three crayons the hostess had provided—blue, green, and red. "Tree trunks are brown," she insisted.

Jessie returned in time to handle the two-year-old's crisis and convince Becca that she could pretend the tree was from *Sesame Street,* so it could be any color.

"Let's go around the table and get to know one another," Marianne said. "Brian and I have been married for eighteen years, and we have three kids—two girls and a boy. Tenth, seventh, and fourth grades. Let's see . . . we met in a family home evening group at the Y. We've lived in American Fork for the last four years. This is our first deployment, and I'm *terrified.*" She said the last with a chuckle, as if trying to make light of it. She turned to Nora to pass the baton of introductions.

"I suppose I'm the grandma of the group," Nora said wryly. But this woman was the furthest thing from a gray-haired, rocking chair–bound granny. "This is our third deployment. My husband served in Desert Storm and had a second tour in Iraq a few years after 9/11.

We have five kids. Dan, my oldest, is an orthodontist in Texas. My two daughters live in Michigan and Ohio with their families. One's married to a lawyer, and the husband of the younger one is finishing grad school. Steven's on a mission in Toronto, and Scott, our baby, started at USU this summer, straight out of high school. I've got an empty nest now."

Kim couldn't help but notice that the daughters were identified only by what their husbands did, as if the women weren't individuals who had their own lives, passions, or activities. They didn't even have their own names. They were almost certainly stay-at-home moms, which took over their lives and even ate up who they were. Exactly what she didn't want to become. But she would anyway.

Jessie and Brenda each took a turn with an introduction. Both had three kids. Both had been married for roughly the same amount of time. Then it was Kim's turn.

She cleared her throat uneasily. "Oh, well. I'm not very interesting. We got married in April, so no kids yet. Justin's hoping to finish school and be a social worker when he gets back, but that'll be awhile yet. I work as a dental assistant."

Oh, and I think I'm pregnant.

Their food arrived right then. Kim took the opportunity to stop talking and dig into her burger and fries.

Chapter 2: Marianne
Chipper

Brian had been gone almost a month—still in Mississippi for training—so he was out of harm's way for the time being, thank heavens. Marianne sat down at the computer to see that his instant messaging icon was blue, which meant he was online. Maybe they could chat.

You there? she typed.

Sure am, cute stuff. How r u?

Marianne smiled at the nickname only Brian used. *We're good,* she wrote back. *McKayla hates her drivers ed teacher. Bailey's loving Beehives. Kevin misses you the most.*

The fact that she could hit ENTER and have her words magically appear on Brian's computer screen gave her a sense of comfort, as if he were really just in the other room. She couldn't hear his voice or see his shape or touch his hand, but they were still connecting. The blessing of technology would get a mention of thanks in her prayer tonight.

Brian typed his answer quickly. *I miss all the kids. And you? How did the first lunch go?*

Ah, the lunch. Marianne thought back to Jessie juggling her kids, Kim sitting so quietly—what was going on in her head? She hardly said a word the entire time. Nora was a sweetheart. Marianne was quite sure that over the next while, she'd be calling on Nora's many years of deployment experience. Then there was Brenda. Sweet girl, from what Marianne could tell. Nora had made sure they all wrote down their phone numbers and addresses so they could stay in touch easier, and she'd sent the contact information to the entire group. Marianne still had trouble remembering which name went with which face, but she knew that it wouldn't be long before they all knew one another intimately.

It went well, I think, she typed. *It'll take time for us all to get to know one another, of course.*

After a minute, Brian replied, *Yeah, it'll take time, but I hope you get to be good friends.*

Me too. Marianne hoped it more for *his* sake that all the women would bond like that. In the weeks since Brian left, he'd already talked a lot about the husbands of the women she'd met today. Justin and Tim were big kidders, always joking around. Rick was quiet but a very hard worker. Brian had an obvious respect for all of them. Colonel Lambert, Nora's husband, was not only a great leader, but also a very spiritual man, encouraging individual and company prayers. Rumor was that Lambert never let his men go on a mission without a prayer first. The idea was a comfort.

If the wives at home became close, it would be a big support to their soldiers while they were gone. But you couldn't force intimacy, and Marianne wondered if having nothing in common besides deployment would be enough to unite them.

Found out something weird, Brian said.

Oh? Marianne smiled in confusion as she typed the word.

Afghanistan is ten and a half hours ahead of Utah. No idea why the extra half hour.

Marianne furrowed her brow and laughed aloud. *That is weird. I'm still getting used to you being two hours ahead during your training. That will totally throw me off!*

She was glad to be discussing something as lighthearted as time zones instead of her other worries. Brian didn't need to know about how she still felt buried under a mountain as she got used to handling the finances, especially with all the paperwork that deployment added to the mound. Not to mention that the garbage disposal was on the fritz, and the downstairs toilet was clogged—*way* past what a plunger could handle. It would need a snake, which promised to be a rather nasty job. She was trying to decide whether to get the plumber's snake from the garage and try to use it herself, hire someone, or beg her home teachers to do it—the first of many, many times she'd call on them in Brian's absence. She didn't want to become a burden too soon.

Then there were the other basic stresses she'd normally unload on Brian in the course of a week, things that now seemed too petty to bother him with, like Bailey getting braces and the accompanying trauma—and drama. Or McKayla's feeling as if she had social leprosy because of her increasing acne. In spite of her protestations that she'd be an outcast because of the "volcanoes erupting on her face," as she put it, the shunning hadn't happened yet; instead, some boy from algebra had asked her to Homecoming.

Which made Marianne the bad guy because she wouldn't let McKayla go to the dance. "I'm six weeks away from sixteen, Mom," she'd said in that whiny voice. "What difference does *six weeks* make?"

McKayla would never have talked to *her dad* that way.

The other kids were feeling stress too. Kevin had failed every spelling test so far this school year. There had only been two, but in the past, he'd always aced spelling. Last year he even won the third grade spelling bee. So how was he forgetting words he had memorized a few months ago? It worried her. Marianne didn't know whether it was because he was anxious about Dad being gone or whether something else was the culprit. Maybe Kevin needed glasses or something—she'd heard that eyesight could affect grades.

Regardless, she'd deal with it herself rather than unloading something on Brian that he couldn't do a thing about.

We're turning in for the night in a few minutes, he said. *What are you doing right now?*

"Sitting alone in the dark, feeling desperately lonely," Marianne whispered to the monitor. But she couldn't tell him that; it would only make him sad. She glanced up at the ceiling, where the kids were asleep in their rooms, theoretically. Funny how *empty* the house felt when they went to bed. Before Brian left, she'd relished the moment the kids were out of her hair. Now, not so much. It was a little *too* empty.

Knowing she should be "doing" something to tell him about, she looked around the room, trying to decide what to tell him. She grabbed the remote and turned on the television. When it flashed on, the last notes of the *Teeger* theme song played out, signaling the beginning of an episode. When the commercial break started, it was a relief; the tune had been almost painful to hear. She and Brian used to watch the detective show together. After slapping the remote on the desk, Marianne planted her fingers on the keyboard.

Just watching Teeger, she wrote. It was true. Now.

Which one? he asked.

Marianne hit the "info" button on the TiVo remote to check. *"Teeger and the Librarian."*

Love that one! Brian said. *Wish I were there watching with you.*

Me too.

The corners of Marianne's eyes burned. Normally, after a hard day, they'd get the kids to bed, and then she and Brian would settle on the couch together to watch something—often *Teeger* or Brian's favorite medical drama. Half the time they'd end up pausing the TiVo in the first half so Marianne could vent her daily stresses. He never seemed to mind the interruptions, and after she was done, she'd curl up next to him with his arm around her and melt.

What she wouldn't give for one more night in his arms. It always made her feel secure. Happy. Safe. An hour in front of *Teeger*—or whatever show, it didn't matter—made her able to go on and face the rest of the week.

The cursor blinked for awhile before either of them wrote again. Marianne wondered if he was remembering their late nights on the couch too.

It's late, Brian said. *I have to turn in now.*

Good night, BRAIN, she wrote, a play on his name that she used sometimes.

Good night, cute stuff. Love you.

A moment later, his icon turned red. Offline. She stared at it for several seconds, willing it to go blue again. When it didn't, she pushed away from the computer desk. Time to turn in. Standing, she reached for the remote and almost turned the television off, since she'd turned it on only for Brian's sake. Instead, she made her way to the couch. She sat down and pulled a decorative pillow onto her lap. Something to hug, anyway. Then she leaned against the side of the couch—rather rough and cold compared to Brian—and watched the opening scene of *Teeger,* where the murder victim was found in the city library. Marianne had seen enough episodes that even though she didn't remember the solution to this one, she knew the formula in the writing. When the camera lingered for a second on the cover of a book on the counter, she knew it would be a major clue.

A few minutes into the show, the stairs creaked, and Marianne looked over to see Bailey coming. "Hey, honey. You okay?" Marianne asked, instinctively pausing the show.

Bailey nodded but came all the way down. "My teeth hurt," she said, her voice sounding muffled. She held her hands up protectively near her checks—but not against them—with her lips splayed to reveal her new silver braces.

"Do you want some Advil?" Marianne asked.

"I just took some like Dr. Porter said I could," Bailey said between her teeth. "But it's not working yet."

Marianne lifted an arm to the side, and Bailey took the invitation to settle beside her mother. Marianne put an arm around Bailey, who cuddled close.

"Do you need any wax for the rough spots?"

Bailey shook her head. "I just want you for a little while."

Silently Marianne unfolded a blanket and spread it over the two of them. Then she resumed the show and stroked Bailey's honey-blonde hair. *I should send her back to bed,* she thought.

But instead, she kissed the crown of Bailey's head and kept watching the show. With her there, Marianne didn't feel quite so alone.

Chapter 3: Nora
Daughter

The phone rang as Nora reached into the fridge for the orange juice. She closed the door and padded in her slippers to the counter, hoping it wasn't someone who needed anything from her, at least for the next hour. She wouldn't be able to say no, but it would take her that long to put herself together even if it was almost noon. It wouldn't do to show up sans makeup, hair flat. There was a reason she maintained the pulled-together, sophisticated image. It spoke of competence. Self-confidence. Strength.

At least no one can tell through the phone that I look like a drowned rat, she thought, smoothing her hair and hoping that her visiting teacher who had unexpectedly rung the doorbell an hour ago hadn't heard her shush the dog.

Nora picked up the receiver. She looked at the caller ID then groaned as she pushed the ON button. "Hi, Mom," she said cheerfully, rubbing her fingertips against her forehead.

"Morning, Nora-honey."

It's still morning in Seattle, Nora realized. *Mom might not care if I'm in my nightgown and unshowered.* She sighed. *Who am I kidding? Yes, she would.*

"How are you doing?" Nora asked. The invitation was the only thing her mother needed to begin chatting like a five-year-old who'd missed her Ritalin.

As Mother went on about last week's dinner at the seniors' center, Nora began putting dishes into the dishwasher, as if her mother could see through the phone and be horrified at the fact that they'd been left out overnight. Why was it that just the sound of her mother's voice was enough to make Nora feel twelve again?

"Naturally, they had me in charge of the food," her mother went on. The assignment made perfect sense. Years ago her mother had owned a catering company, and ever since Dad's retirement—and then his death four years ago—Mother had found every opportunity to put her finger back into cooking and serving at any opportunity. Chances were that she had usurped the job, rather than having it assigned to her.

"But you wouldn't *believe* what happened."

"Oh? What?" Nora asked, only half-listening as she put away the salt and pepper shakers. A crisis for her mother would be something akin to an improperly basted turkey.

"First off, we had a dozen more people show up than expected."

"Wouldn't that be a *good* thing?" Nora asked, thinking how many other phone calls she had endured where her mother pined about how few people showed up to her events.

"Of course. In *theory*," she said. "But not when it means you're going to run out of roast beef."

Oh, of course, Nora thought, rolling her eyes. *How silly of me. Crisis of the first order.*

"Can you *imagine* how awful that would have been? And Joyce Arnold, who had the job of making the rolls, let them rise too long, so they fell and ended up hard as a rock. I had to send Ray out to buy some from a restaurant around the corner, so *that* catastrophe was averted." Her words implied that several other catastrophes had still been imminent.

"Glad to hear it," Nora said, now dampening a dishcloth to wipe down the counters, remembering vaguely that Ray had worked at the senior center as a janitor and noting that she needed to shred that pile of junk mail before anyone saw the clutter. "I'm glad it turned out well."

Nora swiped toast crumbs into her palm and dumped them into the sink then realized her mother wasn't talking anymore. "Mom?" she asked, brushing her palms together to get off the last of the crumbs.

"I'm here, honey," her mother said, but her voice was quiet, tired—

completely unlike her. She said nothing more for several seconds.

"Mother?" Nora asked again, standing straighter. This kind of pause was exactly what preceded her mother's announcement that Nora's father had died. Her insides twisted. "Is something wrong?"

Silence, followed by her mother clearing her throat. "Well, since you asked, there is one little thing I've been meaning to ask you to do for me."

A favor? Is that all? Nora began breathing again. "Anything." She put away the oven mitts and closed the drawer then tucked the phone between her cheek and shoulder so she could still talk. She picked up the ceramic pot from the slow cooker to bring it to the sink to soak the crusted-on soup from yesterday. As she reached the sink, her mother spoke.

"I'm dying, honey."

The slow cooker slipped from Nora's hands and fell into the sink with a clang. She fumbled with the phone then pressed it to her ear. "I'm not sure I heard you right. What did you say?" *Please don't say what I think you did. Please, not that.* Nora again rubbed her fingertips up and down her forehead, waiting. The silence felt like an eternity before her mother repeated the words.

"I think you heard me right, honey. Doctor says I've got three to six months without treatment, a few more if I decide to endure a kind version of torture." She paused, and Nora's mind tumbled about in the silence before her mother spoke again. "I've decided that a couple of extra weeks aren't worth the pain."

"What . . . what's wrong?" Nora heard herself speaking the words, but her mind felt numb. What happened to cooking roast beef for senior citizens? How did her mother jump from that to . . . *this*?

"I've got cancer of the colon. It's spread all through my body, and they can't operate on it. Drugs can't cure it either; they'd only buy a little time."

Nora found herself nodding slowly as she tried to comprehend the information a piece at a time. *As soon as I hang up, I need to call Russell at work,* she thought. *He'll know what to do.*

But Russell wasn't *at* work. He was training in Mississippi, and in a matter of weeks he would be on the other side of the world. That was part of the reason she was still in her pajamas at 11:53 AM. She was pretty much a wreck without Russell's leveling influence—and without even Scott around anymore to keep her going, now that he was gone to college.

"So because of all that, I wanted to ask something of you," her mother went on.

Only then did Nora's mind come back to what had started this thread of the conversation—her mother asking for a favor. Nora had thought she meant something like buying a Mormon Tabernacle Choir CD or her favorite hand lotion, which she couldn't find in Seattle. Since when did "I'm dying" have anything to do with the category of favors?

"What is it?" Nora asked, her throat tight.

"I'd love to live with you for my last weeks."

"Of course. You can stay in Scott's old room." The words came out before Nora had thought them, before she could contemplate all the logistics in getting her mother down to Utah, finding new doctors, watching her get weaker and weaker . . . dying.

And, for a short time, living under the same roof again. She'd think about the ramifications of *that* later.

"Over the summer we turned his room into a guest room. It's close to the bathroom, it's on the main floor, and . . ." Her voice trailed off. In the midst of thinking through the situation logically, her emotions pressed upon her like a weight.

"Thanks, Nora-honey. I don't like the idea of leaving home, but dying away from loved ones would be even worse." Her voice didn't give much clue as to what she was feeling—this could have been a conversation about beets being on sale, for all the emotion her mother put into it.

"My home is always open to you," Nora said, wiping tears from her eyes. With sudden irony, she decided it was a good thing she hadn't put on her makeup yet, or she'd have dark rivers of mascara trailing down her cheeks. "When do you want to come?"

"In a week or two. It'll take me that long to get myself ready to go." Nora could almost see her clasping her hands in pleasure as she went on. "Nora-honey, I don't think I've ever seen the house you're living in right now, have I?"

"No," Nora said. "I don't think you have." She knew full well her mother hadn't been here, because she'd never criticized the colors or the decorations or how Nora liked to hang her pictures an inch or two higher than was supposedly "correct." She scanned the kitchen and great room, suddenly wondering how much deep cleaning she could do in the next few days—curtains, tile grout, carpets, upholstery . . .

A confusing, complicated mixture of emotions swirled inside Nora—worry for her mother, comfort that she was coming where Nora could offer care, dread at the constant nit-picking and criticisms that would inevitably arrive with her.

"I love you," she said softly, meaning it, but also wanting to say it because of the sudden guilt she felt for not being more excited about welcoming her mother under her own roof.

Chapter 4: Brenda
Trying

Brenda arrived at IHOP ten minutes late for the second wives' lunch. She slipped past the hostess, found the table with all the other wives, and slid into her chair. "Sorry I'm late."

"No problem," Nora said, smiling. She slid a menu over to Brenda. "Glad you could make it."

She opened the menu and shook her head. "When I dropped the twins off at the sitter's, they clung to me, screaming as if someone were cutting off a limb. I don't get it; that's so unlike them."

Jessie lowered her menu to the table and nodded. "My kids are acting out, too. They've turned into little horrors. I'd heard kids did that during deployments, but I didn't think it would happen so fast."

She returned to looking over the hamburger menu, but Brenda's head came up. "You think the twins are reacting to their dad being gone? But it's been what, a month and a half? The guys aren't even in country yet."

"Those kinds of details don't matter to little ones," Nora said. She took a sip of water—which had a lemon slice in it—and shook her head. "It always amazes me how quickly children respond to the stress of deployment."

"But Rick's been gone on long business trips before," Brenda pressed. "Last winter he had to fly to Japan for three weeks. None of the kids freaked out like this."

Marianne and Jessie both nodded, agreeing with Brenda. They all turned to Nora expectantly, hoping for help. Nora leaned back and clasped her hands together on the table. "This is different," she said. "What they're reacting to right now is *your* reaction, *your* stress. They can tell that this is different than Daddy's trip to Japan, because Mommy's not reacting the same way to it." She smiled and cocked her head. "Are you?"

Sheepishly Brenda said, "No, of course not. I'm a lot more stressed out than when he was gone in January. How could I not be? I know he won't be back in a few days. Instead, he'll be near the Taliban, possibly getting shot at. As soon as the guys finish their training in Mississippi, I probably won't be able to be in contact with him every day—and definitely not on his cell phone. Or at normal hours because of the time difference, and . . ." Her voice trailed off, and she realized that the server had arrived, notepad poised in the air.

"Are you ready to order?" the server asked.

Brenda hadn't given the menu more than a cursory look, but right now she knew exactly what she wanted—something nice and full of calories. She ordered a big stack of pancakes, complete with hash browns, two fried eggs, and sausage. And a tall glass of orange juice. Comfort food. As she handed over her menu and waited for the other ladies to order, she thought back to how the kids had been acting, and her stomach tightened.

When school started, getting Bradley to his second grade classroom was like trying to walk through tar. The poor kid had acted as if she were leading him to the executioner's block. At the time, she couldn't figure him out; it wasn't as if he were going to a new school or even transitioning to all-day school. Two of his best friends were in the same class, and he'd met the teacher at the back-to-school night and loved her. When he went from kindergarten to first grade, he did fine—and that was a far bigger transition than from first grade to second.

Bradley was quiet, but he rarely showed anxiety or fear. In the past, he always handled the bumps and dips of his young life without complaint. Something had changed, and it worried her.

Then, of course, there were the twins. Dropping them off at her friend Lisa's took fifteen minutes—with Josh still screaming and yelling at her, Tyler with huge tears falling down both cheeks, holding his arms out as if only she could save him from death itself.

She'd tried to comfort and console and persuade and even bribe but had finally left. She threw an apologetic glance toward Lisa as she hurried out the door and closed it behind her, the twins still shrieking inside. Out on the steps, she grabbed the railing and cringed, wondering if she should skip the wives' lunch today. Lisa came to the window and shooed her away, so Brenda ran to the car and drove off without looking back, cranking up the stereo as if that would drown out the sound of her boys' screeching in her head.

The twins were unusually independent for three-year-olds. She'd always been able to leave them anywhere, and they'd hardly give her a wave as they trotted off to find some fun. At eighteen months, they went to Nursery without any fuss.

Now, as she sat there with all the other wives, who were chatting and laughing, she realized why the twins reacted differently last Sunday. Why they wouldn't go into Nursery at all. Instead, as she stood in the open doorway, blocking traffic, they'd each taken one of her legs and held on, refusing to budge—and wailing loud enough to crack crystal if she tried to pry one of them off. They weren't crying; instead it was an angry, terrified scream.

At the time, she'd been stumped as to why.

The server gathered up the rest of the menus and left. During a pause in the conversation, Brenda looked over at Nora. "So the kids are reacting to *me.*"

Nora nodded. "When they sense your stress, it makes them anxious." She smoothed her napkin on the table and addressed the wives together. "This is why it's so important for you all to take good care of yourselves. If you spend this deployment trying to put out fires for everyone else, that's all you'll be doing. And trust me—the fires will only get bigger. By the time your men get home, you'll be on the verge of a total breakdown, and that is *not* what you need, because the year after deployment—that whole reentry process—most definitely has its own challenges."

"So . . . what do we do?" Jessie asked, eyeing the other wives at the table as if asking on their behalf. Brenda and everyone else nodded their agreement on the question.

Nora began scooping ice from her glass and piling it on her plate. "I have sensitive teeth," she explained then went on. "Take care of your kids' mom. They deserve that. And trust me; they'll do so much better when they can see that you're handling the situation well. That means taking a little time for yourself every single week. Coming to lunch with all of us is good, but find something else, too. Go to the temple. Exercise. Get enough sleep. That kind of thing."

"All that stuff takes extra time," Brenda protested. "Isn't that taking *more* time away from the kids when they need extra attention from the one parent that *is* around?"

"Look at it this way," Nora said. "Your kids look to you for reassurance that everything is going to be okay. If you aren't taking measures to be sure that you *are* doing well, they'll sense it all the more."

Brenda sat back. "I hadn't thought of it like that," she said, wondering if her voice sounded tense even while reading *Yertle the Turtle* to the twins last night.

"Look," Nora continued, "if they feel that you're doing okay, they're okay. If you're not, they'll struggle. They might even revert to earlier stages, like no longer sleeping through the night or wetting themselves." She shook her head ruefully. "It's scary, really, how in tune kids can be. They know before you do how you're holding up. You can't fool them."

So that explains the potty-training problem, Brenda thought. Six months ago, the twins were fully trained, but both of them were having accidents again, and sometimes the nasty kind.

Jessie continued to probe Nora for advice on dealing with deployment, especially in regards to kids. Marianne was the only one with teenagers, so she asked about what to do with them. "I swear," she said with a shake of her head. "I thought being a mom to little kids was hard. Hah! Parenthood is much harder and exhausting than it ever was when they were babies."

Brenda wanted to throw a fork at her. Marianne might not have meant it, but she'd single-handedly belittled the problems Jessie and Brenda were dealing with. She'd obviously forgotten how physically, emotionally, and psychologically draining the baby years were.

"I'm sure teenagers come with their own set of issues," Brenda interjected. "Things I can only guess at right now, but if you think you weren't drained and exhausted and at the end of your rope . . . then you don't remember."

"Trust me," Marianne said. "Teens are *much* harder."

Brenda sat back and bit the corner of her lip, trying to keep the tears at bay. It felt as if, in a single sweep, Marianne had just shoved Brenda's problems aside. As if she didn't have the right to feel as if she were hanging on by a single thread simply because she only had three little toddlers instead of three teenagers.

Name the last time your fifteen-year-old finger-painted the wall with blueberry yogurt, dumped a gallon of pancake syrup onto the carpet, or kept you up every single night for months—and then demanded your patience in the morning. There's a reason sleep deprivation is a torture method.

She was sure that older kids brought big challenges, but having her problems brushed aside as silly made her feel about two inches tall.

Brenda listened carefully to Nora's advice, trying to ignore Marianne's supposed stress, coming from a woman who got *six hours* of free time every day with all her kids in school—must be brutal. Jessie added a few questions about keeping the kids' father a part of their lives while he was gone.

When the food arrived, Brenda stopped talking, dumped a huge blob of ketchup on her hash browns, and dug in. Greasy, yes. But so good. With Rick gone, did it really matter if she let herself go? Her eyes nearly rolled into the back of her head with pleasure. She added a little salt. You could never have too much salt, even if it did mean retaining water later.

I'm the reason my kids are freaking out, she thought guiltily, stabbing a fried egg. *I need to get a grip, or we'll all lose our minds.*

Toward the end of lunch, Nora announced that she might miss next week's lunch and would almost certainly miss the one after that. "Of course, I hope don't," she said, selecting a few bills from her wallet for a tip. "I haven't figured out my flight plans yet, but I'll be going up to Washington State next week to bring my mother down. I'm not sure how long it'll all take to get her pulled together. She's coming to live with me."

"Oh, how neat," Marianne said, patting Nora on the shoulder. "You won't be so alone then. I imagine it's been rather strange for you to have that whole house to yourself—having an empty nest *and* a deployment at the same time."

Nora smiled wanly. "It *has* been an adjustment," she said. "But Mother's getting on in years, and her health isn't quite as good as it once was. It's good for her to be near family. Dad died several years ago, and neither of us daughters is in the Northwest anymore. I'm the older one, so it makes sense that I'd take her in."

"We hope you can come next week," Jessie said. "But we'll understand if you're not here."

"I'll let you all know on e-mail what to expect," Nora said, standing. She put her purse strap over her shoulder and smiled down on them. "Ladies, I'm glad we're together in this. Having group support is so important." She wagged a manicured finger. "Promise me that you'll let me know if you need anything. That's what I'm here for. Truly, don't hesitate to call."

"We promise," Marianne said. "Don't we?"

Jessie and Kim murmured yes, and Brenda made do with a noncommittal half-nod. As Nora left, Brenda grunted silently. There was no way in the world she'd ever ask Nora for help. Of course she was sincere in her offer; Brenda didn't doubt that she could swoop into any situation like Wonder Woman, complete with golden wristbands and lasso, and save the day.

Brenda looked through the windows, watching Nora walk past the building toward the parking lot. She looked so composed all the time. Brenda would give a lot to know what her kids were like when they were little—during their father's Desert Storm deployment, maybe. Somehow Brenda couldn't quite picture Nora cleaning up a toddler's poopy accident from the carpet on the stairs, again. She was so calm, collected.

If I were to ask her for help, she'd see what a wreck I am.

She imagined what kind of situation she'd be in to need to call on Nora. Maybe if she got a flat tire. No. Even then, calling Nora was totally out of the question.

No *way* did Nora have a car that looked like Brenda's minivan, a smorgasbord of crushed Cheerios, fruit-snack wrappers, a half-eaten Go-Gurt that had smeared—and dried—onto the upholstery, abandoned crayons crammed between the seats, remnants of spilled sodas, fossilized French fries, and grocery store receipts, plus a box bound for D.I. Cleaning it up had been on her "to do" list for a while now.

No, Nora's car was likely pristine, with nary a crumb or scrap of paper in sight. *She might have a coronary if she were forced to sit in my car,* Brenda thought with a smirk. Then she sighed as she watched the other ladies gather their purses to leave. She shoved one last bite of pancake into her mouth and stood as well.

The van was one more thing she really should get to—one more thing that showed she had totally lost control of her life since Rick left.

I'll get to it, she thought, putting on her jacket. *Eventually. I think.*

Chapter 5: Kim
Growing

Kim paced in her small apartment, going between the bedroom, which had orange shag, and the front room, which sported sculpted aqua carpet. She wrung her hands as she tracked her steps—sixteen to the bedroom, sixteen back—and worried.

This morning she'd started spotting.

What did that mean? Was she miscarrying? Should she go in to see a doctor? If so, could it wait until tomorrow, or was it an emergency? If she waited, would she miscarry for sure? In a horribly guilt-inducing way, that would be a huge relief. She wouldn't have to deal with a pregnancy and baby birth and all that without Justin. But could she live with herself if her baby died and it was her fault?

No one knew she was pregnant. Not even Justin. Not even a doctor yet. She'd been relying on a stupid book. She'd bought it in hopes of learning what was normal, but about all she'd learned from it is that almost any funky symptom could be considered "normal" for pregnancy. Although there *was* no textbook pregnancy, apparently living with your head over the toilet was pretty common. Just her luck that she'd be normal *that* way.

She hadn't opened the book in three weeks because it had pictures and descriptions of what was happening to the baby at every stage. She was okay with that when the embryo was the size of a pea and still looked like a lizard. But the last time she'd opened the book, the life inside her was no longer an embryo; it was now called a fetus. And it had organs and hands and feet and even tooth buds.

It was a tiny person. And *that* was a little too real.

Now she was bleeding. Not heavily. A stabbing feeling began on her right side, and she closed one eye. Cramps couldn't be a good sign.

She wasn't sure what to do; she could always open the book again. It might tell her something, but she didn't want to do that. For one thing, the language in it was technical for someone who'd struggled to graduate high school.

"I should lie down," she said under her breath. She'd heard of women ordered to bed rest during pregnancy. Lying down would probably be a good thing. On her way to the couch, one hand instinctively went to her right side where the cramping was getting worse.

She crossed the room and climbed onto the gold, seventies-style sofa that had swirls in the fabric. Resting on her side, she tucked her knees but was no longer able to comfortably pull them up to her chest. Her swelling tummy, small as it was, got in the way now.

Kim stared at the blank television screen, eyes feeling dry, stinging. What had she been thinking, getting married so quickly? If they'd waited a little, maybe Justin would have been deployed during their engagement, and then she wouldn't be here, alone, pregnant, scared. Terrified.

Mom and Dad warned me not to do anything rash, to "not get swept away with the current." They'd been so against the quick marriage. Kim couldn't very well call them *now* and ask for advice. All she'd get was an earful of "I told you so."

Who else could she turn to? She didn't really know anyone in her ward. She had no idea who her visiting teachers were or even the Relief Society president's name, although someone had pointed her out once, so she recognized her by sight. As soon as they'd moved in, Kim was put into Nursery, so she might as well have been on another planet for as much as she knew any of the other women—but she was closer to the age of the Laurels anyway. Now she spent most of her Sundays trying not to barf because of the little kids' goldfish crackers at snack time. Ugh. The *smell* of those things . . .

But she really needed advice. The bleeding and cramping might be totally normal, nothing to worry about. Or maybe she should be calling 911. Or the right answer could be something between those two extremes. She could always try Google.

If she had someone she could turn to that was *like* a mother . . .

She surprised herself by immediately thinking of the Army wives. She'd known them for a few weeks now, and while they weren't her best friends or anything, she knew they'd help her out—that was sort of the point of their get-togethers, to create a support group so their husbands knew they'd have someone to turn to. Any one of them knew a ton more about pregnancy than she did. Mentally she scanned past the lunch tables, imagining herself telling them about her problem.

Nora? No, she was too old for Kim to feel comfortable talking to.

Brenda? Maybe. But she seemed too stressed out. Kim didn't want to add to that.

Marianne? She was years past her last pregnancy. Someone who was closer to it would probably remember more.

Jessie.

Wait—Jessie's a nurse!

With an odd leap in her chest, Kim sat up. Should she call Jessie? Kim remembered watching her struggling through the restaurant doors with her three little ones that first week. A smile played at the corners of her mouth. Jessie seemed down-to-earth and approachable. She'd had three pregnancies in the last four or five years. *And* she was a nurse. She'd know what to do and wouldn't think Kim was too big of an idiot for asking.

She went into the second bedroom, where the computer was, and pulled up Nora's e-mail that had everyone's contact information. Still uncomfortable from the cramps, she took a deep breath, reached for the phone, and dialed Jessie's number.

After only two rings, the call was answered with a pleasant, "Hello?"

"Jessie? Hi, it's me, Kim. Um, Kim Howett? From the Army wives' lunches?" What if Jessie didn't remember her? Kim was so young compared to the others, so inexperienced, that she half wondered whether the other women had even noticed her presence.

"Of course. Hi, Kim," Jessie said. "What's up?"

"I . . . uh . . ." Kim leaned on her forearm against the desk. "I have a question. You're a nurse, right?"

"Yeah. Is everything okay?"

"I think so," Kim said. "Or, I don't know . . ." How could she say this? "Can you keep a secret?"

"Of course. Kim, is something wrong?" Jessie's voice sounded a bit strained now.

"See, I'm bleeding," Kim began.

"Did you cut yourself?" Jessie asked.

"No, nothing like that. I mean . . ." She sat up and took a deep breath then said the words she'd only thought until now. "I'm pregnant."

Jessie squealed on the other end. "That's fantastic! Congratulations! Wait . . ." She apparently understood how conflicted it must feel to expect a baby with your husband gone.

"Yeah, it's a little tricky right now," Kim said. She sat back, feeling better already after saying the words. That one word—*pregnant*—in particular.

"Wait—you're bleeding?" Jessie cut in, as if rewinding the conversation in her head. "How heavy is it?"

"About like a period," Kim said, suddenly feeling a rush of relief that someone who had half a clue about what to ask was on the other end, helping.

"Are you cramping?"

"Yeah. It started a few minutes ago. Does this mean I'm miscarrying?"

"Not necessarily," Jessie said with an encouraging tone.

Kim felt a strange wave of conflicted emotions—a slice of relief with an equal measure of dread that this pregnancy might not be going away. Miscarriage happened a lot to the women in her family— her mother *and* all her sisters. She still might . . .

Jessie's voice brought Kim back to the moment. "How far along are you?"

"Twelve weeks." Kim hated that she knew without even having to check. Using the chart in her trusty pregnancy book, she'd identified her due date and circled it on the calendar with a red Sharpie. The mark felt like a big target counting down to the end of life as she knew it.

"Okay," Jessie said slowly, as if thinking through the issue. "It might still be nothing."

"What should I do?"

"First of all, we need to get you in to your doctor right away."

Kim felt a little flutter of relief at Jessie's use of *we.* Maybe she'd come. "We need to see what's happening with the baby," Jessie went on. "Where's your doctor's office?"

A flush rose on Kim's cheeks. "I . . . don't have one . . . yet."

After a pause, Jessie said. "Oh."

Kim rushed on. "You're the only person in the world I've told. My parents don't know. I haven't . . . I haven't even told Justin."

"Oh, Kim." Jessie's voice was laced with tenderness. "You don't have to go through this alone."

Suddenly defensive, Kim sat with her back straight, ready to hang up. "Listen, I have my reasons for not telling anyone, all right? Just tell me what to do."

"Sorry," Jessie said. "I can probably get you into the clinic I used to work at."

Kim felt guilty for snapping at Jessie, who was being so generous. "That would be great. Thanks," she said, softening her tone. But the idea of going alone was scary. If Justin were around, she'd drag him. But alone? No way. She needed someone with her who could think straight in the middle of it all. Jessie would know what questions to ask and could explain things to her using words Kim could understand. "Would you come with me?"

"I . . . I guess I could," Jessie said. "Are you sure you want me to?"

"Positive."

"Okay. Give me your address. I'll pick you up. I'll pull a string or two and get you into the clinic. You're in Provo, right? I can be there in twenty minutes or so."

"What about your kids?" Kim asked, already feeling a weight lift.

"They'll be fine. I'll get the Mia Maid next door to come tend. She's trying to save up for a new iPod, so she'll be thrilled for a chance to earn a little money for a couple of hours."

Kim gave her some basic directions then said, "Thanks, Jessie. I really need someone."

"No problem. I'll be right there."

"Um, Jessie?" Kim said, hoping she hadn't hung up yet.

"Yes?"

"Please don't tell anyone."

"Of course I won't, but I think you should—" Jessie protested.

"I'll tell others when I'm ready. You won't say a word?"

Jessie sighed. "Don't worry. I promise."

* * *

Jessie drove Kim to the clinic in American Fork. It was farther away than was necessary, but Kim was happy to go the extra distance if it meant seeing a doctor Jessie knew and trusted.

They filled out a bunch of paperwork, and Kim was suddenly glad she had good health insurance through the military. When she turned the forms back in, the receptionist thanked her and said, "Nurse Practitioner Michaels is running just a few minutes late, but it won't be long."

Kim turned from the desk and walked back to sit beside Jessie, who was flipping through a magazine. "A nurse?" Kim hissed as she sat. "You're taking me to see a *nurse?* No offense, but shouldn't I be seeing a *doctor?*"

"She's not just a nurse," Jessie said casually, flipping a magazine page. "She's a nurse *practitioner.*"

"What's the difference?" Kim was already uncomfortable just *sitting* in the clinic. This new bit of information made her nerves worse.

"They're like normal nurses, only on steroids, educationally speaking," Jessie said. She shook her head. "Okay, that's not the best way to describe it. They're practically doctors. They can prescribe medications and even have their own practices. She's excellent. Trust me."

Kim eyed her warily. "You're sure?"

"I'm sure. She's also a certified midwife—she delivered Joey. I wouldn't have brought you here if I didn't trust her one hundred percent."

That was a little better. Kim gave an accepting nod. She'd see how it went with this nurse person before deciding whether to see someone else.

Within fifteen minutes, a nurse called her name. Kim stood and took two steps before realizing that Jessie was still in her chair.

"Aren't you coming?" Kim asked.

"What, into the exam room?"

"Um, yeah."

"I didn't think so."

"Why not?"

"Because I'm not family. You know, patient privacy laws, and—"

"Oh, come on," Kim said, pulling on her arm. "I want you in there to explain it. I'm clueless, remember?"

In surrender, Jessie set aside the magazine and stood. "All right, I'm coming."

They were brought back to an examination room, where the nurse took Kim's vitals, jotted a few notes into the computer, then left them alone. They waited a few more minutes—which felt like a trimester all by itself—before Nurse Practitioner Michaels came in. She had curly, gray hair cut into a no-nonsense style and wore a simple pair of pearl earrings with her lab coat and tan slacks. She was also shorter than Kim, which was saying something, since Kim was all of five-three.

The shorter woman smiled at Jessie in greeting. "Why hello, Jessie. Tiffany told me you were here. What a great surprise." She glanced at the file in her hand. "Kim, is it?"

"Yep." She wore a weak smile.

"Call me Eleanor. Nice to meet you, Kim. I take it Jessie's family?"

"Um, no," Kim said awkwardly. "But I really want her in here. I . . . I don't have any family around right now."

"And we appreciate you working us in at such short notice," Jessie added.

"Anything for you." She sat on a stool. "All right, then, Kim." She began quizzing her about symptoms—when had the bleeding started, when did the cramps start, how heavy was the bleeding, when was her last period? She did a brief exam, probing Kim's belly and checking the size with a measuring tape. Kim lay on the table, shirt up to her ribs, and Jessie held her hand for support.

"All right. Let's take a look at baby." Eleanor moved a cart into position and squeezed heated jelly onto Kim's stomach before using the wand and eyeing the screen. Every few seconds she paused, clicking some buttons then continuing to probe Kim's tummy. After a while, she turned the screen so Kim could see it. Holding the wand still, she pointed.

"See that movement? It's your baby's heart beating. Nice and strong. Just how we like it."

Kim let out a breath. "So the baby's okay?"

"Sure looks like it," she said. "Do you see the legs here?"

Not trusting herself to speak, Kim nodded. The images on the screen shifted and then came into focus again. There were arms. A head. It looked like a *baby*.

"So can you tell why I'm bleeding?" Kim managed to ask.

"Look here," Eleanor said, moving the wand lower and then pointing at the screen. "That's the placenta."

"Ah," Jessie said in quiet understanding.

"What?" Kim asked, getting up and supporting herself on her elbows.

"You have placenta previa," Eleanor said.

"Is that serious?" Kim looked from Jessie to Eleanor, unsure what to think or feel.

The nurse cleaned the wand, put it away, and then wiped the jelly off Kim's stomach with a white towel. Kim lowered her shirt and sat up, still staring at the monitor.

"In your case, I think you'll be okay," Eleanor said. "Yours looks like type II, which is marginal. It may correct itself. That's great news." She stood and patted Kim on the arm. "As long as you take it easy, I think the bleeding will stop soon. You'll have to be on bed rest for the next couple of weeks, though. And no lifting. That means no laundry, no vacuuming, no going to work."

I guessed that much right, Kim thought, pleased that even as clueless as she was, she'd figured out *one* thing on her own. She'd have to figure out what to do with her job. And how she'd get any laundry done. No worries about dishes or cooking; she'd order in. But she still didn't know what was going on. Feeling like an idiot for not understanding, Kim looked at Jessie, confused.

"Could you explain to her what placenta previa is?" Jessie asked.

Eleanor pushed the ultrasound cart to the side and clasped her hands. "It means that your placenta is down low, covering the cervix. That could be a problem, because during delivery, it would detach and come out before the baby."

Apparently Kim's continued feeling of bewilderment showed on her face, because the older woman added, "That would cut off the baby's oxygen and blood supply. But the good news is that placentas usually move upward during pregnancy, and since yours isn't completely covering the opening, there's a good chance it'll move entirely out of the way. If you take it easy for the next little while, until the bleeding stops, I think you'll be fine."

"Okay, good." Kim began breathing again. "I can handle resting for a while."

"And, since we know to monitor you," Eleanor continued, "if it hasn't moved enough by the time you're full-term, we'll simply take the baby C-section."

Kim's eyes widened. Getting cut open—gutted like a fish—wasn't the most attractive option. The thought made her ill. But as much as she didn't *want* to be a mother, she wasn't so coldhearted that she actually wished the baby would be in danger at birth.

Until now, she'd pictured the baby as a mass of tissue that was making her feel sick all the time and making her pants tight. Now it *looked* real. She'd seen it moving around. She'd seen the heart beat. It was a real person.

Darn it.

Chapter 6: Nora
Return

Nora drove along the winding road that led to her childhood home in Renton, a suburb of Seattle. She always forgot how much of a desert Utah really was until she returned to the Northwest and saw the lush greenery and deep colors she'd grown up with. And the dampness. If it wasn't actually raining, there was a good chance of a drizzle or at least the feeling of walking through mist. As she pulled up to the house and killed the engine, she wished for an umbrella but caught herself and smiled. Around here, carrying an umbrella in anything other than a true downpour was a sure sign of a tourist—or a serious wimp.

She took her purse from the passenger's seat and reached for the door but paused and looked—really looked—at the house. It was gray-blue, with a slanted, asymmetrical roof and a maroon door. The yard was immaculate, something Mother couldn't have kept up on her own and likely couldn't afford, either. But she'd rather go without utilities than have her neighbors see weedy flowerbeds and a lawn in need of a mow. How many more times would Nora see this place? After she brought Mother home to Utah, she'd probably come up here one last time. And that wouldn't be until after her mother had passed, when the estate needed to be taken care of.

With an odd sense of finality, she opened the car door, stepped out, and closed it firmly. After getting her suitcase from the trunk, she headed for the steps that led from the driveway to the front door. The last time she'd come this way, it was during the kids' spring break two and a half years ago. Back then, four of them had walked the pathway, and Russell had carried her luggage. Scott and Steven had bounded ahead to the door. It was the first time they'd visited since Nora's father died. Maybe that was one reason she hadn't wanted to come back—she didn't want to face the house without Dad's gentle presence that tempered Mother's harshness.

Back then, Scott had just gotten his license and had begged to drive from the airport. Russell hadn't allowed it, of course. Scott could barely navigate Alpine City and brief stretches of I-15. No way would they let him attempt Washington interstates.

Steven had been about to graduate from high school and was excited to brag to Grandma about being class salutatorian.

Usually Nora and Russell—and the kids, whoever was home—took a trip up to Washington each year. How had so much time passed since her last trip? Between sending Steven on his mission, Scott graduating from high school and going off to college, Russell's deployment, and her personal general busyness, a convenient time simply hadn't presented itself.

Not that she'd looked for one.

When she reached the door, her hand went to the knob but then froze. She felt out of place, as if she were a stranger. As if she should ring the doorbell of her childhood home. She could almost hear Steven and Scott bursting into the house and finding their grandmother in the dining room. Most times they arrived, Mother sat at the table, looking out the window into the backyard, her hands wrapped around an oversized mug of hot cocoa. The boys' enthusiasm never did wane, even though their grandmother didn't share it.

After a second of indecision, Nora pulled her hand from the doorknob and pushed the doorbell. She waited for a bit before hearing her mother's voice saying, "Coming," from the other side of the door.

She pictured her mother's effort, easing herself down the steps from the living room, and suddenly felt guilty for not simply going in. The house was a split-level, with stairs going up on the left and down on the right from the entryway, which was a setup easier for a young family than an elderly woman. Nora reached for the doorknob. Surely it would be open; Mother always left it unlocked when expecting family. Nora turned it, but she met resistance. It was locked. She breathed out and lowered her chin. She'd guessed right. Mother was making sure her own daughter couldn't barge in on her.

The dead bolt *thunked*, and after a click to unlock the knob, the door opened. Nora, smiling wide, waited expectantly for her mother's face.

"Hi, honey," her mother said. "What took you so long?"

Before Nora could answer, her mother turned her back and was slowly climbing the stairs. "Hi, Mother," Nora said, taken off-guard. She hadn't expected a warm, fuzzy reunion—Mother wasn't like that. But shouldn't there be more than this?

"We landed ten minutes late, and then traffic was pretty nasty," Nora said, lifting her suitcase over the threshold. "Which room do you want me in?"

Her mother paused halfway up the flight of seven steps and peered over her shoulder. "You could have called." She nodded toward the hall on the right side of the house. "Take your old room. I haven't had a chance to put sheets on the bed, but there should be clean ones in the closet."

Nora walked up behind her mother, her luggage thumping each time she had to pause, waiting for her mother to go up the next step. "I did call—from my cell—but you didn't answer." Of course she called. She always called when plans didn't turn out exactly as her mother would—or might—expect them to.

"I thought that was some telemarketer. Didn't recognize the area code."

She didn't recognize the Utah area code? Shaking her head, Nora moved to another topic. "So, how are you feeling?"

Her mother had reached the top now. She shuffled across the carpet in her wool socks and, drawing out her breath, eased herself onto a dining room chair next to her ceramic pink mug. "There's a roast with potatoes and carrots in the fridge we can warm up for a bite."

Message received: it wasn't time to talk about the elephant in the room quite yet.

"I'll heat it up as soon as I get settled," Nora said, wheeling her suitcase down the hall. She was tired from the trip—and suddenly very aware of her age. When she was younger, the flight didn't bother her at all. Now she wanted a long nap. But she'd be making lunch from left-overs instead.

She knew that when Mother said there was food "we" could prepare, it meant Nora.

It always had.

"Aren't you going to do it now?"

"Let me unpack first." As soon as she was in the hall, Nora stuck her tongue out. Then she rolled her eyes at herself. Mother really did bring out the child in her.

Her old room no longer resembled the one she'd grown up in. It had been redecorated, turned into a guest bedroom with entirely new colors and furniture. Nora didn't blame her mother for doing it. The walls were now a neutral tan, but they used to be two shades of purple—perfect for a preteen girl. She hefted the suitcase onto the bed and unzipped it.

She'd brought several days' worth of clothes, including a nice dress, a couple pairs of slacks, and a silk blouse just in case her mother had plans she hadn't told Nora about.

As she hung up her things, she glanced at her watch. The weekly wives' lunch had ended a couple of hours ago, while she was in the air. She sighed, wishing she'd been there instead of somewhere over Idaho at the time. With those women, she felt looked up to, respected, needed.

Here, she was a little girl again, hoping for her mommy's approval.

I'm an old woman, Nora thought, closing the closet door a tad more forcefully than necessary. *I shouldn't have to prove myself to anyone, least of all to my mother.*

But reality said otherwise. Nora knew she'd spend the next couple of days—and who knew how much time back home—trying to please her mother.

At least I'll be at next week's lunch. It was a pleasant thought, and that fact alone made her smile. Who would have thought that Russell's request for her to essentially babysit four younger women would turn into not only something she missed when she couldn't do it, but a place where she felt more comfortable than in her own childhood home?

I could be their mother, she thought. Age aside, they treated her better than her own mother did.

"Are you doing all right in there?" Mother's reedy voice came down the hall.

In other words, what's taking you so long?

"Almost done," Nora called cheerfully. She practically wrenched the zipper off her suitcase as she pulled it shut. Sighing and wishing for a good chat over whatever restaurant food it had been this week, she added, "I'll get that roast right into the oven."

She closed her eyes. This would be a long week. She hoped to be heading back to Utah within a couple of days so she could adjust to Mother being in the house before the next wives' lunch. She *wasn't* going to miss another, even if it meant sneaking out of her own house to do it.

Chapter 7: Kim
Easy Does It

WEDNESDAY, SEPTEMBER 23, 2009

For the first time, Kim arrived at the restaurant—Winger's today—before any of the other wives, surprised at how eager she was to see everyone. She got a corner booth for the group and even ordered drinks for everyone and a Dr. Pepper for herself. No ice in Nora's water. A lemon slice for Jessie's. She was pleased to already know these ladies so well after only a month.

As the heavy door opened with a whoosh of air, Nora came in and looked side to side. Kim waved to catch her eye and felt a sudden rush of excitement at seeing the older woman smile and wave back.

I've missed her, she realized. *I've missed them all. Wow.*

Only weeks before, she'd nearly run away from their first lunch, and here she was looking forward to this one. It surely helped her mood that she'd stayed home last week on doctor's—or rather nurse practitioner's—orders. This was the first time she'd left the apartment in nearly two weeks, except for a quick run to the Laundromat. That was sort of a necessity. And the two baskets weren't *that* heavy.

"Hello, there," Nora said, sliding onto the bench across from her and stopping in front of the glass without the ice. "Is this mine? Thank you for remembering how sensitive my teeth are." She took a quick sip and then said, "It's so good to see you. I missed you last week."

"Oh, I wasn't feeling well," Kim said by way of vague explanation. She wasn't ready to spread the news *quite* yet.

"I'm so sorry to hear that," Nora said. "Are you feeling better?"

"Yeah, a bit," Kim said, smiling. The bleeding had almost stopped. She probably shouldn't be off bed rest quite yet, but she didn't want to miss another lunch, and she'd been *really* good about the whole stay-off-your-feet thing so far, except for the one trip. She'd even skipped out on church and Nursery duty, although no one seemed to notice. If she'd called on her visiting teachers to do it, she'd have needed to explain. Then word would spread to the Relief Society president, and then it could snowball into the entire ward knowing that something was up. The bleeding increased after she did the laundry, but she'd gone straight back to bed—and to watching season three of *Lost* on DVD—right away.

"I missed last week's lunch too." Nora smoothed her napkin on the table. "I went up to Seattle for my mother. It's good to be home again."

"Oh, yeah," Kim said. "She's living with you now, right? How's that going?" She laughed and widened her eyes. "I think my mother and I would kill each other if we had to live together."

Nora chuckled, tilting her head to one side and then the other. "Oh, we're still in the adjustment phase—we're two old women set in our ways—but I'm sure it'll work out."

The restaurant door opened again, and Jessie appeared, with Brenda coming a few yards behind. They came in together then spotted Nora and came their way. After walking about ten feet, her eyes landed on Kim, and she halted mid-step. "Hi . . ." Her voice held mild surprise. Eyes flitting to Nora and then back to Kim, she added, "I didn't expect to see you this week. I thought you were still . . . under the weather."

"Oh, I'm fine," Kim said breezily. She took a drink of her Dr. Pepper and made a point of avoiding Jessie's eyes as she gestured across the table. "Look, I got your water with lemon."

"Thanks," Jessie said, sitting down.

"Brenda, I got you water with ice," Kim said. "I didn't remember if you usually order anything special."

"Oh, plain old water is fine," Brenda said, taking a seat. "Although when the server gets here, I could use some lemonade."

Kim glanced up at Jessie, who had one eyebrow in a high arch as if saying, *What do you think you're doing? Get back to bed, young lady.*

Ignoring the look, Kim lifted her menu and scanned it. "Anyone have any favorite foods here? I don't really know the menu, but my stomach's feeling kind of funny today. I'd better not have anything too spicy." A single eyebrow raise from Jessie showed what *she* thought of Kim's not telling the wives about her "funny" stomach and the reason behind it. Kim's tongue pushed hard against the side of her cheek, but she just smiled back. Jessie wouldn't say anything; she'd promised. Besides, she was a nurse. Even though she wasn't working right now, didn't she have some kind of professional duty to patient privacy?

Kim wasn't about to let Jessie pressure her into saying anything before she was ready. As Marianne arrived a moment later, Kim caught Jessie's eyes again, and they exchanged a knowing look of understanding. "I'm okay," Kim mouthed.

Jessie nodded absently, message received. "Marianne! Come here," she said, scooting over. Marianne shrugged out of her jacket and sat down.

"I already know what I want, so we can order right away," she said, noting the server walking toward them.

They placed their orders, and as they waited for their food, they updated one another on any news they'd gotten from their husbands, especially since the men were now in Afghanistan, so the deployment took on a whole new meaning. They were dealing with the enemy on a regular basis.

But their individual news reports still had some positives. Tim and Justin kept up their pranks, like stealing Brian's clothes from the shower when he was in it. Brenda mentioned a prayer Colonel Lambert offered that meant a lot to Rick. Another soldier wanted to be baptized after Brian had taught him about the Church and had given him a copy of the Book of Mormon he'd brought with him. But underlying all the chitchat was an unspoken anxiety.

Now their men were regularly in harm's way.

When the food arrived, Jessie spread her napkin on her lap and asked, "So Marianne, how did McKayla survive a dateless Homecoming?"

Marianne snorted as she picked up her fork. "Barely, if you believe her side of the story." She rolled her eyes. "She and two of her friends—one who didn't have a date and one whose parents are *also* mean and wouldn't let her go before her sixteenth birthday—dressed up in all black and went out to dinner and a movie."

"All black?" Nora said.

"Said they were in mourning," Marianne explained. "Cute, huh? I know the teenage years are full of drama, but I *swear* I was never that bad."

"I think *I* was," Kim said, a sharp chuckle coming from her throat. There was some laugher behind it but a lot of pain, too. "My parents practically disowned me by the time I moved out." Wondering if she'd revealed a bit too much about her life from just a couple of years ago, she shoved a fry into her mouth and hoped someone else would speak up.

The truth was her mother was probably *still* thinking about disowning her. At twenty, she'd barely exited her teens, so those years of angst were still pretty fresh. She remembered what it was like to not go to senior prom—especially after she'd heard rumors of no fewer than five different guys who planned to ask her to it. *All* of her girl friends went to the dance. Every single one of them—three of them with guys she'd thought were going to ask her out. Staying home that night was humiliating, and the wound still festered. She still had no idea why none of the guys had asked her. The best she could come up with was that they all thought another one would ask, so they all asked different girls.

"Oh, I doubt you were that bad," Marianne said, patting Kim's arm.

Kim wanted to shy away from the touch as if it were her mother's hand. She had an idea of what McKayla was feeling right now—anger at her mother for not letting her go, for sure. But it was probably also a lot of being misunderstood, that her mother didn't *get* how important Homecoming was to her. The way Marianne brushed it aside as something trivial said a lot. Sure, a single date in high school might not mean much when looked at from a grown-up, parent perspective. But Kim knew how much those things mattered when you were in high school. They were everything.

"I bet that night was really hard on her," Kim said, twisting her glass and avoiding Marianne's eyes. "Does she get that you know that?"

"I . . . well . . ." Marianne fumbled for something to say.

Kim's eyes stung. Of course McKayla didn't know her mother understood, because Marianne most definitely *didn't* understand. "It might help if you tell her you're sorry," she suggested.

Nora tilted her head in consideration—as if maybe Kim had a point—but Marianne's brow furrowed. She stabbed her salad, her tone becoming terse as she spoke. "But I'm *not* sorry. She's the one acting disrespectful to me. She's the one who made it out as if this dance was the sun and the moon and that her entire universe almost collapsed on itself. But it was just a stupid dance. One night of her life."

Jessie looked up from cutting her chicken. "But how do you get them to understand how little a dance matters?" She shook her head as if shuddering. "I'm terrified for when Alex and Becca will be teenagers. As toddlers, they already make everything into a soap opera. Can you imagine how bad it'll be in ten or fifteen years?"

"Makes me glad I have all boys," Brenda said with a grin. "They may beat each other up and knock holes in the walls, but there won't be any estrogen-based roller coasters in our house. At least none that don't start with me." She chuckled and took a bite of her burger.

Kim could understand the exasperation all of these women were experiencing—now that she wasn't in high school anymore. Sure, it was a "stupid" dance. Only one night. But prom still impacted her even if it was over two years ago. In some ways, it still mattered. It still stung. One night or not, it was a mark on her emotional calendar that would always be there. But how could she explain that to Marianne without coming across like an immature high school kid? Didn't they remember what it was like?

She sank into her seat as if it might help camouflage her even as she spoke up. "Right now, school and friends *are* her universe. She can't see what you can yet. It may seem silly to you, but I'm sure it was a really big deal to her."

Marianne's fork paused midair. She glanced over. "I guess," she said in a noncommittal tone before putting the bite in her mouth.

Somewhat encouraged, Kim tried again. "Maybe . . . maybe if she knows how much you care about her feelings, she'd be more willing to listen to your advice next time." She shrugged and played with the zipper on her pink hoodie. "I mean, maybe. I would have liked it if my mom had done that."

"It's worth a try." Marianne sighed. "I hate seeing her so upset, and I do feel bad that she's hurting. But it's hard to sympathize when her problems seem so ridiculous."

Nora leaned forward and raised a hand, which always commanded everyone's attention. These were the moments she imparted advice—and so far she'd been right every time. "Kim's got something there."

"Really?" Kim's eyes went wide. She didn't expect Nora, of all people, to defend her.

"Really," Nora said with an encouraging smile. "Think of it this way. Remember when McKayla was learning to walk? That was a big deal. I'm sure she fell and cried with frustration and pain, right?"

Marianne smiled wistfully as if remembering her baby girl and her first steps. "Of course."

"Would you have thought those tears silly or ridiculous? After all, walking is no big deal to *you* anymore. It's easy." Nora raised her eyebrows, and Marianne nodded, getting the point. "Or maybe when she was learning how to print her name in kindergarten. Was that hard for her? Did she ever get frustrated over it? It's easy for *you*. Did you roll your eyes at her then?"

"No, of course not. And you're right." Marianne nodded in surrender. "'Hard' is subjective. McKayla's not a miniature adult, so I shouldn't expect her to act like one."

Feeling bolder, Kim sat straighter and said, "Yeah. Her problems are big to *her*. Someday she'll have bigger ones, and then these things will seem little. But for now, in her world, they matter."

Brenda rubbed her forehead. "You know, sometimes I wish I could go back to those days, only experience them with my current maturity. Wouldn't it be nice to have those kinds of problems *and* be able to deal with them? It would be a cake walk." She shook her head. "I'd take having a dateless Homecoming today if it meant Rick was home, not in harm's way for another ten months."

The table lapsed into quiet agreement, several ladies nodding.

"I think we all would," Nora said, the voice of the group. "This is one of the hardest times you'll ever have. But you know what? You'll also learn things about yourself that you never expected. Each of you will come out the other end stronger, more confident, and amazed at the women you've become. And it will all be because of the challenges deployment put on you. It's a refiner's fire. It feels awfully hot now, but on the other side, just wait. You'll be gold."

Chapter 8: Jessie
Supervision

Thursday, September 24, 2009

Jessie loaded the kids into the minivan and headed over to Kim's place. After seeing her at lunch yesterday, she wasn't about to let the girl do anything else stupid that might put her or her baby at risk. Kim still needed to be horizontal as much as possible.

Jessie parked on the road outside the apartment building and unloaded her crew, juggling the infant carrier, holding Becca's hand, and insisting that Alex hang on to Mommy's pocket. "Alex, get back here. Don't run into the road!" Jessie called, shoving the van door the rest of the way shut with her hip. Alex reluctantly returned and slipped her fingers through Jessie's belt loop. Not her pocket, but close enough. "Good. Now stay on the sidewalk. These are much busier streets than we have around our house."

As they hobbled up the metal stairs of the fourplex, she reflected how very similar this was to the first time she'd met Kim. She'd been juggling the kids the same way then, only going from the van to Chili's. The day could not come fast enough where going somewhere with all of them didn't take as much effort as putting on a Broadway production. Alex jumped up and down on the metal stairs.

"It makes a funny noise. Listen, Mama." Alex screwed up her face and jumped hard with both feet.

"I know, honey. Neat. Come on," Jessie said, trying not to sound impatient.

They passed the first apartment, the carrier bumping against her leg with each step, and reached Kim's wide kitchen window. The eighties-vintage brown curtains were mostly drawn, but through a four-inch crack, Jessie could make out a stack of dishes in the sink. At least Kim hadn't been overdoing it with cleaning up, she thought to herself wryly. As she reached the door, she released Becca's hand and pointed to the other set of stairs with a firm "Don't go near those" and debated whether to put down the baby carrier while she waited for Kim to answer.

But before she even knocked, a shrill noise sounded inside, and the door flew open. The side of Kim's head appeared. She was looking into the kitchen while holding onto the knob and waving the door back and forth as if fanning the room. The shrill noise—the smoke detector—was louder now. Within seconds it stopped, and Kim turned to close the door. Only then did she notice her visitors.

"Oh! Jessie," she said, obviously startled. She gestured toward the kitchen sheepishly. "Stupid toaster always sets off the smoke alarm. Have to air out the place to get it to shut up." She opened the door and waved them in. "Come in."

"Thanks," Jessie said, ushering the kids inside. Becca had both hands over her ears and tears welling in her eyes. "It's okay, sweetie. The sound won't come back. Let's go in."

Jessie had to take Becca's arm to lead her over the threshold then turned back to Alex, who was eyeing the metal steps as if they beckoned to her. "Come on in, Alex. Now." With a regretful sigh, the little girl obeyed. As the apartment door closed behind them, Jessie added, "Sorry to descend on you like this." Once at the couch, she immediately pulled out all kinds of tools of the trade from the diaper bag: a rattle for the baby, two packs of fruit snacks for the older girls, plus a board book for Becca and some crayons and a coloring book for Alex. When all three kids were happily settled, she turned to her hostess, who looked at her blankly.

"Wow," Kim said, sitting opposite on the matching, seventies-style gold love seat. The upholstery on it looked brand new. Must be made of that polyester stuff that never wore out, Jessie figured. Kim eyed the kids and then Jessie. "You're good."

"Oh, you learn," Jessie said with a shrug. "Mothers have to be more prepared than Boy Scouts."

They watched the kids for a second before Kim asked, "So . . . what brings you here?"

"I wanted to be sure you're doing all right," Jessie said. She took in Kim's appearance—white T-shirt, pink sweat pants, her hair in a sloppy ponytail. No makeup. That was all good; it probably meant Kim hadn't been up and around too much. And at the very least, it was an indication that she hadn't gone to work. She might not have even left the house for grocery shopping.

"I'm doing good," Kim said. "The nausea's going away. My jeans are getting really uncomfortable, though. That's why I wear sweats most of the time."

"What about the bleeding?" Jessie asked. No reason to beat around the bush.

"It's good," Kim said evasively.

"Good as in *gone* or good as in *going away* or good as in *not too heavy*?"

When Kim looked at the ceiling, not answering, Jessie pressed on. "Have you talked to Eleanor about it?"

Kim grunted. "What are you, my mother? I said it's *fine*." Kim stood and went to the fridge. She yanked the door open and withdrew a can of soda. She seemed to hesitate for a second then pulled out a second one.

"Look . . . I'm sorry," Jessie said. "After lunch yesterday, I worried that maybe you were overdoing it. I want you to take care of yourself."

"And the baby," Kim added. She handed Jessie one of the cans, popped open her own, and sat on the far corner of the love seat, one arm folded across her chest.

"Well, yeah. Of course."

"I'm fine." Kim leveled a stare at Jessie, who raised her palms in surrender.

"Okay. I was just checking." Her hands slapped against her thighs, and she looked around. "But as long as I'm here, can I do anything for you? Run some errands, vacuum, take a few loads of laundry with me?"

Kim raked her fingers through her hair. "Sure. If you want." She stared off into the corner. Jessie shifted uncomfortably. Joey began fussing, and Jessie thankfully turned her attention to him.

"It's okay, buddy," she soothed, rocking the carrier. She fished into the diaper bag for a cracker for him to gum. It quieted him right away.

But then Becca got tired of her board book and climbed into her lap. The little girl put her pudgy hands on Jessie's cheeks and declared, "Mama, I wanna go."

"I know. We'll go soon." Jessie pulled Becca's hands away and turned her around on her lap. Her attention reverted to Kim. "Now, give me all your laundry and a list of things to get at the store."

Kim looked incredulous. "Are you serious? You've got kids climbing all over you, and you want to worry about me?"

It was true. Becca had wriggled back around and thrown her arms around Jessie, and now Alex climbed up behind her mother and seemed to be scaling Everest in the form of Jessie's back. Jessie again pulled their arms off her neck so she could actually breathe and said, "Let me. Please?"

"All right," Kim said with a shake of her head. "It's your life." Kim stood and headed for a back room, where Jessie assumed the laundry was kept. Jessie extricated herself from the girls and hurried after.

"Don't carry any baskets," Jessie warned. "I'll do that."

The bedroom had an unmade bed, clothes scattered about, and a few takeout containers lying around. Kim turned and folded her arms as the girls tagged along and Joey began shrieking because he could no longer see his family. "Jess, how do you think you're going to carry a laundry basket *and* deal with your kids?"

Jessie grinned. "You get to watch the kids while I walk the laundry out to the car."

"Oh . . . okay," Kim said hesitantly—as if she were terrified of touching a child.

"As long as you promise to lie down the minute I'm back inside," Jessie added quickly. "I'll even make you some more toast before we go out so you don't have to get up for that."

Jessie followed Kim into the room, stepping over a pair of discarded high heels and a stack of books on her way to the closet. Kim pointed to it. "Most of the dirty stuff is in there." She began scooping clothes from the floor and dumping them into the basket.

When it was full, she paused and turned back to Jessie. After a second, she finally spit out, "Really. Why are you doing this?"

"Because I care. I'm a nurse and a mom. It comes with the territory." She shrugged and smiled. "And I have an idea of how hard this must be for you."

Kim's eyes grew watery. She looked away and tracked the white wall down to the floor. "Thanks for coming," she said thickly. She seemed about to say something else but then must have thought better of it, because she clamped her mouth shut.

"What?" Jessie touched her arm. "What's wrong?"

"Can you keep a secret?" Kim asked.

"I'm already keeping one, remember?" Jessie said, smiling wryly. "But I'm game for another."

Kim took a few steps back and sat on the bed. Jessie followed suit. Joey had quieted from the other room—maybe he'd found his Binky—and the girls both climbed onto the bed and began jumping. The two women abandoned the mattress and sat on the floor to avoid the jouncing and keep the toddlers happy.

"I feel like something's wrong with me," Kim began.

Immediately, Jessie's mind went to the medical side of things. "Should we have Eleanor check you? What are your symptoms?"

"It's not that." Kim sniffed and gazed out the window over Jessie's shoulder.

"Then what?"

"I've never, *ever* wanted to be a mom. I've never liked kids. Even when I was a little girl, I didn't like playing with dolls. I *hate* cooking. I don't even know how to sew on a button." She hugged herself tight. "Almost every lesson I heard in Young Women was something I couldn't relate to. Half the activities were things like, 'Ooh, let's learn to bake bread or quilt or can peaches.' I hated it all."

Jessie pulled her knees to her chest and tried to think of what to say. "There are different kinds of women and moms, each with their own strengths and weaknesses. Just because you don't like quilting doesn't mean you won't be a good mom."

"But shouldn't I love those things just because I'm a girl? What kind of excuse for a woman *am* I?"

A lump formed in Jessie's throat. She'd asked herself that same question lots of times. While she'd always wanted kids and loved being a mom, motherhood—as much as she loved it—didn't fill her up one hundred percent. She'd always needed a few nursing hours here and there to fill up the rest of herself. Going a couple of months without those hours had been hard since Tim left. What did that say about her as a mom?

Then there was her less-than-stellar marriage. She'd married Tim thinking that their wedding marked the beginning of happily-ever-after. They'd gotten married in the right place by the right authority. Didn't that mean they were entitled to some kind of warranty?

What kind of woman was *she* when she was happier now than she'd been in years and knew full well it was because her husband wasn't around? She couldn't relate to the "marital bliss" idea—and wondered where she'd gone astray. There wasn't much she could do about it. She wouldn't violate her covenants, and Tim hadn't violated his. No grounds for divorce.

Kim tilted her head to catch her eye. "Jess? You okay?"

She put on a smile and returned to the present. "Nothing's wrong with you. Every woman is different." She put a hand over Kim's. "Having a baby is scary, but you know what? I have a feeling that when this baby gets here, you'll fall head-over-heels in love with it and won't be able to imagine *not* being a mom."

"You think so?" Kim's voice held a shade of hope.

"I think so," Jessie said with a nod.

I wish I could say the same for me. She could imagine all too well *not* being a wife. And liking it. The fact ashamed her.

But as long as she kept busy helping Kim, she wouldn't have to think too much about it.

Chapter 9: Brenda
Discovery

Saturday, October 3, 2009

As Brenda pulled into a parking spot at Discovery Park in Pleasant Grove, she pointed toward the boy standing beside Marianne at the park entrance. "Look, Bradley. That must be Kevin."

"He's the one a little older than me, right?" Bradley asked.

"Right," Brenda said. She hardly got the car stopped before Bradley and the twins had unbuckled themselves, tumbled out of the minivan, and bolted toward the huge, all-wood playground.

"Cool!" Bradley yelled over his shoulder, pointing to one end of the park. "Look, Mom! That part looks like a giant volcano or something!"

Brenda was about call out to Bradley and officially introduce him to Kevin, but the two boys apparently had an instant connection and ran off together toward the wooden volcano.

The other wives were already there as well, gathered on the benches at the entrance. This week's lunch was at a park on a weekend rather than at a restaurant during the school day. The idea was for their kids to meet one another. Brenda waved at the wives as she hurried after the twins. She showed them the southern side of the park, which was more suited to their preschool age than the big tire swing and other activities on the north end, where their big brother had run off to. Then, with the twins playing in the wooden T-Rex head and roaring at one another, she plopped on a bench, grateful for the shade trees behind her.

"We made it," she announced breathlessly.

"How long do you think they'll be happy out there?" Jessie nodded toward the wooden beehives in the younger kid area, where Alex and Becca were playing hide-and-seek.

Marianne shaded her eyes as she watched the kids. "I'm guessing they'll play a good hour before getting tired and realizing they're hungry. This is a fun park. Lots to do." Her older daughters were watching out for the toddlers, obviously enamored with their job of babysitting.

Jessie sighed with contentment and jounced her youngest on her lap. "I have to say, it's *so nice* to be able to sit here with just the baby instead of having to run around after the girls. Your daughters are lifesavers."

"They're happy to do it," Marianne said.

Bailey was showing Alex how to use the pipes at different areas to talk to each other, and Alex was laughing hysterically at something Bailey must have said through one of them.

Nora stood and stretched. "It's good to be outside in the sun." She headed for the walkway into the play area. "I'll go see if Brenda's boys would like a granny to play with."

"Thanks, Nora," Brenda said, impressed. There had been a time when she, too, enjoyed racing after kids and playing with them. She'd done more of that stuff when Tyler was three. But having twins drained every last bit of energy out of her. Of course, she shouldn't have been surprised that Wonder Woman Nora jumped into the fray. All she needed was the lasso and golden tiara.

She'd probably even fit into Lynda Carter's costume, Brenda thought dismally as she watched Nora walk off. *And I'm a tub of lard.*

Jessie and Marianne started chatting about some shoe sale they'd both stumbled on, and Brenda listened, not contributing because she really wasn't much of a shoe person. Good thing, because she couldn't afford anything pricier than a fifteen-dollar pair of sneakers at Payless.

After a minute, she noticed Kim, who sat facing the little kid area, watching something over there. "I think I'll go help Nora with Brenda's twins," Kim said suddenly, standing up.

Marianne and Jessie's conversation stopped mid-syllable. Jessie paused and gave what seemed to be a significant—somewhat perplexed but maybe impressed, too?—look at Kim, who smiled back nervously.

"Thanks," Brenda said, unsure of what had transpired between Kim and Jessie. Something had, no question, but she supposed it wasn't any of her business.

Jessie's nose crinkled up. She lifted Joey's bottom to her nose then made a face. "Oooh, he's ripe. Gotta change the little guy." She headed for the parking lot, leaving just Marianne sitting opposite Brenda.

They sat in awkward silence for a minute, Brenda trying to decide whether to force herself into starting up a conversation or if she could wait until Jessie returned to act as a conversational buffer. The plain and sad truth was that Brenda didn't connect with Marianne. They were in different stages—the teen years versus the toddler years—and, judging by that one conversation they had at lunch awhile back, Marianne apparently looked down on Brenda for thinking that she had a stressful life with three little ones.

It's so much harder with teens, is it? Brenda thought. Not only was the idea devastating—was there *never* a point where motherhood got easier?—but it was as if Marianne had been trivializing what Brenda went through every day.

What could the two of them talk about? Anything Brenda brought up would be something Marianne had gone through nearly a decade ago. Either she'd brush it off as a silly topic, or she'd bestow her mature "wisdom" about it. In reality, Brenda could use some advice on *re*-potty-training the twins, but she wasn't about to ask Marianne for it. Nora would be a better resource. Even though she was in the grandmother stage, she wouldn't put Brenda down for struggling with the twins' having at least ten accidents every day between the two of them. Their regression went back to the deployment, she was sure. Before Rick left, the house hadn't seen a yellow puddle in nearly four months.

"Um, Brenda?"

Marianne's voice pulled her out of her thoughts with a soft tone, making her instantly contrite for such negative feelings. "Yeah?"

"I've been thinking a lot about something I said a few weeks ago."

Stiffening, Brenda was quite sure she knew which conversation Marianne meant. The same one *she'd* been thinking about. "Uh-huh?" she said hesitantly.

"I'm afraid I owe you an apology. It was unfair of me to belittle you like that."

All the emotions from that lunch rushed back, and it was a struggle for Brenda to say, "Um, that's okay. Thanks."

"Last week, Nora kind of touched me, you know, with what she said about how kids' problems are big to them?"

Okay, so was Marianne comparing Brenda to a child? Her forehead wrinkled in dismay and confusion. She didn't say anything, letting Marianne continue.

"What Nora and Kim said got me thinking about how you really can't judge another person's trials. Trials are trials, you know? For me, the teenage years really *are* hard—much harder than the baby years were. But then, that could be because I've got holy terrors as teenagers, and I never had a baby with colic or reflux or chronic ear infections or anything like that. Heck, McKayla slept through the night when she was three months old."

One side of Brenda's mouth curved up a bit at that. Maybe Marianne wasn't so bad.

"I've been trying to sort out why it's harder for me now—because I think it really is," Marianne continued. "But I also realized that I wasn't really remembering the struggles of the baby years. There were times when I was barely hanging on, trying to get through a few more hours until bedtime."

Brenda smiled wider. *She remembers. A little.*

Marianne shifted on the bench, leaning closer to Brenda. "See, I think I figured out part of it. When kids are little, the stress is mostly physical. They ask so much of you between nighttime feedings and diaper changes and naps and baths. It's physically draining keeping up with them and cleaning their messes and all that. When they're older, they can dress themselves, feed themselves, clean up after themselves, and sleep all night. A lot of the physical stress goes away. Right?"

"Right," Brenda said, not sure where Marianne was going with this but willing to give her a chance to redeem herself further.

"But see, all that physical stuff is pretty black and white. Either the baby has a full tummy or she's hungry. Either she's got a clean diaper or a stinky one. Either she's bathed or she's filthy. The mom is on a hamster wheel to get it all done, but there's a pretty clear to-do list." She paused as if in thought. "And that's where the stress comes in when they're older. You have all kinds of new problems, with school and peer pressure and spiritual things—but there *isn't* a to-do list on how to deal with any of it. Nothing's clear-cut anymore."

Marianne shook her head and threw her hands up. "Suddenly your kid is old enough to make mistakes that can hurt other people, influence their own futures, and here you are, expected to guide them through this labyrinth when *you* don't even know which direction they should go sometimes. And the few times you *do* know which way to turn, your kid doesn't want to go that way—and you can't make them. You can't send them to time-out anymore. You can't do their homework for them. You can't be there when they're faced with friends trying to get them to do something totally stupid and life-changing. You can't implant a testimony into their hearts. You teach them the best you can then sit back, biting your nails, hoping that when all is said and done, they turn out all right."

When Marianne finished, she had tears in her eyes. She shook her head and sniffed. "Sorry." She rubbed at her eyes with the back of her finger then looked at the wooden walkway. "It's been a hard week with McKayla."

Brenda felt a flood of compassion for Marianne. They were both mothers in different stages, experiencing very different things, but in the end, they were both on the same team, striving for the same thing—a bright and happy future for their children. Marianne was right: teens had the power to make decisions that could drastically change their own lives and others' lives.

Marianne's words brought to mind an incident from Brenda's high school years, something she hadn't thought about in ages—a massive car accident involving five students from her senior class. All but one of the teens in the car died, and that one had major injuries that led to multiple surgeries and years of physical therapy. Slick roads and excessive speed were blamed. In the blink of an eye, five families were changed forever.

She thought about Bradley behind a wheel in eight and a half years, propelling a huge steel weapon down neighborhood streets. The image made her stomach lurch.

And then there was the spiritual side of things. What if her boys never got personal testimonies? As their mother, she could take them to church and read scriptures with them and pray and hold regular family home evenings, but in the end, she couldn't give them her testimony. That was a personal possession they had to find for themselves. What if one of them fell away from the Church when he grew up? Her heart would break.

Cleaning up potty accidents suddenly sounded preferable.

"I never thought of it like that," she said, chuckling through sudden emotion. "Now I almost wish they'd stay little, where I can control their world and make sure they're safe. When they get older, I'll be a basket case."

"You'll do fine," Marianne said. "Remember, it's not like you'll get a fifteen-year-old overnight. They grow up a year at a time."

A pause followed, and then Brenda asked, "But it goes awfully fast, doesn't it?"

"It does," Marianne agreed, gazing at her daughters walking Alex and Becca across a wooden bridge and making it bounce. It made the little girls howl with laughter.

Jessie followed close behind, resting Joey on one hip, apparently done with the diaper change and having fun with her kids. Marianne's youngest, Kevin, trailed after Jessie, looking up at her with apparent stars in his eyes. His first crush.

"I think he's smitten," Marianne said wanly then turned back to face Brenda. "Sometimes when they're little, though, there are times when it feels like the baby years will never end, doesn't it?"

"Yeah." Brenda smiled. A finger to the corner of her eye came away wet.

She remembers. Now.

"Yeah, it does."

Chapter 10: Jessie
Relief—and Guilt

"Marianne, are you all right?" Nora asked over lunch, a clump of Appleby's oriental chicken salad perched on her fork.

Jessie hadn't noticed anything amiss with Marianne. She looked over and realized that, yes, she did look drawn, and she had blue-tinged circles under her eyes.

Marianne smiled weakly. "Oh, I'm all right. I'm just not sleeping well."

That explains it, Jessie thought, dragging a fry through a puddle of ketchup. *We're all under stress, though.*

"It's hard to change your sleeping patterns after so many years of sleeping beside someone else, you know?" Marianne sighed and twisted her glass side to side, staring at the bubbles rising in her soda. "Brian always has his arm around me as I fall asleep. I didn't realize how it relaxed me at night—not until he was gone. I've tried imagining him being there—holding me—but it doesn't work that well when his side of the bed is empty and cold. His pillowcase doesn't even smell like him anymore." She lifted one shoulder in a shrug. "You'd think that after two and a half months I'd be used to it already, but it's one more thing to adapt to, right?"

"Yeah, I guess so," Jessie said, nodding sympathetically with the rest of the group. She wasn't about to mention that she loved having the bed to herself. Tim always stole the covers and snored. And because she ran cold, he'd never let her snuggle close.

"Sheesh!" he'd say, pulling his feet away from her icy toes. "I'm not your radiator." Did it ever occur to him that if he'd let her have some covers, maybe she wouldn't try to warm up on *him*?

Now that he wasn't in the bed, Jessie slept better than she ever had since their wedding day. Sure, she missed him, in a way. She loved him, so she worried about his safety and had anxiety about what would happen to their little family if he were killed or wounded in action. But she hadn't reached the point of wishing he were both out of danger *and* home.

"What about dinners, though?" Jessie threw out, hoping to lighten the dreary mood around the table. "That's one small bright spot in all this, right? No more trying to have a hot meal on the table when Daddy gets home from work." She waited for the reaction, hoping the other women would agree with her.

To her relief, Brenda chuckled. "Rick would freak out if he knew how often I'm feeding the kids macaroni and cheese or peanut butter and jam sandwiches."

"Or letting them scrounge for a snack from the pantry," Marianne said, as if it were a confession.

Brenda laughed out loud, putting down her drink before she spilled it. "I've got a plastic bin on the bottom shelf of the pantry that's for snacks they can grab anytime they want. All the neighborhood kids know about it and come over for fruit snacks and goldfish crackers."

"Me too!" Jessie said, laughing so hard she snorted. "They don't realize that half the time, that's also their dinner."

After the laughter died down, Nora chimed in. "I'm missing Russell *because* of dinners. Over the last year, he started cooking, and I cleaned up." She leaned back and sighed, a contented look on her face. "I can tell you, after cooking every night for thirty-five years, it's been wonderful to have someone else do it. Now I have to cook for myself again." She leaned forward and picked at her salad some more.

The entire table seemed to grow quiet as, presumably, the wives thought of all the things they missed about their husbands. Everyone but Jessie. With two of the women on one side of the table and three on the other, she was the one hanging out on the end, almost like a fifth wheel.

And I am the fifth wheel, she realized. *I'm the only one not really missing her husband. I worry about him. But that's not the same thing.*

She remembered what Kim had said before: *What kind of excuse for a woman am I?*

What was wrong with her? Why had she expected the other women to react the same way she did? She had come to lunch today thinking that they could all laugh at the things their husbands did that drove them crazy—and how nice it was to have a break from it all. Already she had a lengthy—and growing—mental list of the kinds of things she assumed the others would share with her.

Leaving his smelly clothes on the floor.

Rarely eating with her and the kids at the table and leaving early when he did—and always expecting her to put his dishes away.

Never ever helping with the housework—and complaining like a martyr if she asked him to do something as simple as take the garbage out.

Not helping with the kids unless she asked specifically—and again, she'd get the martyr act every time.

Taking months to get any basic home repairs done. She might be able to make the time shorter if she became a nag, but she didn't want to be one, so she rarely asked more than twice. Sometimes she went ahead and taught herself how to do the repair. The time she fixed a broken tile on the bathroom floor suddenly annoyed Tim.

"I could have done it so you couldn't even tell where the broken one used to be," he said.

Then you should have done it yourself sometime in the last six months, she said to herself, wanting to storm off. Instead she said, "It had been a while, and I wanted it fixed. I thought I did a pretty good job." She had walked out at that point, not wanting to linger and see the continued disappointment on Tim's face. Sure, he *could* have fixed it beautifully. But he didn't. Jessie didn't want to wait until next year—or whenever he was finally in the mood to do it—especially when there were plenty of other home maintenance things waiting for Tim's attention.

But the worst was the mental and emotional games, the way he manipulated everything into sounding like it was *her* fault, losing his temper over trivial things. She could never predict what would set him off, and she often double- and triple-checked scenarios, walking on proverbial egg shells and smashing them regardless of how careful she tried to be.

"Oh, I need to go," Kim said, pulling Jessie back to the present as she glanced at her watch. "I have to be back to work in twenty minutes." She dug into her purse and withdrew a ten-dollar bill. "Will you guys take care of my tab?"

"Of course," Jessie said, taking the money as Kim pushed her chair back and got up. Everyone else was at eye level with her stomach as she hitched her purse over her shoulder.

Nora stared at her obviously round and protruding tummy and smiled. No way could it mean anything but what Jessie already knew it was.

Nora pointed at it with her fork and raised her eyebrows. "Kim?" she said, the tines bobbing up and down. "Do you have something to tell us?"

Kim's hands flew to cover her swollen belly, where her scrubs were tight. She and Jessie exchanged looks. She smiled sympathetically and shrugged to show that she'd kept the secret and to remind Kim that it would have had to come out sometime.

"I—um . . ." Kim closed her eyes and sighed. Her body slumped. "Yeah. I'm almost four months along."

The other ladies followed the announcement with cheers of excitement and congratulations. Jessie pretended it was all news to her.

"Of course, this isn't the way I would have planned it," Kim went on. "You know, seeing as how Justin won't be here until the baby's crawling or something, but—"

"But it's so exciting!" Brenda said. "You'll be a great mom."

"When are you due?" Nora interjected.

"Late March. The twenty-fourth." Kim swallowed and laughed nervously. "It was . . . a surprise."

"Don't you worry about a thing; we'll all help you," Jessie said.

"Of course we will," said Marianne. "Good gracious, girl, why did you keep this a secret from us for so long?"

Kim laughed awkwardly. "Thanks, guys," she said, playing with the key chain to avoid answering Marianne's question. "I'd better go now. See you all next week. We're at what, Los Hermanos next time? The Provo one, right, not the one in Pleasant Grove?"

"Yep," Brenda said. "I'll be there early to down as much of their salsa as I can manage."

As Jessie watched Kim leave, she suddenly realized that Kim hadn't joined in the conversation about all the things they missed about their soldiers. Jessie knew Kim was nervous about the pregnancy, and that might explain the behavior. Maybe she felt the same way Jessie did—a bit of relief that Justin was gone, that she could call her life her own again? On the other hand, Kim hadn't been married long enough for any real peeves about her husband to form; the deployment orders had arrived on the heels of their honeymoon.

Seeing Kim leave for work brought back all those times it had felt like Tim kept Jessie on a leash. It was glorious to go out to lunch without having to account for when she'd be back; her mother was babysitting until she got home, whenever that would be. Heck, if she wanted to, she could go shopping right now. She could go to a movie after that and then visit a museum. And Tim would never know, so he'd never be able to bug her about it. If he made home more pleasant for her, maybe she'd want to hurry home instead of stay out longer and be late.

Today all she'd have to do was call her mom and ask if she could take care of the kids for the rest of the day. Mom wouldn't bat an eye—and she wouldn't grill Jessie about where she was going and when she planned to return.

Freedom. *That's* what she was feeling. Sure, her evenings could be long and lonely. At times she missed Tim's smell and went into the bathroom just to open his bottle of cologne and sniff it. She loved his eyes, his smile. His kisses. But there was so much more she didn't miss.

That accusatory look on his face. The terse tone in his voice. The oppressive air, pushing down on her as she walked around, trying not to crack those stupid eggshells.

I feel like an imposter in this group, she thought, putting on a smile and continuing to chat with the other three ladies as they finished their meals. They'd never know how she really felt. As far as they were concerned, she and Tim were perfectly happy, and they had an ideal marriage.

She'd keep the truth to herself.

Chapter 11: Kim
Confession

The computer chimed, and Kim leaned forward to read Justin's instant message.

Miss u.

She smiled, feeling giddy as if she were flirting with her boyfriend over the Internet. Sometimes that's what it felt like—as if she and Justin were still dating, since they'd been married for such a short time when he left. Sitting in a pair of Justin's old sweats, she set aside her bowl of Kellogg's Frosted Flakes—tonight's dinner—to respond.

Miss u 2.

She pressed ENTER and sat back with her bowl. She scooped a bite as she waited for Justin's next response. He'd said he had about fifteen minutes before needing to report on duty. It was morning for him—well after breakfast—but bedtime for her.

After all the talk about husbands at today's lunch, she missed Justin even more than usual. The apartment felt bigger, emptier. And there was a little worm of guilt in her chest that she still hadn't told him about the baby. The wives all knew now. It was "high time" her husband knew, as her mother would say. At least, she'd say that if *she* knew.

Legs crossed, Kim bobbed one foot up and down, sending one Pooh Bear slipper bouncing. Justin bought them for her at Disneyland on their honeymoon. He'd almost gone for the *101 Dalmatians* ones, but she'd talked him out of it, saying that they were a little too close to something Cruella DeVille would wear.

Justin is typing, the screen announced. She got a little thrill in her middle, exactly as she had when they were dating and she'd stay up for hours at night instant messaging him. She glanced at her wedding ring, a visual reminder that she was, in fact, already his wife, not just flirting with a guy she'd met a year and a half ago.

The program paused, and she got impatient. He was probably interrupted by someone. She pictured one of the wives' husbands walking past and talking with Justin then moving on before he could get back to the keyboard.

As she waited, her hand went to her swelling tummy, and she pressed her lips together, hard. She was *more* than married to Justin—she was having his baby. She needed to tell him, but how, this late in the game? She wouldn't be able to share in his excitement, not when she still felt so conflicted about the baby in the first place.

She could still hardly believe that there was a life growing inside her. *I'm too young,* she thought. When she missed a period back in July, she hadn't been all that concerned. Life had been topsy-turvy then, what with being newly married, moving into their apartment, and then—wham!—getting Justin's deployment orders and shipping him off for a year. With all that going on, it would have been more surprising if her cycle *hadn't* been out of whack, so she didn't think much of it and didn't mention it to Justin either.

When she missed her period the first week of August right after he left, she brushed away the worry, not even taking a home test. Pregnancy might explain why she'd felt so *off* lately, but Justin leaving could have also explained it.

Ever since her older sisters got married, Kim had assumed she'd have trouble having kids, because her sisters did. Getting pregnant so fast was a shock, but she still assumed that since her sister Lori had had three miscarriages before carrying a baby to term, and her other sister, Jana, miscarried twice, that she'd follow suit the first time around at least. Even under all her nerves, she hadn't been too worried at first that this pregnancy would last, so why tell Justin about it?

Biology class aside, Kim hadn't believed that getting pregnant would happen so fast—especially when they had planned *against* it.

Even science is only ninety-nine percent effective when used correctly, she reminded herself. And she wasn't one hundred percent sure she'd been faithful about her pill, which only stacked the odds against her.

Justin's message came though.

We're having a big party for Halloween.

Already? Kim asked.

We're only planning it now, Justin typed after a minute. *Something to look forward to.*

Good idea, she said. *What are you planning?*

Some of the guys are making a piñata using a bunch of hard candy they got from care packages. Anything soft like chocolate melts before it gets here.

Kim had no big plans for Halloween, at least not yet. She hadn't thought three weeks ahead. But suddenly she realized that in a couple of years, Halloween would mean dressing up her kid as a pirate or a princess and walking around the neighborhood with a hollow plastic pumpkin. It didn't feel like all that many years ago when *she* was the one dressing up and going door to door.

She put her fingers on the keyboard and typed back. *Sounds fun.* What would he think of the care package she sent yesterday? There wasn't much he could donate to a piñata from it, just some of his favorite things—sour cream and onion Pringles, a box of Lucky Charms, the newest book by James Patterson, and some calamine lotion for the tick bites.

Real exciting stuff. She rolled her eyes at herself. She should come up with something better to send him next time.

You have any plans for Halloween? Justin asked.

Not much, she typed. *Answering the doorbell with a bowl of chocolate, I guess. Assuming I don't eat it first. Haha.*

As she and Justin chatted, she kept trying to find a way to work in the baby news. Ever since the wives' lunch earlier that day, she'd known she had to say something. She'd put it off for too long, living in denial, thinking that if she followed her sisters' footsteps, he'd never have to know, that this whole situation would go away on its own.

But every day, the baby was getting bigger and older. She'd started feeling kicks and small movements. All signs pointed to a healthy, normal pregnancy. She *had* to tell him. And when she did, how would she explain why she didn't say anything earlier?

What kind of horrible person did that make her, that she just assumed the problem would go away? That she saw a baby as a problem? Guilt ate at her from the inside out for thinking that. *What kind of mother doesn't want her baby?*

A lot of people didn't tell anyone they were expecting until the "danger" had passed, right? But "anyone" didn't include a woman's husband. And she'd passed the "danger" point—plus "Free Parking" and "Go"—some time ago.

Justin wrote about how he was now wearing a "Nacho Libre" mask on missions and how Tim had gotten hosed down on his birthday last week.

At least his birthday is in the fall. I'm hoping the tradition doesn't keep up—getting hosed down on my birthday in January would be killer.

I didn't know it got that cold over there, Kim wrote back.

The weather here isn't too different from Utah, Justin wrote. *Some of the mountains even look like home. So, yeah, it'll be pretty cold in January.*

Kim shuddered at the idea of getting hosed down during a Utah winter. *Remind me to send you some of those heat packs in your birthday package!*

Enough about me, Justin typed back. *Anything new over there?*

The question seemed to glow in neon letters. This was it, she thought. Time to make the big announcement.

Hands trembling, Kim typed, *Actually, there is something new.*

As soon as she hit ENTER, she pulled her fingers off the keyboard as if from a hot pan. How could she tell her husband about their baby in something as impersonal as an instant message? The news should be more special than that. Justin wanted to be a dad more than almost anything. Besides, an instant message made her readily available for his reaction. She didn't want to be there for the anger over her being almost halfway along without his knowing.

When she didn't type more, Justin came back with, *Oh? What?*

She panicked. She had to tell him something. Just not about the baby.

I'm going to redo our room, she wrote hurriedly. She hadn't had any plans of the kind, but she did now. *No worries—I won't make it too girlie.*

She added a smiley-face emoticon then sat back in the chair and breathed out shakily. She *still* had to find a way to tell him. An idea came to her. In a couple of weeks she'd have the ultrasound. She could get a picture of the baby printed out and mail *that* to him in her next care package. It'd be a great way for him to find out—actually *seeing* his baby. He'd even have a picture to hang beside his bed. Maybe it would show the baby's profile, its hand or foot. She'd be able to tell him whether they were having a boy or a girl.

I guess if the room doesn't end up purple or pink, I can't complain, Justin replied.

No worries, she wrote, hoping he'd read a light tone in her words. *That would clash with the orange shag.*

Then no *floral bedspread, k?*

K.

Gotta get to work now. Luv u. G'night.

Guilt washing over her again, Kim typed, *Luv u 2. Be safe.* She waited for a moment to be sure he wasn't going to send one more message. When he didn't, she sighed and whispered, "Oh, and Justin, you're going to be a daddy."

She lowered her eyes, feeling them burn with emotion, then touched her belly. "You're going to have a great dad. At least you'll get one good parent."

Kim reached for the mouse to close the program right when *Justin is typing* popped back up. The program dinged, and a new message appeared.

U still there?

She swallowed, wondering if this was a sign that she needed to tell him. Now.

Yep, she typed then sat back and held her breath. Maybe he didn't have to go to work after all. They could chat for a few more minutes.

? 4 u, Justin wrote.

Assuming he had something in mind for her to send him—like a CD or a U.S. treat—she looked for her notebook where she kept the list of things he'd asked for. The computer dinged again. She looked over.

Cl. Lambert just congratulated me. What's going on?

For a moment, Kim's lungs couldn't get air. She jumped to her feet and paced the room, hands over her mouth. She kept repeating a word she'd promised herself she'd stop using. *Of course* the wives would tell their husbands about the baby. There was no reason for them to think they shouldn't. But already? They'd known for just a few hours, for crying out loud.

It made sense that Justin's commanding officer was the first to mention it to Justin—Nora was probably pining for her grandkids and spilled the news to her husband the first chance she got.

"What do I say? What do I say?" she asked the ceiling.

The computer dinged again, and she found herself pulled close to read the text.

Is it true?

She dropped to the chair and nodded. "Yes," she said as she typed the same word, then hit ENTER and held her breath. Her fingers rushed on. *I didn't realize it until you were gone, and then I wanted to be sure I wouldn't lose it.* With her pinkie finger hovering over ENTER, she stopped herself. That wasn't entirely true.

She erased the message, but before she could replace it with anything else, a message from him popped up.

Why didn't you tell me?

She was tempted to retype what she'd written before, but Justin deserved better.

Didn't know how. At least that was honest.

Why not?

Why didn't she know how to tell him? How much time did he have? She couldn't go into all the reasons in an online chat; they were complicated. A phone call would be better. Even an e-mail. But chatting? No. Not when she couldn't put some thought into it or hear his voice to know his reaction. Even *she* didn't understand all of the reasons she'd kept the secret to herself.

How could she answer without him regretting that he married someone who didn't fit the "good Mormon girl" mold? Scared, confused, she debated what to say. The silence between them stretched out for more than a minute, Kim typing a word or a phrase and then deleting it.

Probably as a result of her hesitation, Justin finally wrote a single line. *Is it mine?*

Her jaw went slack. She hadn't for one minute thought his mind would go *there*. Who did he think he married?

Of course it's yours, she wrote, muttering, "Idiot." *I'm due in March. Do the math.* This time she sent the message with a smack of her finger and a bit of anger.

She watched the blinking cursor, which seemed accusatory, as if it were saying, "That—was—rude—that—was—rude."

"Fine," she said, feeling guilty. She sat up to the keyboard again. Her hands hovered above the keys, but she didn't know what to say. Finally she let her fingertips drop into place, and she wrote what she'd wanted to say for months.

I'm so scared. I don't want to go through this without you. Tears trickled down her cheeks, and she swiped one cheek and then the other with the back of her hand.

It's OK. Love you, babe, Justin wrote back. *You're going to be an awesome mom.*

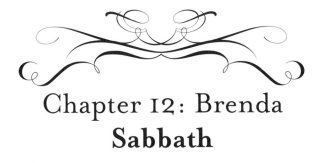

Chapter 12: Brenda
Sabbath

The men were on a dangerous mission protecting yet another supply convoy going close to a battlefront—that's all Rick could tell her—and worry ate at her insides, forming an empty pit in her chest. She'd gotten used to the fact that for a lot of her waking hours, Rick was asleep. So when night came in her part of the world, he was in the middle of his day. Chances were good that if he got hurt, it would be while she lay in bed, asleep.

That fact kept her from sleeping a lot of the time.

Tonight she stayed up late, hoping that Rick would be able to e-mail one last time before they left. Sometime around twelve thirty, she sat in the kitchen, staring at the phone, willing it to ring and be him on the other end so she could hear his voice again, tell him she loved him one more time.

As far as she was concerned, the world stopped spinning on its axis when they talked and began turning again only after they hung up. Hanging up was the worst. Every time, she paid for the joy she felt during the call when her emotions crashed to the ground.

They always said, "I love you," and meant it—deeply—because it could be the last time either heard the other's voice in this life.

But he hadn't called. Would she ever hear the low rumble then big breath he'd take when he laughed?

Even after she knew he wouldn't be calling, she stayed up another hour, writing an e-mail so that when he did return from the mission—

whenever that was—he'd have a message waiting for him the moment he got to a computer with Internet access.

She was so wound up that after sending it, she still couldn't sleep. She wandered the house, rechecking windows and doors. She looked in on the kids. Bradley had cried himself to sleep again; she could tell from the dry streaks on his cheeks.

She went downstairs and watched a pay-per-view movie—a romantic comedy that made her cry. The premise was silly and the dialogue beyond cheesy, but it made her miss Rick even more.

Around three thirty, she climbed into bed and tried to sleep. Every few minutes—after trying to keep images at bay of kafiyah-clad men with rifles and RPGs aimed at the convoy—she opened her eyes, only to see the numbers on the clock going by without her nodding off once. The numbers moved too quickly toward morning, and she started to panic that if she didn't get to sleep right away, she'd be a zombie again tomorrow. But worry over fatigue only kept her more awake.

When she first lay down, she had four hours until her alarm would go off. Then three. *If I get to sleep soon,* she thought, *I could still get a solid three hours of sleep.* It wouldn't be enough, not by a long shot, but she'd survive. If she fell asleep *right now.*

But no matter how hard she tried, she couldn't drift off. The clock ticked by, mocking . . . only two more hours before she had to get up . . . now one and a half . . .

Now she was down to one. One hour. That's all the time she had left to get herself and the kids to church. The digital readout flickered to a new number. Fifty-nine minutes. She'd gone a third night without sleep. At this rate, she'd collapse from sheer physical exhaustion.

Church is in less than an hour. She pressed her eyes closed, shutting out the world. *I can't do it.*

As if on cue, the twins barreled into the room and jumped on her bed. "Morning, Mama!" Josh yelled, throwing his arms around her.

Brenda nearly burst into tears but caught herself and held him tight. "Morning, buddy," she said, sitting up and mussing his hair.

Tyler jumped all across the bed, falling every few seconds as he stumbled on the sheets. "Yay! You're 'wake!"

Looking at their dear faces, she knew that in spite of everything, they'd get into their Sunday best and head to the chapel.

Church isn't something we stop doing when life gets hard, she'd told the boys many times. *It's something we do even more when things get tough.*

But oh, how she yearned to stay home. She knew all too well what sacrament meeting would consist of: wrestling the kids by herself—totally sleep-deprived—while watching all the intact families sitting peacefully on a pew, mother and father working together to keep the little ones happily reverent. And if the twins wouldn't go to Nursery again, then what? She'd spend both of the next hours with them—and twelve other kids with snotty noses whining for more Teddy Grahams and doing the actions to "The Itsy, Bitsy Spider." She'd rather be with the adults, where she might have half a chance of regaining a shred of sanity.

Even if the boys behaved, she wouldn't hear so much as a word, because her mind would be on the other side of the world with a group of soldiers trying to avoid terrorists who were trying their best to destroy the U.S. Army and kill her husband.

I'm whining again, she told herself. *Whining doesn't solve anything.* But sometimes it made her feel a little better for the moment.

"Is it church day?" Tyler asked, bouncing on his knees.

She sighed. "Yes, it's Sunday." Brenda threw off her comforter and wondered if she'd manage to get into the shower this morning. An hour—fifty-four minutes, she corrected herself—was cutting it close. It would all depend on how breakfast and getting the boys dressed went. She climbed out of bed and marshaled the troops.

"So do you guys want pancakes or waffles?" she called, heading for the kitchen. The freezer still had some of both toaster pancakes and toaster waffles. Either would be a fast breakfast. The twins ran after her, and they both voted for pancakes. Bradley reclined on the couch, looking half-awake. "Hey, my man," Brenda said as cheerfully as she could manage. Nora's advice not to let the kids read her stress was about the only thing that kept her from falling into pieces around the boys lately. "How do pancakes sound?" Bradley sleepily mumbled something that she took for an affirmative answer, so she pulled them out of the freezer and popped them into the toaster.

She casually walked over to the computer in the corner of the kitchen to check for anything Rick might have sent overnight. *Modern technology is a serious blessing and a curse,* she thought as she turned the switch to boot it up. She felt as if a leash tied her to the computer. Her need to check e-mail was almost an addiction. The computer seemed to take forever, and she wished she hadn't turned it off last night. The only reason she had was so that she wouldn't be tempted to keep checking it over and over again. She downloaded her new messages.

No word from Rick. Of course not. They'd left last night and wouldn't be back for a few days. She couldn't help feeling disappointed anyway as she returned to the pancakes that had just popped up. Knowing he was okay would have made going to church somewhat bearable.

Forty-eight minutes later—after a maple-syrup lake crisis and a fifteen-minute hunt for a missing pair of church shoes that she could have *sworn* were on the floor beside Tyler's dresser when he went to bed—a shower was clearly out of the question. Brenda threw her hair into a hasty ponytail and donned a sweater and skirt. She applied a little mascara, knowing how scary she looked without it. Makeup on her face was a public service. Then she shepherded the boys to the car. The moment they were all buckled in, she remembered the church bag still in the closet. They wouldn't survive two minutes in the chapel without it.

"Everyone stay in your seats!" she called to them as she jumped out of the van, throwing the twins a look—and one specifically at Tyler that threatened a life without Legos if he disobeyed. He could unbuckle himself now, and that was becoming a liability while driving.

She raced back inside. She grabbed the church bag and threw it onto the kitchen table. Rifling through it, she tossed out last week's garbage—drawings on scratch paper, two macaroni necklaces made in Nursery, and several fruit-snacks wrappers. Good—the bag still had enough crayons, paper, and coloring books. She ran to the pantry and scrambled for food the twins would need to get through the meeting without causing too much of a ruckus. More fruit snacks, two granola bars, and a plastic container of Cheerios.

I'll train them all to go without snacks as soon as I have a husband to help again, she promised herself as she tossed the goodies into the bag and ran back to the car. To her amazement, the boys had actually obeyed this time and were still buckled. She whispered a thank-you heavenward as she turned the key.

She arrived inside the chapel during the last verse of the sacrament hymn, half dragging Tyler and Josh with a hand each and jerking her head in an effort to get Bradley to hurry up. The only pew open was the short one on the side, front row—the one with a good five feet ahead of it before the wooden paneling of the stand. *Great.* Plenty of space for the twins to run around. That kind of seating arrangement bordered on circus-ville, but it was better than resorting to the metal chairs in the overflow. Up here, dropped crayons hit padded seats and carpet. In the cultural hall, they reverberated after smacking metal chairs and landing on the wooden floor. Plus, benches couldn't be moved—screeching as they went—either. A pew always trumped overflow. Even the front bench.

As she ushered the kids forward, most of the women she passed gave her sympathetic smiles, but one woman raised her eyebrows and blew out a breath that looked suspiciously like a snort.

Hey, I'm here, Brenda wanted to say. *Give me at least that much credit.*

When Rick was home, they'd had a rule that the boys couldn't break out the coloring pages, the *Friend* magazine, or any snacks until *after* the sacrament had been passed. The rule was aimed at teaching the kids at least some self-control and reverence.

But with Rick gone, a *lot* of rules had been bent. Or shattered.

As soon as Josh sat down, he dug inside her bag and pulled out the Cheerios. Brenda reached over to help open the lid. If she said he couldn't have any, she'd end up with a screaming child on her hands. Then what? She couldn't very well take him out to the hall and leave the other two boys here alone, not when Bradley was liable to put Tyler into a headlock.

But Josh assumed she was taking the container. He yanked it away and gave her a nasty look. "I *want* some!" he said—loudly—right as the deacons reached for their sacrament trays. His voice echoed off the walls.

Brenda put a finger to her lips. "Shhh! You can have some," she whispered. "Let me help you open it."

She reached for the container again. Josh was already trying to pull off the lid. It released with a sudden jerk, sending cereal bits flying through the air in a shower. Brenda sucked in her breath, watching the little Os dropping to the ground in slow motion like whole-grain snowflakes. When they hit the ground, she flew into action, dropping to her knees and scooping them in front of the pew, the aisle, under the bench.

She glanced up to see where the deacons were—one would be on them in about five seconds—so she sat on the bench again and waited for the bread. Sister Mallard shook her head and seemed to sniff. Brenda looked away and tried not to cry. When the bread arrived, the deacon crunched a piece of cereal under his shoe. He held out the tray, and she hesitated for a second, knowing she didn't feel at all charitable toward Sister Mallard over there.

I'm not exactly in a humble and repentant mood. But she was trying her best, and she needed to have the Spirit with her for the upcoming week more than ever.

Her fingers pinched a piece of the white bread and placed it into her mouth. She passed the tray to the boys but had to tap them on the shoulder to get their attention away from the Spider-Man action figures they'd somehow smuggled in. She handed the tray back to the deacon.

She sighed, wondering if she should confiscate Spider-Man. The boys knew the rules. *I'm trying. Doesn't that count for something? Why is it so hard?*

The meeting's topic was about fathers and a father's role in presiding and helping the mother with her duties. About fathers' blessings and fathers' interviews and father-child activities. After two youth speakers and the first adult speaker, Brenda wanted to stand up and scream. She couldn't help but glance around the room at all the happy families, at the wives who were tucked into the crook of their husbands' arms. Some had the kids spread out between them so the two could tag-team to keep the little ones quiet. She knew that there were several single mothers in the room, but she didn't see any offhand. Somewhere in the back of her mind she knew she had blinders on; she didn't see the single moms because it was the families with dads that drew her attention and made her ache. The knowledge wasn't comforting, because single mothers lived a different life than she did. She had no doubt that they were very stressed—likely in ways she couldn't imagine. But she doubted they lived in a cloud of constant, paralyzing fear.

Josh stole a crayon from Tyler, who retaliated by grabbing a handful of his twin's hair and pulling as hard as he could. Josh turned red and screamed loud enough to shatter eardrums. Bradley, as the mature elder brother, tried to pry Tyler's hand off, but it only made him pull harder and made Josh scream louder. Brenda intervened quickly but not quickly enough. All eyes had shifted to the chaos on the front left pew. Holding a screaming Josh to her chest, she felt sick inside.

Sister Hunter, a woman with two teenage daughters, motioned for one of her girls, Kylie, to cross the aisle. She slipped onto the bench and whispered, "I'll stay with them so you can take him out."

Brenda looked at Sister Hunter, who motioned for the side door inches away. "Go," she mouthed.

Smiling her gratitude to both daughter and mother, Brenda hurried out of the chapel, throwing the congregation apologetic looks. In the foyer, she collapsed on a couch, hardly aware of the other people sitting near her. She rocked Josh on her lap until his screams settled into sobs. His little body shook, and Brenda found that hers did too. When he quieted further, she leaned down and looked him in the eye. "You okay now?"

He nodded and sniffed. "Tyler hurt me."

"I know, buddy. I know." She rubbed his back and took a deep breath then looked at the chapel doors. She needed to get back in there and spell Kylie. Who knew *what* Tyler and Bradley were up to. A Mia Maid was unlikely to be able to handle them if they really wanted to up the ante. But Brenda dreaded going back in.

Sister Harrison, whom Brenda just noticed sitting blithely across from her the whole time, smiled. She didn't know the woman all that well, but she smiled back and kept rocking Josh.

"Must be hard having your husband gone," Sister Harrison said.

"Yes, it is," Brenda said simply. She was too tired to try discussing deployment with someone she hardly knew. A few sentences would never be enough.

The woman shook her head disdainfully. "It's so stupid that we're still in Iraq. I mean, so many people are losing their lives, and for what?"

Brenda gritted her teeth. She was in no mood for a political discussion about the Iraq situation. And it hurt that everyone automatically assumed that Rick was in Iraq. No one remembered that there was another war going on. One targeted at a group bent on destroying the United States.

"My husband is in Afghanistan." She left it at that and walked around the corner with Josh to the drinking fountain before she could say anything she'd regret. She let him have a drink then stood indecisively in the hall, not wanting to return to the couch and the Iraq conversation but not wanting to go into sacrament meeting, either.

The chapel doors opened, and Sister Hunter slipped out. To Brenda's relief, she was alone and not toting Tyler behind her.

Sister Hunter went over to Brenda in the hall. "How's the little guy?" she asked, touching Josh's head.

"I'm not little," he shot back.

"Apparently he's fine," Brenda said with a strained smile. "I suppose I should go back in. Thank you so much for having Kylie help out."

"It's no problem at all," Sister Hunter said. She noticed the trash can beside the drinking fountain and emptied a handful of Cheerios into it.

Somehow Brenda knew that Sister Hunter had cleaned them from the carpet. "Thanks for that, too. I can't seem to do anything right lately."

Sister Hunter looked directly into Brenda's eyes and said, "Hey, you're doing great in spite of a tough time. You're here. Every week."

Brenda nearly choked on the sudden emotion that washed through her. "Thanks," she managed. That's what she'd been telling herself, but thinking it didn't mean much compared to hearing the same words from someone else, from a woman she admired. "It's hard, though."

"I know," Sister Hunter said. She patted Brenda's hand, and before heading back to the chapel, she added, "My father fought in Vietnam. Mom had a really rough time of it." Her eyes looked a little glassy. She looked ready to go back in but first paused. "Remember, you have a date on the calendar when he'll be coming home. Hang onto the hope that this will end." She lowered her eyes then turned around and quickly walked back inside the doors.

Brenda watched her go, shame flowing through her. How had

she forgotten that Sister Hunter was divorced? She'd raised her children—alone—for close to ten years now. But Brenda didn't recall her ever complaining about it, even though *she* didn't have a light—a hope—at the end of the tunnel, a date when *her* husband would come marching home and make things all better. She'd come to church every week too. Even when it was hard.

More now than before, Brenda wished she could call out another thanks. But Sister Hunter was inside already; it would have to wait. She took a cleansing breath then said, "Okay, buddy. Let's go back in." To her surprise, Josh went along without protest. He took her hand and followed her in.

The rest of the meeting didn't go one-hundred-percent smoothly, but Kylie stayed on their bench to help. Tyler seemed enchanted by her, and that was fine with Brenda. Sticking close to Kylie would keep him from picking another fight with his brothers.

The last talk was about ways women could honor their husbands— and of course, every single method the speaker discussed required the husband being present in the home. It made Brenda want to throw darts. *I'm overreacting,* she told herself. *It's the fatigue making me think and act like this. Get a grip.*

As she gathered up her things after the meeting, Sister Hunter shot her a smile. "You're here," she mouthed as she headed up the aisle.

Brenda returned the smile. *I'm here,* she thought. *I hope that counts for something, because I don't know how much longer I'll last . . . and we're not even halfway through this deployment. How does she do it when divorce never ends? I'll be better when Rick's back on base.*

"Come on, boys," she said. "Let's get you to class."

She took Bradley straight to the Primary room, knowing that getting the twins into Nursery might take a little time. *A few more weeks, and they'll be Sunbeams,* she thought. She hoped they'd go into junior Primary easily.

Kylie appeared out of nowhere. "Do you want me to take them into Nursery?" she asked, reaching out for Tyler's hand. With stars in his eyes, he took her hand, and Josh followed happily behind his brother. Brenda watched the miracle but didn't dare believe it right away. When the door closed behind them, she waited for one of the boys to start their shrieks, but there was nothing. She peeked through the tiny window in the Nursery door and could see Kylie sitting on a chair, reading to Tyler while Josh made the two Spider-Man figures fight each other.

Brenda breathed a grateful sigh of relief. She hitched her bag higher on her shoulder and turned away, realizing that she might get to attend Sunday School with the grown-ups for once. On the way there, Bishop Morgan stopped her.

"Sister McKewan, I've been thinking about you," he said.

"Oh?" For half a second, she wondered if she'd be getting a new calling. The bishop wouldn't do that to her while Rick was gone, would he?

"You've been on my mind a lot lately." Bishop Morgan inclined his head. "How are you doing? Really?"

"Fine." But the moment the word came out, the floodgates opened. She couldn't speak. Tears built up and tumbled down her cheeks.

"What would help?"

Besides Rick coming home? She shrugged. "I don't know."

"I'm going to tell Sister Peterson that you need a few meals this week, all right?"

She nodded mutely, swallowed hard, then managed, "That would be nice."

"And we'll arrange babysitting so you can get to the temple this week. Would you like that?"

Oh, boy, would she. "I could really use that. Thank you," she said, still crying.

"How about tomorrow?"

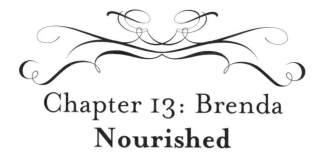

Chapter 13: Brenda
Nourished

The doorbell rang at a quarter to nine. Brenda was already in a dress and had her temple clothes in their bag when she answered the door. As tired as she was—she'd chalked up yet another near-sleepless night on her growing tally—she'd gotten up with the sun. No point in lying in bed when she was too anxious to nod off.

She hadn't known who would be coming to babysit and didn't ask her visiting teachers to do it either—they helped her often enough as it was, often tending during the wives' lunches. Brenda was simply told that a sister in the ward would come in time for her to attend one of the Monday sessions, since it was only a half day at the Provo Temple. It was nice to find Sister Hunter on the other side of the door, beaming and carrying a *Blue's Clues* DVD and a jumbo bag of Skittles.

"The twins will adore you," Brenda said, pointing at the loot as she stepped aside to let Sister Hunter in.

"I figured I should come prepared. It's been a little while since I've had small ones of my own." She lifted the canvas bag she held in the other hand and shook it. "I brought along Kylie's babysitting kit she made in Young Women, so I've got flannel board stories and craft projects, and I don't know what else. We should stay busy." She grinned.

"The twins are a handful," Brenda warned. "I hope for your sake there's no glitter in that bag."

"I guess we'll find out," Sister Hunter said, trying to peer inside. "But I'll keep that in mind. Now you go on out of here. Stay out as long as you like. Go to lunch after. I can pick up Bradley from school if you need me to." When Brenda raised her eyebrows, Sister Hunter insisted. "You look worn out. Take a break, as much time as you need."

"Well, I might get a bite after," Brenda mused. She did look pretty terrible, she knew—makeup could hide only so much of the blue rings under her eyes. "Hailey Barker has carpool this week, so she'll bring Bradley home." She picked up her temple bag and grabbed her purse. "Thank you."

The twins ran into the room, threw their arms around her waist to say good-bye, then turned on Sister Hunter. "Can we eat those now?" Tyler demanded, pointing to the Skittles.

Sister Hunter waved silently to Brenda, who slipped out the door. The twins would be souped up on sugar when she got back, but for now she didn't care one bit.

Forty-five minutes later, she was sitting in the chapel of the temple, wearing her white dress and reveling in the peace and quiet of the room, the deep hum of the organ as it played hymns. She'd always appreciated how strongly she could feel the Spirit in the temple, but today she took in other things as well, like how clean it was—such a contrast to the cluttered mess her house was right now. The quiet helped to make her feel at ease and relaxed. No one would bother her here. No one expected anything from her.

There would be only peace—something she needed so badly.

The next two hours were as close to heaven on earth as she could get. The session went smoothly, quickly, and she wished it would take longer. Before she knew it, she had stepped into the celestial room. She crossed over to one of the white wingback chairs against one wall and with a sigh of relief—as if she were really coming home—sat down and leaned against the side of the chair.

She closed her eyes, bowed her head, folded her arms, and offered a heartfelt prayer for her husband, who was still in danger until he got back to camp, for their three children, and for strength and wisdom for herself so she could know what to do and how to be there for her children during this time.

As she prayed, head bowed, her breathing eased into a gentle rhythm. The muscles in her neck and shoulders released their hold. Her exhaustion gave way, and for the first time in four days, Brenda was blessed by slipping into a quiet, easy, dreamless sleep.

Chapter 14: Marianne
Urgency

MONDAY, OCTOBER 12, 2009, 10:00 PM

Why do I even bother trying to have family home evening? Marianne wondered. She was in the kitchen, cleaning up the root-beer-float mess from refreshment time. In theory, all the kids were in bed.

Realistically, Kevin was probably the only one asleep by now. Bailey *might* be if she didn't have her nose tucked into that bluish book with the water people riding a wave—whatever it was called—that she had picked up at the library the other day. And McKayla . . . well, *she* was most certainly still awake. She claimed to have AP U.S. History homework to do, but considering how McKayla didn't care about school anymore, odds were she wasn't actually doing it. The girl was probably waiting for her mother to go to sleep so she could sneak out again with Jake.

At least I know his name now, Marianne thought, scrubbing melted ice cream off the counter with short, vicious strokes. Lately McKayla had been sneaking out at night with someone, and when Marianne had tried calling her friends' parents, none knew anything about it. It took the cops bringing McKayla home at two o'clock one night last week—when Marianne hadn't even known she was gone—for her to learn the guy's name.

Getting a knock at the door in the middle of the night during deployment was enough to give Marianne a heart attack. She'd answered the door with her stomach in her throat, worried that she'd see two men in uniform. Of course, she had. But they'd been wearing dark blue police uniforms, not green Army ones. Instead of telling her bad news about her husband, they were dragging her teenage daughter home from a party with underage drinking. Marianne wanted to strangle McKayla.

Jake had come by several times since then. He wasn't the kind of boy she'd envisioned that her daughter would eventually fall for. Even in the looks department, she didn't get it. He wore black eyeliner and had six ear piercings—four in one ear, two in the other, plus one in his left eyebrow. While the look wasn't something she necessarily approved of, it wouldn't have freaked her out by itself. One of the best actors of Marianne's high school class had dressed a bit like a Goth in his day, and he turned out fine. He served a mission—sans earrings— and, last she heard, he was in a bishopric. He'd gone through an "eccentric" period, but he'd never been an all-out rebel, and he graduated high school with honors.

But Jake was another story. In the days since she'd first met him, she'd found that he constantly smelled of pot. He used words that made her want to duct-tape his mouth shut. He had no respect for any authority, including the police. He had a juvenile record. He had dropped out of high school and had no plans for college. Everything about him was a giant red flag, but McKayla would have none of it.

"You're judging him, Mom," she'd said after the cops had left. "Do you think Christ would have told Jake to go away because he got his tongue pierced?"

His tongue, too. Wonderful.

How could her daughter twist the concept of righteous judgment so far on its head?

As Marianne cleaned up from the root-beer floats, she wondered whether tonight's family home evening lesson had helped at all. She'd intentionally made eye contact with Bailey and Kevin so McKayla wouldn't feel attacked. She talked about how we love everyone but how we also have to make good choices and not let other people pull us away from the right path. She talked about Lehi's dream of the rod of iron and how easy it was to let go and either get lost in the mists or end up in the great and spacious building.

"Do we hate the people in the great and spacious building?" she asked. "Of course not. Lehi loved all his sons, including Laman and Lemuel, but no matter how much he loved them, he couldn't join them.

We have to stand fast with what we know is right, no matter what."

"No matter what," young Kevin echoed with a single, matter-of-fact nod.

McKayla had sat in the corner of the couch, arms folded tightly across her chest. The corners of her mouth pulled down in a hard line, and she glared at Marianne. She knew what her mother was trying to do, and she didn't appreciate it.

Marianne rinsed out the washcloth, started the dishwasher, then pulled out the broom. No sooner did the bristles meet linoleum than a thought jumped into her mind.

Pray for Brian.

The words came with force. Her arms froze, and she stared at the floor in shock. It came again.

Pray. Now. You don't have time to wait.

A paralyzing feeling of peril, of imminent danger, clutched her chest. Heart thudding against her ribcage, she leaned the broom against a corner of the counter and scurried to the living room, where she dropped to her knees by the couch. Voice shaky, she whispered a prayer, pouring her heart into every word, pleading for the safety of her husband.

Right this minute, Brian was under fire. She knew it.

"Keep thine angels round about him. His mission in this life isn't over yet. Protect him; watch over him. Guide his actions that he and his men may be safe." She went on and on, repeating similar sentiments, pleading for Brian to come out alive of whatever situation he was in. She wished she knew exactly what was going on, wished she didn't feel so helpless, that she could do more for her husband than offer a prayer.

Brian needs more. Pray with your children.

Marianne's eyes popped open in surprise. Brian's life depended on it. Somehow she knew it in her core. She closed her prayer and hopped to her feet, frantic. There was no time to lose. It didn't matter that the kids were in bed already. Every second counted. She took the stairs two at a time and threw open their bedroom doors. "Wake up, everyone. Come here, now. We need to pray for Dad." Her voice was breathy, and her heart pounded painfully in her throat.

Kevin squinted at the hall light. "What?"

"Come here, now. We need to pray for Dad. Girls, you, too."

Without any further prompting, Kevin crawled out of bed and joined her. Bailey came a moment later, passing McKayla in their shared room.

"You coming?" Bailey asked her older sister.

"I don't need to be told when to pray," McKayla growled.

"Please join the rest of the family." Marianne tried to sound patient, but her heart was thudding so hard it was difficult.

"You can't force me."

"Fine," Marianne said. She swallowed against the dryness in her throat. She *couldn't* force McKayla to do anything. But at least she could pray with her other two children. The feeling of urgency continued; there wasn't time right now for a mother-daughter heart-to-heart talk.

"Let's go to the living room," she said, ushering Kevin and Bailey down the stairs.

They knelt in a circle around the coffee table, and one by one they took turns praying for Brian's safety. For those brief minutes, Marianne was in a sacred place. When Bailey finished her prayer, the three of them knelt in quiet silence, looking at one another for several seconds. Marianne didn't want to leave the circle.

Finally Kevin spoke up quietly. "Mom, why did we need to do this now?"

"I'm not sure," she said. It was mostly true; she didn't know specifics. All she was sure of was that Brian was in danger and desperately needed their prayers. But she didn't want to scare her kids. "I felt like Dad needed us right now, and the best way we can give him support is by praying."

"Cool." Kevin seemed to be studying the wood grain of the coffee table. Then he said, "I think he'll be okay."

"I think so too." Marianne opened her arms and took her two youngest children into them. She held on tight, smelling their hair, feeling their sweet limbs hugging her. Her eyes stung. "I love you guys so much."

"We love you too, Mom," Bailey said, her voice quavering a bit.

"Thanks for praying with me." Marianne released them and sniffed. "Good night, guys."

"Good night," they chorused as they headed slowly back up to their rooms.

Marianne stayed on her knees for a minute, trying to feel the Spirit, letting it soak into her bones. Maybe it would tell her whether they'd done enough. Was the threat gone? Would Brian be safe now?

No other urgent thoughts pressed on her mind. She tried to hang on to the peace she'd felt a moment ago during the prayers, but it was hard. The urgent, frightening feeling had been so strong before that it was hard to shake. Trembling, she got to her feet and went down to the computer in the family room. She needed to e-mail Brian tonight, even though she wouldn't be hearing from him until the convoy returned to the base.

Chapter 15: Nora
Venting

Tuesday, October 13, 2009

Nora sat down to scribble out her frustrations in a spiral note-book. In three months, she'd already filled four of them with "letters" to Russell, and she had a feeling that she'd be using up a truckload more before he got home.

Thanks to her mother, Nora felt an inch away from the loony bin.

She wrote all kinds of things on the lined pages. She documented what daily life was like caring for her mother during cancer and what it was like being the "mother," in a sense, of the wives group. They really did need a matronly shoulder like hers, and she was bound and determined to give it to them.

This was her third deployment, after all. During the first one, she would have given her eye teeth for the kind of advice and help she could now give these young wives starting out. Watching out for them had been Russell's idea to begin with, but she embraced the role now. They needed her.

Although she began each entry in the notebook with, "Dear Russell," she never mailed the letters or copied the entries into e-mails. Most likely, her husband would never see these words even after he got home. She had no plans to share them with anyone. She might not even keep them that long. Maybe she'd burn them. It might feel good to watch the evidence of her frustrations go up in flames and smoke.

The pages were filled with all kinds of things—the bare bones of her raw emotions and stresses. Things she didn't want to reveal even to her sweet husband. He might think less of her if he knew how petty she could be. Besides, she told herself, Russell had enough to worry about over there; he didn't need to have *her* anxieties and worries compounding the problem.

And she wouldn't—couldn't—write them in her regular journal. That cream-colored, hardbound book with the painting of Christ on the cover was for posterity. At least, that's what she believed. You write a journal so that you can pass on your wisdom and knowledge to future generations and so, in the next life, angels can quote from it. Or some such.

She most certainly didn't want her children, grandchildren, great-grandchildren—and who knew how far beyond—reading her whining complaints. Angels wouldn't be quoting references to Mother's irritability in her last days or Nora's latest bunion pain or how she couldn't get the darn computer to work or how the house seemed to be falling apart—the guest bathroom faucet was leaking *again*—without Russell home to fix things. She wrote all of it down, her pen flashing under the speed. Her handwriting at this rate was truly atrocious, but it didn't matter if the words weren't the least bit legible because no one would ever read them.

She saved her good penmanship for thank-you notes. And for her real journal, where she'd soon be chronicling the last tender moments of her mother's life and thoughts about mortality, the spirit world, and the reality of the Atonement and future resurrection. Topics much more suitable for descendants to read.

Today she unloaded more of her mental garbage—the stuff she simply *had* to get out and clear her mind of. She scribbled about the annoying crack in the windshield that came when a semi threw a big rock into it yesterday. Mother's insistence that the thermostat was set too hot. And then too cold. And then too hot again. Using a blanket and slippers, which could be removed or put back on at any time, was apparently not going to happen. Mother always did insist on the least convenient solution to things.

Writing out all the petty feelings in black ink helped Nora to leave the emotion on the page. After a writing session—time she often stole when her mother was napping—she slipped the notebook back into the high cupboard where Mother couldn't reach it and felt lighter when she walked away.

But leaving all her emotions on the page also made sure that she never vented where it wouldn't be appropriate, where it could be seen . . . like with Russell. Or with her mother. Or, worse, with the wives, who needed to see strength and serenity.

The notebook was a safe place where she didn't have to pretend.

But even with all her writings, today even the notebook didn't seem to be enough of a release valve. Was there something else she could write down to let it go? Today she couldn't even pretend she was talking to Russell, because instead of staying on base and giving the orders, somehow he'd ended up commanding a mission.

He was a colonel, for crying out loud. This deployment was supposed to be easier on her, because Russell would be the one back at the base, planning the missions and telling others what to do. He shouldn't be anywhere near enemy fire. The fear and nausea she felt during his first two deployments returned in full force. She suddenly had greater compassion for what the other wives went through regularly. In a sense, she'd forgotten how debilitating the worry was.

Russell, of course, couldn't give her the details about where he was and what he was doing, but his going had something to do with one of the men getting violently ill and another being injured by an RPG hitting a Humvee, so Russell volunteered to take the latter's place. That was something Russell would do.

He'd better not take the convoy on after dark, she thought. Doing so was against regulations, but no one would question a colonel if he wanted to skirt the rule by driving for an hour in the dark so they didn't have to camp out with the ticks in the desert. It would be a lot like how Russell had insisted they drive straight to Washington from Utah in one day even when they had little ones. By the time they arrived at her parents' house, the kids were little better than rabid animals. Poor baby Scott was screaming himself hoarse.

This time, pressing forward could get Russell killed. Under the cloak of darkness, without any warning, the enemy could easily fire at his Humvee, or the convoy could drive right over an IED. She hated that acronym. It stood for "improvised explosive device"—any bomb cobbled together from whatever deadly ingredients the enemy had on hand. The resulting explosions were ugly and deadly. Humvees could often withstand a lateral strike like an RPG. The vehicle would get beat up, but it would probably protect the men, or *most* of them, if hit. On the other hand, it was far more vulnerable from the bottom. Which meant that driving over an IED or landmine . . .

She pictured Russell's vehicle hitting an explosive, a bright flash of light, bodies torn apart . . .

She shook her head to chase away the image then closed her eyes and rested her head in her left hand, trying to think of something else, sending a prayer heavenward that Russell would be able to get the convoy delivery there and back without incident.

She had shoved her fingers into her hair—hair that really needed the roots touched up. She'd gotten a lot grayer over the last two months than in the previous two years combined. Her hair could also use a wash.

To get her mind off Russell being under enemy fire, she wrote about something utterly trivial—her beauty routine.

I don't know why it's so hard to get myself going in the mornings. For years I never skipped exercising on a weekday, but this month I think I've skipped more days than I've gotten onto the treadmill. I can't get myself out of bed.

And since I'm not exercising and getting sweaty, I don't shower every single day. My hair can tell. When did I become the woman who has visible roots?

I didn't react this way to the other deployments. Why am I falling apart now?

Things were different this time. It was the first deployment where she wasn't spending time with women her age, other wives who knew exactly what she was going through. She envied Marianne, Brenda, Jessie, and Kim. They had what she did for the other two deployments. When she heard them expressing frustrations and supporting one another, it gave her a melancholy ache in her chest. She used to be part of that kind of circle.

This time around, she couldn't completely inject herself into the circle, because they needed a go-to person. If she were a complete equal, they wouldn't have her to take care of them. Before this mission, she hadn't felt the need to have a sounding board for her worries. Not with Russell's rank keeping him safe.

The situation with the wives was good for the other women, but it made Nora's notebooks that much more important.

She ran a hand through her hair again, knowing she couldn't possibly go out looking like this. Pen hovering over the page, she wondered if she'd better put the notebook away, finally take a shower, and put on her face and clothes in case someone dropped by or she had to run to the doctor or pharmacy.

She could be herself on the page, but that self really shouldn't make sudden public appearances. Getting herself presentable should have taken priority over the notebook. She decided to just write a little more, this time to her beloved.

Russell, I hope you're safe. I hope you aren't wounded or worse. I wish you were safely home. Not just at the base, but here, under this roof. I could use you here now. You always stood up for me around Mom. I wish I had the guts to do that. Come home to me.

She closed the notebook, and her head dropped to her hands on top of it. Next time Russell called, she'd be so relieved to hear his voice. She wouldn't ask for advice on dealing with her mother— that would mean telling him the kinds of things she'd been forced to endure hearing. So far, she'd managed to keep her mother's health vague whenever he asked about it.

"Oh, she's about the same," she'd tell him. "Nothing much new."

And that was *mostly* the truth. Mom was getting slowly worse, but nothing much changed from one day to the next.

Nora went to the computer in the kitchen, where Russell used to spend his time doing work or checking e-mail. She sat in the leather chair and stroked the armrests, imagining his thick, muscular arms on them, wishing she could feel him near her. He was in wonderful shape for a man his age. He looked better now than when they had married. She leaned back into the chair, which was still molded to his shape. She liked that.

She looked at the monitor, hoping that maybe he was up in the middle of the night and online right now. Of course the instant messaging program said he wasn't there.

"Nora? Where are you, Nora?" Her mother's voice came from down the hall. Her walker scraped against one wall as she moved it forward. Nora gritted her teeth, imagining the new scratches her mother was leaving.

"Nora, honey, you need to touch up the walls here," her mother suddenly called, as if she had read her daughter's mind. Her mother's bony hand pointed around the hall corner, waving at a particularly big gouge. "You've got all kinds of scuffs. I'm surprised you don't take care of this place better. It's such a nice house."

Nora opened her mouth to protest—to remind her mother that *she* was the one who made the scuffs with the walker, for Pete's sake—but then clamped her teeth together. Contradicting her would only incite an argument, which would leave the subject of touch-up paint real fast and move on to Nora's other shortcomings in housekeeping, past mothering, and who knew what else.

She glanced at the kitchen table and realized that the notebook was still there. *She is* not *going to read that,* Nora thought fiercely. She strode to the table and snatched it up then opened a cupboard and shoved it onto a high shelf. She closed the cupboard with a snap as her mother entered the room.

"What's all that banging about?" she asked. "If you're cleaning up the kitchen, you're doing a sad job of it. No wonder Scott went so far away to college."

Now Nora wanted to *really* slam something. Hard.

Instead, she lifted her chin and asked, "Do you need something to eat?"

Her mother didn't answer right away. She always did like making people wait. She shuffled across the carpet, pulled out a chair at the kitchen table, and sat down, her bones creaking with the slow movement. Once comfortably settled, she clasped her hands on the tabletop and said, "I'd like some orange juice if it isn't too much trouble."

"Sure," Nora said, moving toward the fridge.

"Pulp free, mind you. Those little bits get stuck in my dentures. And some toast. Not as dark as you made it last time but a little more butter than you usually put on, if you please."

Facing the fridge, Nora closed her eyes. "Of course, Mother."

Chapter 16: Jessie
Herself

Wednesday, October 14, 2009

Sitting with the other Army wives at a table outside Sonic in Orem, Jessie took a bite of chicken from her salad, pleased with her meal choice. In the last four weeks, she'd lost five pounds. The month before that, it was only two. But a couple more pounds off, and she'd be able to fit into her favorite jeans again.

Using a pink sauce–laden french fry, Brenda pointed at Jessie's dressing-free salad. "So what's up with all the healthy eating lately? I figure this is the one meal I can really splurge on during the week."

Jessie shrugged but couldn't help smiling a bit. "Trying to lose a little weight."

"Well, it's working," Marianne said. "You look great."

"You can tell already?" Jessie asked. A pleased flush came to her cheeks.

"Uh, yeah," Kim said. "Your face looks thinner."

"Yes!" With one hand, Jessie pumped the air. "It feels so good, like I'm getting my life back in control, you know?"

Brenda swallowed another bite of fry. "I *don't* know, actually. But I'm impressed. Ever since our guys left, having control over my life has meant keeping the boys in clean underwear. If I can do that regularly, it's a success. You amaze me."

"Thanks," Jessie said, skewering a tomato. Their admiration felt good. Having her clothes looser felt even better.

But it was more than that, and she couldn't explain to the women why she was finally able to get on the weight-loss wagon for real this time. She'd tried for years, hating her post-baby, flabby body. At times, she'd taken up running again, but Tim made fat jokes and remarked on what she was eating. He said it was supposed to motivate her.

Instead, it hurt her and ticked her off. She stopped eating junk food in front of him, but then she'd just eat it when he wasn't around—and hide the packaging so he'd never know. She hadn't realized until he left—until he wasn't there harping about her fat rear—that in her heart of hearts, she really didn't want to lose the weight, because that would mean Tim had won, that his fat jokes had worked.

But now . . . he wasn't around. If she wanted to eat a bowl of ice cream, he wasn't there to tell her that it'd stick to her already blubbery thighs. If she turned away from the junk food, *she* won.

She could lose all the weight she wanted while he was gone; she was sure of it. All forty pounds of it. Her only worry right now was what would happen when Tim got home. Could she keep it off, or would she gain it back because a skinny wife was what he wanted, and it would mean that he'd won after all?

"I think I've *gained* three pounds just this week," Brenda said, swirling her fries into more sauce. "This last convoy mission has had me scared spitless, and I'm afraid I ate my stress." She sat up straighter as if a thought occurred to her. "None of you have heard back from your men today, have you?"

Everyone shook their heads, and no one said anything for a minute, not even Nora, who usually had uplifting words to bestow. Jessie wondered why she was so quiet today then remembered that Colonel Lambert had actually *gone* on the convoy this time. No wonder.

"I don't know why I've been so stressed out about this particular mission, but I have been," Marianne said. "I mean, I know our men aren't actually fighting in battle situations, right? When they left, that was a comfort to me. They're bringing supplies to the guys who are doing the heavy fighting. Sure, convoys are still targets, but . . ."

"This one has had me freaking out too," Kim said. "The bigger this baby gets, the more I worry that it'll grow up without a dad. I mean, the poor thing has to deal with me as its mom. The least it deserves is a decent dad." She laughed as if she were joking, but she caught Jessie's eye. They both knew she was serious.

"I went four nights without sleeping this week," Brenda said wearily, as if reliving the strain.

Jessie felt a bit on the outside of this particular conversation. She hadn't given the latest convoy much more thought than the others Tim had been on. It was several days where she didn't have to come up with something to say in an e-mail to him. She certainly hoped he was safe. She prayed for that every day. And yes, a part of her was always anxious that something would happen to her husband and she'd raise her kids as a single mom. But having him gone was still a *break* from all his . . . idiosyncrasies. It was nice.

It wasn't like he helped with the kids when he was home anyway. Taking care of his needs on top of the kids' was like having a fourth child around the house—extra work for her. She envied the wives who found deployment hard in part because they'd lost their partner in parenting. She'd never *had* one.

Her iPhone dinged in her purse. She ignored it. That particular chime didn't mean she had an incoming call; it meant an e-mail had arrived. She should have turned that off for lunch so it wouldn't make noise every time she got some retailer's newsletter or whatever.

"Is that a call?" Nora asked, inclining her head to Jessie's purse.

"No, it means I have a new e-mail," Jessie said.

"You have a Blackberry?" Kim asked.

"No. An iPhone," Jessie said.

"Cool. Can I see it? Justin wants one. I was thinking about getting him one when he gets home."

"Sure." Jessie pulled it out of her purse and unlocked it. Kim went around the table and sat beside her, looking over her shoulder as Jessie demonstrated. "So you click here to browse the Internet." She explained how the buttons worked, how to bring up a new page, go back, increase and decrease the image size with nothing but a small movement of the fingers.

"There are some fun games on it, too," Jessie said, demonstrating. "Tim downloaded one where you tilt the phone to get a ball through a maze. It's wild how real it feels. Okay, and here's my e-mail."

"There's one from Tim!" Kim yelped with excitement. All the wives' eyes widened.

"What does it say?" Marianne demanded, her voice strained but even.

"Yeah, are they all back safely?" Brenda said.

Only Nora didn't say a word at first. She closed her eyes briefly as if saying a quick prayer then opened them and smiled at Jessie. "They're back, then?" she asked calmly.

Jessie clicked the message open, heart pounding. Her eyes hurriedly took in the message, searching for news. After two lines, she glanced up and nodded. "All five made it back."

A collective sigh went around the table, and tensions visibly eased.

"Thank the Lord," Nora whispered.

Jessie reread the full message, slower now. "They did have some trouble on the return trip, though," she said, reading on. She grimaced at the story. "Oh, wow."

"What?" Marianne said, her voice suddenly hoarse. "What happened?"

"Yesterday morning, one of the Humvees was hit by an RPG. Took out the tower and killed another soldier. Not one of ours," Jessie added quickly.

"Anything else?" Brenda pressed.

"Minor injuries for Justin," Jessie said, glancing over at Kim. "Just some shrapnel in his arm. They're not even sending him away to treat it. Tim says he'll be back in action in another week or two."

Jessie paused. She swallowed then raised her eyes to Marianne's, which looked haunted, as if she already knew. "Brian's fine, but the RPG barely missed him. According to Tim, if Brian had been sitting six inches to the right, he'd probably be dead."

Marianne shuddered, and tears suddenly filled her eyes. "Tuesday morning for them means Monday night for us. I *knew* Brian was in danger. I *knew* it."

"But he's safe now," Nora said, putting an arm around Marianne, who was falling apart, as if she could no longer stand it now that the pressure of the last few days was gone. She lowered her head into her hands on the table and sobbed.

"He's safe," Jessie said, echoing Nora.

"I know," Marianne said. "But he almost . . ."

Jessie nodded. She looked around the table. The other wives' faces were pale, drawn. Kim looked a bit spooked, surely knowing that Justin was lucky to have such minor injuries.

It was as if they all understood now that even though they'd worried about their men—lost sleep over their safety—they'd been deceiving themselves. They'd all thought how lucky they were that the men hadn't been assigned to a combat division. The fighting was where the really risky stuff happened, right? Sure, *most* of the risky stuff happened on the front lines, but not all. They knew that now.

Jessie didn't tell them the last part of Tim's e-mail, because it would only make things worse. But it confirmed what she had suspected.

Being part of a delivery convoy is one of the most dangerous jobs over here. It's almost as bad as battle itself. Some days I wonder if I'll make it out of here alive.

Chapter 17: Kim
Junior

B renda volunteered her house for a group Halloween party, so on Saturday afternoon, Kim drove to Spanish Fork and wound her way through the subdivision to find the right house—a simple, taupe-colored, split-level home with a bay window. It looked very much like the taupe-colored one next door and the mauve one next to that. Three cars she recognized were already parked out front. Kim pulled behind Nora's Taurus then grabbed her purse and a small bag from the passenger-side floor.

A cement sidewalk led to a gate in a chain-link fence that had white privacy slats. Orange and black balloons streamed from the opening, marking the entryway to the backyard party. There was already a nip in the air, and the flowering plum trees next to the sidewalk had lost most of their leaves. But the kids out back didn't seem to notice the chill as they chased one another across the ample yard, squealing and giggling in their costumes.

Kim noticed a pirate, a princess, Thing 1 and Thing 2, and Dorothy from *The Wizard of Oz*. It took her a minute to connect each costume to each child. Brenda's twins were Thing 1 and Thing 2. One of Marianne's daughters was Dorothy—Kim could never keep Bailey and McKayla straight. The pirate was either Bradley, Brenda's oldest, or Kevin, Marianne's youngest. The princess had to be Jessie's daughter Alex.

"Hey, Kim!" Brenda came over, toting a cupcake with orange icing and a jack-o-lantern face made from candy corns. "Here you go."

Kim took the treat and picked off a candy corn with her teeth, effectively making the face one-eyed and lopsided. "Thanks. Looks like everyone's having fun."

"Oh, they are." Brenda looked over at the kids, who were playing some game they had probably invented themselves. The flush in her cheeks was from more than the cool air; Kim could see the glow of love for her kids in her face and wondered if, in a few years, she'd have that same look while watching her own kid running around in some store-bought superhero costume. The chances of her actually making a costume from scratch were about as likely as her growing her own tomatoes and canning them.

Then again, over the last few months, her best friends had become women who were much older than she was—something else she would have bet against ever happening. And she was going to be a mom. Strange things were turning her life on its head.

Maybe someday she'd plant a tomato bush. Or something.

The pirate raced up to Brenda. "Can we go trick-or-treating *yet?*" he pled achingly.

"Not yet," his mother said. She took his shoulders and turned him around. "We'll be playing some games soon. Go hang out with Kevin."

"But he's *bored,*" Bradley insisted. "His costume looks dorky without the box." Kevin had come up behind him and nodded emphatically. He wore all black: a turtleneck, jeans, and shoes.

"What are you?" Kim asked.

"A Lego," he said. "But you can't tell without the rest of the costume, and I can't run around and play games with it on."

"Show her," Marianne said, coming over, sipping a mug of apple cider. "It turned out really great, if I say so myself."

Kevin put on a bright red, spray-painted cardboard box with arm and head holes. Six jumbo plastic cups were glued to the front in two rows like the bumps on a Lego block. He put on a hat that looked the same: red with four smaller red cups. He really did look like a Lego now.

"Now *that* is a cool costume," Kim said with an approving nod.

"Thanks," Kevin said, grinning. "I won Most Original Costume at school. So can we go yet?" He turned to his mother and Brenda, arms outstretched.

"I said one more hour," Brenda said. "After we get back, we'll have dinner inside. I've got a killer tortilla soup in the Crock-Pot." She added the last part for Kim and Marianne.

"Sounds great," Kim said. "All of them have really cute costumes. You guys are really creative."

Jessie came out of the house at that point, carrying a dirty diaper in one hand and Joey in the other arm. He was bundled up in a furry Tigger costume. "My version of creative is going to Costco and plunking down fifteen bucks for something already made," she said, depositing the diaper into the trash can.

"Come get yourself a drink," Brenda said, ushering Kim to the table set up on the cement pad.

Nora sat next to the table, drinking cider. She nodded toward Kim's bag, something no one else seemed to have noticed. "What's in there?" she asked. "A costume for your little one to wear next year?"

The plastic handles of the department store bag suddenly felt hot in Kim's hand. "Sort of," she said. "It's actually something I thought I'd send to Justin, but I wanted your opinion on it first."

She sat on a white plastic outdoor chair and put the bag on her lap, surprised that her hands were trembling with anticipation. Her ultrasound had been yesterday, and as it was, it had taken a lot *not* to spill the news in a group e-mail.

"Yesterday I got this," she said, showing an envelope that held a printout of the ultrasound image. She opened it and pulled out the picture.

"Yes!" Jessie cried, hurrying to her side. A wave of excitement swept over the women, and Brenda clapped her hands and scurried over. "Does this mean you know what you're having?"

Jessie grabbed the picture and squinted at it. "Okay, I was always bad at deciphering these things. What am I looking at?"

"A boy," Kim said, grinning. She could already picture Justin playing catch with their son, dressing him up in Utah Jazz clothes and indoctrinating him on Cougars versus Utes. Even though Justin himself wasn't a graduate of either school, he bled blue.

In the middle of it all, she had a brief flash in her head of Justin wounded and bandaged from the last convoy. She sucked in her breath and had to remind herself that it was only flesh wounds, that he'd be fine. He wasn't even being sent to an Army hospital to recuperate. But in a way, she wished he were wounded *just* enough to come home. Then he'd be out of danger *and* be with her when the baby came.

The wives squealed and cheered and gathered around the picture for a better look. "Here's the side of his face," Kim said, pointing to another picture and then handing it to Jessie. She dug into the bag for the rest of what she'd brought. "I thought I'd tell Justin what we're having by sending him this."

She held up an infant-sized shirt, pants, and baseball cap—all in camouflage.

"Oh, that's priceless!" Jessie surrendered the picture to Brenda and came over to look at the tiny soldier clothes. "He'll love it. What a great idea." She lowered her voice and whispered, "Does he . . ."

Kim inclined her head toward Jessie and whispered, "Of course." As if such a question were silly. It felt natural to think so . . . now. What a difference a few weeks made. What a difference when you had friends who cared about you and supported you.

"You know," Kim said, louder, so the group could hear. "It's probably a good thing we're having a boy first."

"Oh? How's that?" Nora asked, taking her turn looking at the picture.

"I imagine Justin would be so overprotective of a girl that he'd lock her up until she turned thirty. And then he'd guard her bedroom with an M-16 and chase off any boys trying to so much as look at her. Maybe having a boy first will break him in for the next one."

The ladies laughed, and Kim folded up the clothes to put back into the bag. It wasn't until she slid the cap in that her hand froze with a realization. She'd talked about having *another* child—maybe a girl—as if it were a foregone conclusion, something she wouldn't even mind doing.

I did say I'd have two, she reminded herself as she placed the bag onto the cement pad. But she'd referred so casually to a future with multiple children.

Wow.

The whole "woman in Zion" role—attributes of the woman Justin thought he'd married—seemed to be slowly starting to fit, an inch at a time. Maybe, just maybe, by the time Justin came home, she would be almost to the point of feeling like she was *normal*. She would probably never fit it completely—and in some ways, she didn't want to fit the typical woman's role—but "normal"? That sounded good.

Maybe there was hope that she wouldn't totally mess up her kid's life.

Chapter 18: Brenda
In It Together

Brenda twisted her paper napkin—the object of her nervous energy—into a tight point. "I thought I'd be doing better after that one really awful mission, but I can't seem to get myself together."

"You're no better at all?" Marianne asked, concern in her voice.

"Well, a little," Brenda conceded. It *had* been a few weeks. She wasn't a total basket case. "I have good days. Halloween was a ball—it got me totally distracted, and I felt great all day. And I've slept okay, for the most part. But I never know when another bad day will come, and I feel like I'm on the verge of a wreck *all* the time." She twisted so hard that the napkin tip broke off. This week's lunch was at Mimi's Café in Orem, and they were lucky enough to get a secluded table, away from noise and listening ears. The wooden decor and country-style curtains made the place feel homey. "Does it ever get easier?"

The four younger wives all turned to Nora for an answer, knowing she was the person Brenda meant the question for, even if it was technically rhetorical.

Nora dragged her fork tines across a piece of watermelon, not looking at any of the wives. "Honestly? No, deployment doesn't get any easier. And when you hit the year mark, you'll be *so* ready to have it over." She chuckled. "I remember in previous deployments how passing the year mark made the whole thing feel like an overdue pregnancy."

Groans erupted; everyone there who'd gone through childbirth knew what *that* felt like, and Kim could relate on some level too.

Nora ate her watermelon pensively, swallowed, and spoke again, her brow knit together, her mouth pressed into a grim line. "You also need to be ready for *after*. The boys will come home with a whole new set of problems. In some ways, I'm grateful that Russell's back on base telling the others what to do this time. For his two other deployments, he was in the thick of it and saw a lot of ugly stuff. It affected him—us—for quite a while."

Brenda felt as if she were suddenly falling out of a plane without a parachute. Nora usually gave them wisdom and comfort. This time, all she could offer was basically, "It won't get any easier," possibly that, "It'll only get worse," and, "The end *won't* be the end."

How depressing.

"I can't think that far ahead," Brenda said. "Right now, it's one day at a time."

"That's all you can and should do," Nora said. "Don't think about all the months to come and all the things you'll need to deal with then. Just get through *today*."

With a nod, Brenda said, "There are days when I feel like I'm doing all right personally, and like you said they would, my boys do okay too. But no matter what, sometimes they manage to come up with their own worries."

"Kids are rather good at that," Jessie remarked dryly. She broke off a piece of muffin and stared at the chocolate chips in it. "The other day, Becca said, 'Mama, I love Dada. Dada all gone.' And then she waved good-bye all matter-of-factly. About broke my heart. How do you explain to a two-and-a-half-year-old where her daddy is and why he's gone?" She popped the muffin into her mouth. "I've tried. She doesn't get it."

"And how do you explain it without scaring the daylights out of them?" Brenda said, her voice going up a notch.

"Exactly!" Jessie said. "You can't lie and say that for sure everything will be all right, but anything else freaks them out. Before Tim left, if Alex had a nightmare, it was about things like a witch under her bed or an alligator in her closet. Now it's bad guys shooting her daddy with big guns. And I can't tell her that those bad guys don't exist. They're *real*. Imaginary monsters were easier to deal with."

"Bradley's having the toughest time of it," Brenda said quietly. "The twins don't get what's happening, no matter how I try to explain. They really miss their dad—Josh sees pictures of Rick, and no matter how many times I correct him, he thinks it's Uncle Tony. And I think Tyler's starting to forget Rick altogether. But Bradley . . . he thinks Rick doesn't love us anymore, and *that's* why he's gone. I explain where his dad is, what he's doing, and why, but it's always, 'If Daddy really loved me, he wouldn't have missed all my soccer games,' or something like that. How will he handle Christmas and his birthday without Dad?"

A tear rolled down her cheek, and she brushed it away with her fingertips. Deployment was complicated enough for adults to comprehend and deal with; it was nearly impossible for kids to figure out.

"My kids can point to a map and show you exactly where their dad is," Jessie said with a nod. "But that doesn't mean they have any real idea how far away it is or what he's doing."

"Or how long a year is," Marianne added.

"I don't know what to tell you," Nora said with a shrug. "It's tough. I'm sure you've learned this one already, but for me, my greatest strength during deployment has always come from prayer. Some days during Desert Storm, when the kids were little, I don't think I stopped praying from the moment I woke up until my head hit the pillow at night. And sometimes I didn't stop even then, because I'd be too worried to sleep. Prayer is the only way you're going to survive—and the only way to know what to do for your kids."

Around the table, heads bobbed in agreement. Even Kim's. She was rarely vocal during the lunches, but today she piped up.

"Obviously, I don't have kids yet, but for the first time in my life, I'm praying—harder than ever." She sniffed and smiled. "This may sound totally stupid to you guys, since you're all these huge spiritual giants and returned missionaries and everything . . ."

Everyone shook their heads, with murmurs of "No, we aren't" and "Don't sell yourself short."

Jessie snorted and added, "Hardly."

"You are—a lot more than I am, anyway," Kim insisted. "But right now I'm closer to the Spirit than I've ever been, and I doubt anything but coping with Justin in Afghanistan could have done that. As much as I hate it all—especially being pregnant alone and worried all the time—at least this one good thing has come of it. I feel like I finally 'get' the gospel for the first time in my life."

The table lapsed into a reverent silence as they all let Kim's words sink in. The only sounds were utensils on dishes and cups clanking on the table.

After several seconds, Marianne, who sat beside Brenda, spoke up from her reverie. "I wish McKayla would learn the same thing right now instead of going the other direction." She lowered her chin, putting her forehead into her hand. A little sob escaped.

Brenda put an arm around her, and Marianne turned into her friend's embrace. "What's happened?" Brenda asked gently, concerned at Marianne's sudden break.

At first, she didn't answer. She cried for a minute, choked on a couple of sobs, then pulled back and wiped both hands across her cheeks to dry them. "Sorry," she said with a disdainful shake of her head. "This is so unlike me."

Nora leaned across the table and put her hand over Marianne's. "But what's wrong? You can tell us."

"It's McKayla. She's been doing all kinds of stupid things. It started out with sneaking out of the house at night. Then the cops brought her home—and I hadn't even known she was gone. She smelled of alcohol."

"Oh, I'm so sorry," Jessie said, her face crinkled with concern.

"Last night when I went to check on her," Marianne went on, "she was gone again, and she didn't take her cell phone with her either. I called all her friends' parents, but none of them knew anything—and all of *their* kids were home. I'm pretty sure she was with her new boyfriend, Jake, who's creepy scary. Last night, I drove all around, looking for her at parks and any hangout I could think of. When I got home, she was already in bed. She had no idea I'd been out looking for her, and she denied everything when I went into her room. She must think I'm a total idiot—she swore she'd never had a drink in her life, but it was on her breath again. And then . . . I noticed something sticking out in her jeans pocket she'd left on the floor when she put her pajamas on."

Brenda and Jessie exchanged foreboding looks. Brenda had a feeling she knew what was coming.

"It was a baggy of OxyContin pills."

A collective intake of breath surrounded the table. Marianne looked at the ceiling and shuddered. "How can she be so stupid? We had a talk—not the calmest on my end—and she blamed everything on Brian being gone. If he really loved us, she said, he wouldn't have left." She glanced at Brenda, and they all nodded, as if recognizing the similarity between Bradley's and McKayla's thoughts. "She doesn't believe in the Church anymore, because wouldn't God know that she needs her dad during high school? He wouldn't take her dad away." She lowered her head. "She's always been a daddy's girl, so ever since she could reach for him, I've played second fiddle. Having Brian gone is *killing* her." She looked up, gazing at Kim, pleading for help. "What can I do so she'll turn away from drinking and drugs and . . ." She shuddered. "And stop looking for male attention in the wrong places?"

Kim looked side to side as if stunned that Marianne really wanted her opinion. "I wish I had a good answer," Kim said, verging on tears herself. "At that age, I don't know if anything could have gotten through to me if I'd decided to do drugs and stuff. I did sneak out a few times, but I didn't do anything else." She twisted her glass thoughtfully. "Sounds like she really needs her dad around."

Marianne shrugged helplessly. "But I can't give her that. I worry that she'll end up in jail or pregnant . . . or worse. Those drugs . . . what else has she used that I don't know about? How often has she snuck out before I found out she was doing it? I feel so stupid. I thought the biggest problems I had with her were a few bad grades and her whining about not going to the stupid Homecoming dance. I can't believe I missed seeing all *this*. She needs counseling—that's what she needs. But I don't know if I can get her there."

Everyone sat still, listening to Marianne, as if they knew that she needed to spill it all out. Brenda's eyes burned with tears, and she ached for Marianne—the woman she'd felt so much irritation for not so long ago. And she had to admit—maple syrup in the carpet didn't hold a candle to this. Now she felt closer to Marianne than she did to her own sister.

"If Brian were here," Marianne went on, "she wouldn't be acting up this way. I know that. So now *I'm* starting to resent him being all gung-ho about the Army. I'm mad that he didn't get out when he had the chance a couple of years ago, that he left us right when she needed him. I'm afraid that if she drives her life into a ditch, I'll blame Brian for it."

She closed her eyes, and her lips trembled. "Isn't that terrible?"

"It's not terrible," Nora said quietly. "It's real. It's painful. And it's not easy. But we're here for you."

Marianne nodded, unable to speak, and as if on cue, all five women leaned forward and shared a group embrace, every eye and cheek wet, every heart full.

Chapter 19: Marianne
Aid

"McKayla? Sweetie? Can I come in so we can talk about it?"

"No." Her single word was like a sharp stab.

Marianne stood outside the bedroom door, praying to know what to do. Bailey stood beside her, hoping to get inside to get her homework. But McKayla wasn't opening their shared bedroom door for anyone.

She tried again. "Brother Davis isn't coming over for another hour. If you don't want a blessing when he gets here, that's fine. Come out so you and I can talk. And so Bailey can get her homework."

Bangs sounded from the other side of the door, and a second later, it flew open. McKayla appeared just long enough to shove Bailey's bright pink book bag into the hall before she slammed the door shut again. Marianne and Bailey both jumped at the noise.

"I said no!" McKayla bellowed from the other side. "There's nothing wrong with me. And if I'm going to get a blessing from anyone, it's going to be from *Dad,* not from some doofus who doesn't even know me."

Brother Davis isn't a doofus, and he deserves your respect. Marianne had to catch herself from yelling the words; defending their home teacher would only throw fuel on the fire right now. If there was any hope of getting through to McKayla, she had to deal with one issue at a time, not push her farther away with each outburst. She turned to Bailey, who still stood in the hallway, wide-eyed and clutching her bag to her chest.

"Why don't you do your homework down in the family room?" Marianne suggested under her breath, ushering Bailey toward the stairs. "I'll be down in a minute if you need help with your math."

With Bailey and Kevin both downstairs, Marianne tried again. "McKayla, we both know you're going through a rough time right now. A priesthood blessing could help."

"Nothing is wrong with me," McKayla snapped through the door.

Marianne clenched her teeth, trying to rein in her own anger. Several "things" were wrong with McKayla and her life right now. So many of her choices were leading her into deeper, darker waters—a place from which she wouldn't be able to escape if she didn't make a course correction soon. Nora had mentioned a great therapist friend named Deborah who specialized in both teen girls and military families, and Marianne had every intention of taking McKayla to her—but how helpful would counseling be when the patient was unwilling to participate openly? She'd hoped that McKayla would agree to a blessing and that maybe it would soften her enough to be more open to therapy.

"I'm not coming out," McKayla called. "So don't waste your breath."

"Just *think* about it," Marianne said. "I'll be downstairs if you want to talk."

"Don't count on it," McKayla said. Something hit the door—probably a shoe.

Marianne wanted to burst into the room and shake some sense into her daughter. But she knew from experience that the more frustration and anger she showed, the more McKayla pulled away. So she only pretended to kick the door and shake her fist in frustration, gritting her teeth. The impudent little brat.

Breathing out heavily, Marianne headed downstairs. Kevin was on one side of the couch, watching *Teenage Mutant Ninja Turtles* while Bailey worked on her homework on the other end. Marianne made a beeline to the computer, hoping that Brian might have sent an e-mail since she'd checked last. He hadn't, of course. It was a little early in the morning his time for that. But there was one from Nora. It included the therapist's number then continued.

I talked to Deborah yesterday like you asked me to, and she says she had a cancellation for Thursday at three. She's usually booked three weeks in advance, so I jumped at the chance and asked her to hold that spot for McKayla. Let her know if that works for you.

The other wives and I want to help with babysitting and meals while you're helping McKayla. I'll be running to the grocery store tomorrow. Let me know what I can pick up for you. I'll be buying food for you whether you ask for it or not. You might as well place an order so I'll get stuff your kids will eat!

I'll bring it all by around noon tomorrow—and while I'm there, I'll pick up some laundry to do for you. (Yes, I will. Don't argue with me.)

And so you know, all of us wives will be holding a fast for McKayla. We're starting by ourselves on Tuesday after lunch, and we'll break our fasts together at lunch Wednesday at Café Rio. I think we're going to the one over by your house.

Take care and know we love you.

Nora

Marianne's face contorted with emotion at the outpouring of support. It was almost as if Nora could see the bare fridge and the mountain of dirty clothes in the laundry room. In light of McKayla's issues—like her latest stupidity with skipping out on entire days of school, making Marianne frantic with worry—it was a struggle to get the basics taken care of. And with her attention and energy focused on McKayla, the younger children were feeling the strain. Bailey was acting out with preteen temper tantrums, and Kevin was emotional and sulky. She knew they both needed her attention. She felt torn into far too many pieces. There wasn't enough of her to go around. If only Brian were here.

She glanced up at the "compose mail" icon and bit the inside of her lip. How much should Brian be told? In the beginning, she hadn't told him anything. At first, McKayla's behavior was disrespectful, but it wasn't anything alarming—sneaking out wasn't unheard of for teens, and neither was dating someone parents didn't approve of. She'd thought that refusing to let McKayla go to Homecoming was bad. Now the girl was not only dating a boy when she was barely sixteen, but dating someone downright unacceptable. She was also failing school, going to wild parties, and now she was doing drugs . . .

Her behavior was escalating by the week. Brian *needed* to know some of it. And he did know parts, bits and pieces, at least. But Marianne worried about telling him too much and making him worried when he had no control over what was happening at home. Back in August, McKayla had e-mailed Brian regularly, but that had trickled off—the chances that she'd tell her dad what she was doing were pretty much nil anyway. For weeks Marianne had felt alone as she dealt with the whole thing. Why had she hesitated telling the wives about it?

What a relief it was to have their support now that she'd opened up. Not one of them judged her for the situation. She judged herself harshly enough as it was, beating herself up with thoughts of how a better mother could raise up a righteous daughter who never strayed this far from the path.

Marianne reread Nora's e-mail, this time having to wipe her eyes several times to make the image clear again. When Brian left, she'd thought that having her parents nearby and neighbors willing to help would be plenty. But now . . . she couldn't imagine how she'd get by without the wives.

She called Deborah's office and left a message on the voice mail to confirm the appointment for Thursday. Then she replied to Nora, thanking her for her offer to help and taking her up on it, something that still felt foreign to do even months after Brian had left.

I could use someone to keep tabs on the kids during McKayla's appointment on Thursday. And yes, I could really use some groceries as well.

She ran up to the kitchen and grabbed her shopping list then copied down the most urgent items—eggs, bread, peanut butter, toilet paper, butter, apples, and a case of macaroni and cheese. They went through a lot of that as the kids fended for themselves lately. She made a hot meal once or twice a week if they were lucky. They were old enough to make their own dinners if they were simple. She felt a bit guilty for not being a "good mom," but with her current stress—and without a husband to cook for—dinner was one thing she'd let fall to the wayside.

I have a load or two of laundry I'd be more than happy to give you. Thank you so much for your help! And please thank the other wives, too. I'll be fasting with you tomorrow.

As she sent the message, the doorbell rang. Marianne grabbed a tissue from a box on the desk and wiped her face, hoping she didn't have makeup smeared all down her cheeks. She hurried up to the door to find Brother Davis and his son Matt on the other side.

"Good evening, Sister Gardner," he said, holding out a plate of warm rolls. "My wife sent these when she heard I was coming over."

"Thanks," Marianne said, taking them. "They smell divine." Someone else taking care of her felt good. She wasn't sure the family would even have dinner tonight. Now they'd at least have homemade rolls. Maybe she'd crack open a couple cans of chicken noodle and call it good.

Brother Davis and his priest-aged son stepped inside when she held the door open. "So is McKayla ready?"

Marianne glanced up the stairs. "I can check, but I don't think she's receptive to having a blessing right now. She's never had one from anyone but her dad. I meant to call and tell you . . ." She'd meant to call him if McKayla refused. She'd gone downstairs and hoped for the best, and when she got Nora's e-mail, the idea of calling Brother Davis hadn't made an appearance in her head.

He nodded in understanding. "Must be hard for her. And you. But in that case, is there anything Matt and I can do for you while we're here?"

Marianne's eyes pricked with tears again.

For crying out loud, will I never be able to get control of myself?

With a nod, she said, "Actually, I think *I* could use a blessing, if you don't mind."

"Not at all." Brother Davis retrieved a chair from the kitchen table. Matt sat on the couch and folded his arms.

Marianne gestured for Bailey and Kevin to join them in the living room. "I'm getting a blessing," she told them when they sat on the couch. "If you want one too, I'm sure Brother Davis will give you one."

"I'd be happy to give them blessings as well," he said as Marianne sat on the chair. "So Sister Gardner, what's your full name?"

Marianne closed her eyes and breathed deeply. A calm already began to descend over her as she tilted her head so he could hear.

Anytime she said her maiden name, it gave her an odd sense of comfort, as if it were a reminder of who she'd been and the family who loved her and would always be there for her. It was the same today.

"It's Marianne Elliott Gardner."

Chapter 20: Kim
Common Ground

Lunch at Café Rio would be their last until after Thanksgiving. Kim arrived at the same time as Jessie. Kim got her food first and took a pink chair at a bright green table as they waited for the others to arrive. Jessie sat down a moment later. They purposely chose a corner so they could inconspicuously say a group prayer and break their fast for McKayla together.

Kim's chimichanga taunted her. Being pregnant, she couldn't fast like the others, but she couldn't very well eat in front of them before they broke their fasts. Nora and Brenda came over with their trays a few minutes later, and Marianne arrived last. When she made her way through the line, she sat down at their table with a grin on her face.

"You guys are a sight for sore eyes," Marianne said, scooting in. "You're wonderful. That's all there is to it. Thanks for fasting for McKayla." She sniffed then laughed. "And I've *got* to stop getting all weepy."

Nora reached out and took Marianne's hand in one of hers and Brenda's in the other. Everyone else followed suit to create a ring. Nora acted as the voice of the group in prayer. She whispered the words, and everyone leaned in to hear as she ended their fast and asked for comfort, courage, and clarity for McKayla to see the correct path and to made good choices, to have her heart softened that she might be willing to accept the help being offered her.

"Amen," everyone murmured then squeezed hands and pulled apart.

"Thank you," Marianne whispered, picking up her fork. "I'm going to miss you all over Thanksgiving."

"You won't be getting rid of us that easily," Nora said with a grin. "We won't be having lunch, but we're helping out with babysitting and errands, right?"

"Right," Marianne said. "But hopefully not for long. You have enough stress on your plates. I can't believe how generous you all are." She shook her head and fanned her eyes. "Enough of this emotional stuff. I've been feeling so down lately, I need some cheerful talk."

Kim had barely taken her third bite when the pain started. She pressed a hand to her chest and grimaced. Maybe she shouldn't have put quite so much salsa on her chimichanga. Or maybe Café Rio wasn't the best place for her to pick for today's wives lunch. But the food had never bothered her before. Then again, almost *any* food upset her stomach nowadays. Even Ritz crackers, if she ate too many.

"Are you okay?" Jessie asked, narrowing her eyes, forkful of shredded beef poised midair.

"I'm fine." Kim squinted one eye as the worst of it ebbed. "It's just heartburn." A ripple of murmurs and nods went around the table as Kim searched her purse for her antacids, which she always kept on hand.

Brenda groaned with a memory. "I got heartburn so bad with the twins I couldn't sleep at night. I had piles of pillows stacked high enough I was practically sitting—didn't help—and I swear I went through a bottle of Tums every couple of days."

"Oh, me too," Marianne said, putting down her drink. It was as if Kim's heartburn were opening up a conversation topic for everyone, something they could all relate to and use to avoid thinking about McKayla for a while. Marianne pretended to shudder. "There's a reason they call it 'heartburn.' I thought I'd die."

Kim found the bottle of Tums. "This is my best friend lately," she said, rattling it. The women laughed.

"I don't think I ever had much heartburn during pregnancies," Jessie said thoughtfully. "For me, it was urinary tract infections, yeast infections, and the occasional gall bladder attack."

"Oooh. Sounds like fun," Kim said. "I don't envy *that.*" She popped two tablets into her mouth and closed the lid.

"Oh, trust me—it was a party," Jessie said with a chuckle.

"What about you?" Marianne asked, turning to Nora. "What were your pregnancies like?"

Nora smiled wanly, her fork trailing through the green chili sauce on her burrito. "Well, I lived by the toilet for the first three and a half months. I'd lose so much weight, the doctor would threaten to send me to the hospital." She shook her head at the memory. "But I couldn't let *that* happen, because, except for the first time around, I always had at least one other little one to take care of."

"How awful!" Marianne said. "I was sick but not *that* sick. Of course, I do tend to get horrendous, weeklong headaches when I'm pregnant, but I don't usually live with my head in the toilet."

It was as if a dam had been released. The look on Marianne's face was one of relief; Kim guessed that she'd been thinking of nothing but McKayla for days. The four of them discussed all kinds of pregnancy ailments—apparently Jessie had also once had the symptoms of hydro-nephrosis—whatever that was—but it turned out to be something else. Brenda was ordered to bed rest with the twins. Nora was in a car accident while expecting her first and had to hobble around eight months pregnant with a cast on her foot.

"I gained nearly sixty pounds that pregnancy because I couldn't move or exercise," she told them.

Marianne always had horrendous sciatica pain—not great for someone living in a split-level house who needed to navigate stairs a lot.

Kim put in her two bits here and there, commiserating with throwing up, having a superhuman sense of smell—the odor of bacon and many other things now made her want to wretch—and other aches and complaints that went along with having a baby.

As the women continued, Kim found herself sitting back, a smile curving her mouth. She wasn't smiling because the others had experienced any of those things, but because talking about pregnancy ailments made her feel less alone. These women had gone through the same things that she was dealing with and more.

It was also a reminder that women throughout history had borne children and come out the other side with stories to tell—even if they wore a few battle scars as a result. She could get through this. For the first time, she really fit in with the wives. She was just like the rest of them.

Kim felt a poke in her tummy, rounder now that she'd passed the five-month mark. She reached down and rested her palm over the spot where the baby had moved, waiting for another kick. They were getting stronger every day now, and she was finally looking pregnant; people no longer avoided asking whether she was having a baby for fear that she'd just gained weight. Her tummy looked like a small, tight basketball under her shirt.

She was in the middle of what her doctor called the "golden weeks" of pregnancy: after the nasty morning sickness—which Kim thought of as "any-time-of-the-day-or-night sickness"—but before the baby had grown so big that moving and sleeping were uncomfortable.

Jessie talked about how being a nurse made pregnancy worries worse—she knew way too much about what *could* go wrong and panicked over all kinds of little symptoms.

As the ladies talked, Kim stroked her belly.

Who are you? she silently asked. *Do you have any idea what you're getting into?*

She lowered her eyes, hoping—but not really expecting—the other wives to admit to their feelings of total inadequacy, to say that at some point, maybe they hadn't *wanted* to be pregnant, even if the feeling was for a fleeting moment. But all she heard from them was how each baby was a "blessing."

She looked at Marianne, who seemed tired all the time. Especially lately with McKayla's problems. If this baby had been a girl—or if she had a girl next—would the two of them ever run into these kinds of things? Would her own daughter yell at her and fail school and do drugs? How would things be for her and her son in fifteen or sixteen years?

"As difficult as pregnancy is for me, I really can't complain," Marianne said. "According to the doctors, I shouldn't even have had one child, let alone three. I wanted more, but it's a miracle I got what I did."

"Oh?" Nora asked, her brow raised. She placed a sympathetic hand on Marianne's. "I'm so sorry. Infertility can be such a trial."

"It was," Marianne said. "We were almost to the point of wondering if we'd ever have a baby the old-fashioned way. Brian was considering adoption when I finally got pregnant with McKayla." She smiled wistfully, and somehow Kim knew that Marianne was remembering the magic of her first pregnancy, her first baby. It was a sad irony that the same baby was causing so much stress—and wasn't so innocent anymore.

"I never ever wanted to be anything but a mom," Marianne said, staring at her plate as if she could see the past there. "Even as a young woman, when I had friends planning these great careers and choosing majors in college, I didn't know what to pick. I wanted nothing but to be a mom. I'm so glad I get to be." She raised her eyes and looked right at Kim. "It's the hardest job in the world, but it's also the best one."

"Here, here," Nora said, raising her glass of lemon water. Everyone else raised theirs in a toast to motherhood. Kim raised her root beer and mechanically bumped the paper cup against the others.

So Marianne was born to be a mother, Kim thought. *And she almost didn't become one. I never wanted to be a mom, and it just happened.*

As the wives continued with stories about ultrasounds, swollen ankles, and labor, Kim clasped her hands together and rested them on her belly. *I'm sorry,* she thought, directing the message to her baby. She was starting to want the baby—a little bit—but she wanted it when Justin was here. The reality of a baby during deployment was terrifying.

She put on a plastic smile for the rest of the lunch, still enjoying all the funny chitchat—which had gone on to episiotomy horror stories and epidurals—but wondered what was wrong with her when the basic instinct she should have been born with . . . didn't exist.

She began playing with her salad, using her fork to move around pieces of lettuce and tomato on her giant chimichanga, which was way too big for her to get down, especially now that her stomach was getting squished. At meals, she ate until she was ready to pop but could only get down half of a normal meal. But that didn't amount to much food, so within an hour, she'd be starving again. Might as well bring it home and warm it up later.

"You know how women often get into labor and pregnancy stories when they gather?" Marianne suddenly said.

Several of the women laughed. Jessie swallowed and waved her fork as she said, "Tim hates that. Whenever that happens with him around, he turns to the guys in the room and starts quoting his favorite James Bond scenes."

"Rick would totally get into that." Brenda laughed.

When the murmurs died down, Marianne continued. "It occurred to me that the reason women love to share those stories is because most women have had babies and can relate. It's common ground for them." She looked around the table at each woman, one by one—including Kim—and said, "That's why I'm so glad I have all of you. This is the only place I have common ground. No one else understands what it's like during deployment. I need you guys."

Jessie nodded, her mouth pressed tightly as if she were angry. She stabbed her fork into a pile of lettuce. "To be honest, it really gets under my skin when women try to relate with what we're going through. 'Oh, it must be so hard to be the only one to take care of the kids,'" Jessie said with a high-pitched, annoying voice. "'I did that for a month when my husband was out of the country on business. It was *so* hard.'" She rolled her eyes.

"Oh, and let me guess, 'it's exactly like being a single mom,' right?" Nora piped in. Everyone guffawed, having heard *that* one more times than any of them could count. Nora smiled knowingly. "Of course, that's what we thought going in, didn't we?"

They all nodded. Even Kim, because in some ways, she'd thought that being pregnant while Justin was gone would feel like being a single, pregnant woman. It didn't feel like that. She wasn't single. She was very much married, and her husband was dodging bullets.

"You know what would be nice?" Brenda asked. She was normally so calm and pensive, but now her eyes sparkled. "To carry around a big, flashing neon sign that says HUSBAND DEPLOYED. BACK OFF!"

Marianne was taking a drink and almost spurted soda out of her nose. She grabbed a napkin and held it to her face, but before she got her laughter completely under control, she added, "Or how about DON'T BOTHER. YOU JUST DON'T GET IT!"

Everyone nearly bowled over. Brenda wiped tears from her eyes and kept giggling, as if a stress valve had been opened, and now she couldn't close it back up.

Kim brought her straw to her mouth and drank some root beer. This was nice. She was glad she came to that first lunch in August. She might be nearly ten years younger than the next youngest wife, but in ways that really mattered, she fit right in.

Chapter 21: Nora
Insufficient

Nora and her mother left their latest doctor visit exhausted and ravenous. What should have been a one-hour outing turned into three, thanks to a patient whom the doctor had been delayed with at the hospital. If she'd made Thanksgiving dinner last week, she'd have had plenty of leftovers still to use, but she hadn't done that.

Dan and his wife had invited Nora down to Texas for the holiday, but she couldn't very well travel with her mother. The other children either couldn't make it to Utah or had the holiday with their in-laws this year. Except for Scott, who insisted that he had too many papers to write to come down. Nora had a suspicion that the reality was he didn't want to leave his new girlfriend for the weekend.

It was all just as well. She didn't want to worry the kids about their grandmother yet. They knew Grandma was sick. Nora would tell them *how* sick when she felt ready to. The new year would be a good time. Their Thanksgiving was a simple, quiet affair differing little from their everyday lives except for the small turkey and pie.

On the way home from the appointment, the car moved through snow, the sound of slush thrown by the tires rhythmic in the silence.

"We're driving too fast," her mother protested. "You're going to lose control on the ice."

"The roads aren't slippery," Nora said. "They're only slushy. And I'm going a little *under* the speed limit."

They passed Wendy's, and Nora's stomach gurgled. She would have preferred to pull in and get the two of them fresh salads, but that wouldn't do for her mother. "What a waste of money, when you can make food for yourself at home," she'd say if Nora were to suggest such a thing. Sure, making lunch at home might be cheaper—possibly tastier and most likely healthier—but sometimes it was nice to pay more for a little convenience, something Nora's life lacked of late.

All she did was take care of her mother, visit the wives on Wednesdays, and coordinate whatever help they needed throughout the week. She did as many errands for them as was possible, a number that was getting fewer all the time as her mother's health declined. But Nora wanted to care for them as Russell had asked her to—and now, as she *wanted* to—but without them knowing that her mother didn't have much time left.

But caring for Mother meant that she was mostly helping coordinate assistance for the Army wives rather than doing it herself—figuring out schedules, assigning babysitting, making phone calls, doing only an occasional grocery errand.

They pulled into the garage, where Nora helped her mother out of the car and into the house. In the kitchen, her mother settled onto a chair to wait for lunch. Nora knelt at her mother's feet to get her shoes off, one at a time, and set them aside.

Then she went to the fridge, where she pulled out some hard-boiled eggs. "How about an egg-salad sandwich?" she asked, knowing they were her mother's favorite.

"Well, I suppose that would do. As long as it isn't too dry," her mother said, smoothing her skirt. "A good egg salad is plenty moist. There's almost nothing worse than a *dry* one." She pursed her face as if she had bitten into a lemon.

"Got it. Not dry," Nora said with a forced smile, her back to the table. As she peeled the eggs, she threw a glance over her shoulder. With any luck, her mother would take a nap after getting something to eat, leaving Nora with a couple of hours to herself.

A few minutes later, she placed two plates on the kitchen table, onto the new place mats her mother had bought at Target the other day. "No reason to live like a peasant even if no one else is watching," her mother had insisted.

"Here you go, Mom," Nora said, pulling out a chair and sitting down. "Egg salad on whole wheat. I used a teaspoon of Dijon mustard, exactly how you like it."

Her mother picked up a triangle of sandwich, hands shaking slightly with the effort. Nora had to stop herself from reaching out to help—she'd tried that once before and had received a reprimand for it along the lines of, "Goodness, I'm not a child, dear. I can feed myself."

Nora took a bite of her own sandwich and chewed, the silence between them thick as she waited for her mother's verdict.

"Not too bad," she murmured, sucking a crumb through her dentures. "A little moister than I prefer, but I suppose one can't be too picky."

Or too grateful, Nora thought dismally. *If I had used a teaspoon less mayonnaise, she'd have complained that it was too dry.*

Neither said much else as they ate. Nora had slipped plastic bendy straws into both of their glasses of water. Her mother's bendy straw was to make drinking easier by removing the need to lift the heavy glass. Nora hoped to prevent another spill. The last one had embarrassed her mother and upset Nora—as if it had been her fault. Better to take precautions than to be caught unaware, she figured. But she used a straw too, not wanting to draw attention to the reason behind her mother's.

Nora finished off her sandwich, and after her mother didn't eat more than a few nibbles, she was half-tempted to eat Mother's too. But that would never do. It wasn't polite *or* hygienic.

The horrors.

"Would you like to read or watch some television or something?" Nora asked, praying her mother would suggest a nap on her own. If Nora vocalized the idea, her mother was liable to insist that she wasn't tired *all* the time, for goodness sake, and she didn't need any Mollycoddling, either.

Her mother gently pushed her plate forward a couple of inches—her nonverbal cue that she was finished with her meal. "My head's got a nasty, tight feeling," she said, touching her forehead, which was crinkled, likely with fatigue or pain or both. "I think I'll lie down for a few minutes."

In other words, she's taking a nap, Nora thought, exulting. But aloud, she said casually, "Can I get you anything? One of your pain pills to help your head, maybe?" She knew full well that her head wasn't the only source of her mother's pain, but it was the only one she'd likely admit to.

Pressing her hands on the tabletop, her mother caught her balance and breath. She raised a hand, as if about to wave away the idea of painkillers but then nodded. "I suppose I could use a little something. Maybe a Tylenol. I don't want to put anything into my body like those crazy drugs the doctor prescribed."

"Of course," Nora said, scurrying to comply. She shook two caplets into her palm from the bottle on the counter and refilled her mother's water glass. She handed them over, wondering how intense the pain would have to grow before her mother broke down and swallowed one of the more powerful painkillers. Today the doctor had been surprised that she hadn't taken any of them; he'd clearly assumed she'd be on them regularly like all his other patients who were in their final weeks.

He'd given Nora a look that clearly showed his concern for her mother's well-being then added, "She's going to be experiencing a lot of . . . *discomfort,*" he said, eyeing Nora and emphasizing the last word as if he really meant something else. Like agony.

"I'll try to get her to take them," Nora promised, knowing it sounded weak but also knowing that with someone as stubborn as her mother, "try" was the best anyone could do. Now, looking at her, Nora could see the discomfort in her face already as she stood there by the table. The pain seemed to pinch her eyes at the corners and draw her mouth into a tight knot. Tylenol surely couldn't do more than take off the edge, if that.

"Are you sure you don't want a Lortab? Or a Percocet?" Nora reached for the window sill, where several bottles sat. "Dr. Davenport says—"

"Thank you, but no thank you," her mother said staunchly. "I don't want to have a fuzzy mind." For a woman with little strength, she sure sounded like a drill sergeant. Nora decided that next time she'd give Mother a Lortab without saying what it was and see if she'd take it.

After swallowing the pills, her mother took the walker from Nora's hands and gripped the handles then shuffled down the hall in her stocking feet. A moment later Nora heard the soft click of the bedroom door then let out a breath she had been holding.

Two hours, all to herself.

She hadn't felt such relief since she had her second baby and looked forward to the precious afternoon hours when both of them were asleep at the same time. But first she'd better clean up the kitchen. She spent a few minutes tidying up the small lunch mess, making sure to leave nary a crumb or a speck of eggshell behind. Part of the process included finishing up her mother's sandwich, after all.

It's perfect—not at all too moist, she thought with satisfaction. She brushed her palms together over the sink to get rid of any crumbs then put the plate into the dishwasher.

She went to the living room, where she picked up a novel she had set aside a week ago and curled up with it on the couch. A chapter into it, however, Nora's eyes began to pull shut. Her muscles—her very bones—ached for sleep. She let her bookmark fall into place and the pages shut on themselves. Her eyes closed, and she breathed deeply, her body relishing the feeling of relaxation—something she hadn't experienced much of since Russell left, and certainly not since her mother had moved in.

She was in the hazy place between wakefulness and sleep when she felt something warm and heavy being placed over her. Curious, but fighting drowsiness, she tilted her head on the pillow and cracked an eye open.

Her mother stood above her, arranging a quilt over her resting form. Nora didn't move. She closed her eyes tightly as a lump formed in her throat, and a tear leaked onto the couch pillow beneath her head. Her mother gently tucked the blanket around her, making sure no cold air could reach her then tucked the top under Nora's chin.

Not once did Nora want to tell her to stop, that *she* wasn't a child, that she could put a blanket over herself just fine, thank you very much.

Instead, she let herself remember what it was like when she was young and her mother had tucked her in at night—and wished that during her teenage bout with scarlet fever that she hadn't resented such simple gestures of kindness.

Her mother leaned down and kissed Nora's temple then stroked her hair as if she were that little girl again. Without a word, she padded back down the hall. Only after the click of the door sounded did Nora lift a finger to her face and wipe away the tears.

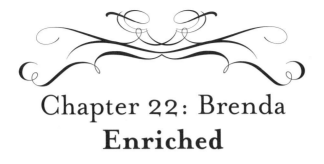

Chapter 22: Brenda
Enriched

Brenda entered the building for December's quarterly Relief Society Christmas meeting a few minutes before six o'clock. She dropped the kids off at the Nursery, where Josh and Tyler both clung to her pant legs and whined. "Mommy, I wanna stay with you!"

You've been with me all day long, she thought, *and I need a break.* But a Relief Society meeting wasn't exactly a "break" for someone who really wanted to hide in a cave, all alone, where no one could see her and where she didn't have to pretend all was well. Tonight would require smiling and being pleasant and chatting with other women— all things she didn't have the energy for. A real "break" would be a three-day nap with no one needing her for anything and someone else taking care of the kids and the house—and a promise that while she rested, Rick would be protected, safe.

Her fifteen-minute, accidental nap in the temple was the best sleep she'd had in months. It wasn't something she could very well repeat anytime she wanted to, although the idea of curling up in some small room inside those walls sounded like literal heaven on earth.

The next-best thing to de-stress was tomorrow's lunch, the first since Thanksgiving. It couldn't arrive fast enough—those were the one and only times during the week that she looked forward to leaving the house, the one time she made sure her hair was washed and she wore some makeup. She'd gone a couple of weeks without seeing them. She'd felt guilty for bowing out of helping Marianne with babysitting, after all, because she didn't have it in her to do one more thing, not on top of Thanksgiving, Christmas preparations, the boys, and that little deployment thing.

Another bit of guilt wiggled in when she saw Bradley had quietly settled into playing with a wooden train in a corner of the room. He'd withdrawn a lot of late—he was so quiet now. She should spend more time with him, but the twins were giving her a run for her money, and the squeaky wheels always got the extra attention.

Nora was right: deployment only got worse, at least during the holiday season. How could she get herself and the kids through Christmas without Daddy? For Thanksgiving, she had the hardest time not being snide with thoughts about things she should be grateful for.

I'm grateful for my husband. Oh, wait. He's not here.

I'm grateful for this food. That took me all day to prepare and that the boys won't eat.

I'm grateful for my children. Who are about to give me a nervous breakdown.

I'm grateful for this great country I live in. That my husband is away defending.

It was all so irrational, she knew. Deep down she figured she should probably go see Dr. Hoffman, who'd prescribed the antidepressants that got her through a very dark bout of postpartum depression after the twins were born. What she felt now was eerily similar to the hopeless place she'd been in then.

A Nursery worker extricated Tyler while another distracted both him and Josh with a set of dump trucks. Their red eyes stopped crying—temporarily, at least. Brenda reached for the doorknob. Josh caught her movement. He threw out his arm toward her and wailed. Tyler copied his twin. *It's not worth it,* she thought, tempted to pick them up and march right back home.

But she couldn't do that; she had to at least go to the Christmas program. Rick would be calling tomorrow, and he'd ask how it had gone. She had skipped the last quarterly meeting, and he had sounded disappointed when he heard about it.

"I thought women needed to hang out with other women," he'd said. "You know, that whole feminine bonding thing."

"We do . . . theoretically," Brenda had said. *Unless they're on the verge of clinical depression and would rather hole up until spring than see anyone.*

"Go to the Christmas activity," Rick insisted. "For my sake. Please? You'll have fun. I want you to enjoy the holiday season with some sisters from the ward."

He was right, of course. She'd spent too much time hiding in the house, going out only for groceries, carpool, and the weekly lunches.

As a Nursery worker distracted the twins yet again with the truck, making beeping and crashing noises as she drove it up and down his arms, Brenda slipped out of the room. The door closed quietly behind her. In a moment she would be going into the cultural hall and facing all those people. Dread descended on her like a heavy cloak. Just doing her hair and makeup—and putting on something nicer than sweats and a T-shirt—had taken their toll on her energy. She didn't want to go through with being smiley and energetic all night—a complete act.

How much do you want to bet that Nora's personally catering her ward's Relief Society activity? I want to go home, she thought miserably. *Nothing here feels like Christmas.*

But how could it feel like Christmas with Rick gone? This was the first one in ten years for which they wouldn't be together.

She folded her arms tightly across her chest and leaned against the wall. What she wouldn't give for a tall cup of hot cocoa with a pile of whipped cream fresh from the can. That and a stack of chocolate chip cookies, the fireplace, and a warm quilt. She'd stare into the gas-made flames of the fireplace as she sat in the darkness and nursed her worries and fears while the kids slept. Assuming they slept. Assuming Bradley didn't wake up yet again with those nightmares of bad guys shooting Daddy.

I wonder how similar his nightmares are to mine, Brenda thought miserably as she straightened and forced herself to move toward the cultural hall.

Outside the open door, she paused, forcing a smile onto her face so that when she stepped in, no one would think anything was amiss.

She knew she'd invariably get hit with comments like "Oh, you're so strong" and "I couldn't be as brave as you are" or "I couldn't do it."

Hah. On all counts. She hadn't admitted even to Sister Hunter or the Relief Society president, Sister Peterson, that she felt ready to implode half the time. She wasn't doing any of this because she was strong or even because she had a choice in the matter. She was scared, all day, all night. And if she had one more conversation with Tina Eldridge or any other woman in the ward who said they could totally relate to her because "my husband travels a lot," she might have to scream.

You just don't get it! Brenda was sorely tempted of late to actually use Marianne's new motto in conversation. It fit so well.

We all had misperceptions, she reminded herself. Brenda almost laughed aloud at how ridiculous some of those thoughts seemed now. Being apart from Rick and parenting alone were two tiny slices of the burden.

No one warned her about the constant worry and fear—the virtual obsession—with finding out if her husband was safe, injured . . . alive. The relief she'd feel at getting an e-mail saying he was fine. For now. This hour. When he clicked SEND a minute ago. But those communications were a brief fix, like a hit for a drug addict, because it never solved anything. The worry always kicked in again until the *next* e-mail, the *next* chance he got to instant message or call home.

Then there was the constant gut-level panic when the doorbell rang. Every time, Brenda steadied her hand before answering, never letting herself look through the peephole first. There might be a military uniform on the other side, bearing the worst news of her life. Of course, it never had been . . . so far. Instead, it was a neighbor, a ward member, or one of Bradley's buddies from down the street wanting to play.

It's not the same, Brenda always wanted to say to Tina Eldridge when the "travel" conversation came up. *Your husband gets to sleep in a warm, safe hotel room instead of a tent in the sand. Yours travels on commercial airlines. Mine travels in the line of Taliban fire, on roads with IEDs that they might drive over without seeing and be blown to bits. Or a bomb might be disguised to look like a dead body. So as they drive by, some softhearted soldier wants to care for it and then is vaporized when he touches it.*

Brenda entered the cultural hall, which was decorated with lit Christmas trees. Quilt batting was tucked beneath them to look like snow. Shining red orbs and garland of gold covered the trees. Round tables with green tablecloths had centerpieces made of cinnamon-scented pinecones, pine boughs, and ribbon that matched the trees, red and gold. Carols wafted through the air from a CD. The place felt cheerful, festive, warm.

So unlike anything Rick is experiencing at this same moment. Brenda knew without doing the math what time it was in Afghanistan—four thirty in the morning. Right now he'd still be asleep. Was his bed at the base tonight, or was he out in the field somewhere, using an old box in the sand as his mattress? Was he so bitten by ticks that he was nearly driven mad by the itching and couldn't sleep at all?

Or *was* he asleep? If he had seen enemy fire today, he could be injured . . . or worse.

She shuddered and plastered the smile on her face even firmer. *I must look like the Joker,* she thought, but it was the only way to face everyone without crying.

Rick was fine, she assured herself. There hadn't been any reports of soldier deaths today—and she had checked all the online wires to be sure, as she did every day. Plus, none of the other wives had reported a military communications blackout. Whenever you ran into one of those, you knew with relative certainly that someone had been killed.

He's fine. Enjoy yourself at least a little so you can tell Rick about it.

A quick scan of the room revealed a few tables that were half full. Brenda made her way to one with lots of young mothers chatting animatedly. Their noise might help drown out her own silence and get her distracted from her worries for at least a few minutes. Maybe she could get herself to pitch in a story or two about potty training or whatever the topic du jour was.

She pulled the metal chair out and slipped off her coat, which she hung on the chair back, then sat down. The women were talking about things their husbands did that drove them crazy—letting gas fly at inopportune moments, watching sports like a zombie, swearing in front of the kids. Tears pricked at Brenda's eyes. She couldn't contribute to *this* conversation. Why couldn't they be swapping labor stories like the wives had last month? Not long ago she could have laughed along with them about toilet seats being left up, but now . . . now she'd give almost anything to accidentally sit in the water if it meant Rick was home.

Safe.

The evening officially began with an opening song and prayer, and then the time was turned over to a guest speaker who had a slide show and spoke about the first Christmas. His voice droned on, and although Brenda tried to concentrate on his words, she couldn't do much besides imagine what Rick's Christmas would be like.

Would her package arrive in time? Would he like the things she sent? Would he be able to call or e-mail? Would the soldiers get Christmas day off? The Taliban certainly didn't respect Christian holidays. Would they try to bomb the base on one?

Brenda's cell phone suddenly rang, blaring a Smash Mouth song from *Shrek* throughout the hall—a ring Rick had picked out for her. Flushing red, she snatched the phone from her purse, silenced it, and raced out the back doors to answer.

The caller ID registered a number she didn't recognize, and she had a sinking feeling in her middle. Maybe it was someone official. Maybe it was news about Rick. As she flipped the phone open, she hurried to the foyer where she could speak quietly. "Hello?"

"Darlene?"

Brenda gritted her teeth with annoyance. "You have the wrong number," she said evenly. She hung up without waiting for a response then put her phone on *vibrate* like she should have before. She was embarrassed in there for a wrong number? She dropped to the navy blue couch with the pink floral design and looked around. The foyer didn't have its lights on; only the hall ones splashed their glow into the foyer, which remained dim. Brenda looked in the direction of the cultural hall.

I should go back in, she thought, but she didn't make a move to do so. Instead, she flipped her phone open again and started playing with its features to wile away the time, delaying the moment she went inside. A few people walked past her as she pressed buttons, and since she appeared busy, none stopped to talk to her. *Good,* she thought. *I don't want any attention out of pity.* She scrolled through the calendar, took a few random pictures of her shoes, then wrote a whining text message and deleted it before selecting a person to send it to.

She exited the menus and shut the phone, dropping her face into her hands and massaging her eyes. Taking a deep breath, she raised her head. Her gaze landed on the chapel door, which stood open, revealing only darkness and the shapes of some pews inside. Without giving it much thought, Brenda stood and found herself walking to the door. The dimness seemed to beckon her like a hiding place where no one would be able to bother her tonight. A safe haven. Two steps inside, the temperature seemed to drop. She hugged herself as she went farther in and sat on a side pew.

She stared at the front of the chapel, the middle spot on the wall above the choir seats. In cathedrals she had visited, a crucifix always hung in that spot, beneath which worshipers knelt and prayed to their god. While she had never liked the image of a suffering Christ—especially the weak, vanquished-looking ones often on crucifixes—she somehow wished there were something up front she could use as a focus for her prayers. Because without intending to, without realizing it consciously at first, a prayer was growing in her heart.

Lord, I'm so alone. Sad. Worried. I can't bear this by myself. I can't keep being both parents to our children. Most of all, protect my husband and bring him home.

The complete silence of the chapel enveloped Brenda in a blanket of stillness. The peace of the room slowly filtered into her bones—not as strongly as it might have in the temple, but a quiet strength was there nonetheless.

She glanced across the way, where the far door to the chapel was also open to the other foyer. Light spilled in from the side, as well as . . .

Brenda started at what looked like a life-size image of Christ walking toward her, right into the chapel. She narrowed her eyes, staring at the image. It took a moment to realize that it was a reflection on the outside glass doors of a painting on the wall. She sat back, hands running up and down her arms, which were suddenly covered with a layer of goosebumps. She was unable to stop staring at the image. Christ reached His hand toward her. He had love in His eyes. He seemed ready to walk right in and sit down with her, hold her, and let her cry in His embrace.

A trembling hand went to her lips as she tried to ward off tears.

Thank you, she silently prayed. *Thank you.*

She stayed in the chapel for several more minutes until she was pretty sure she didn't look like she'd been crying. Then she slipped in the back way to the cultural hall, with a smaller—albeit this time genuine—smile.

Chapter 23: Marianne
Merry

WEDNESDAY, DECEMBER 16, 2009

It was about a week before Christmas when the wives had their last lunch before the holiday. They all agreed that next Wednesday, the day before Christmas Eve, would be too close and crazy to squeeze it in. They met at Porter's Place in Lehi, a rustic joint paying homage to the almost mythical Church history hero Porter Rockwell.

Marianne arrived carrying a small laundry basket with four cellophane-wrapped gifts inside, each containing peach-scented bath salts that she'd made herself, plus a cucumber mask, a foot soak, a bath pillow, and an eye mask. She'd given herself the very same gift. Hers was at home next to the tub, ready for her to enjoy when she got home. All of the wives needed to spend a little time relaxing, alone, she figured. Over the last several weeks, they'd gone above and beyond to help her out because of McKayla. They deserved a little pampering for Christmas. She couldn't wait to pass out the presents; she almost didn't care about the food, although she'd heard that Porter's cooked a great steak.

The hostess led her through the antique wood–paneled restaurant to a set of narrow, rickety-looking stairs. Marianne paused at the base and adjusted the basket so she could actually see the steep line of steps to avoid tripping. At the top, the young woman gestured into a narrow room with its own private door. Today's lunch would be fun, with no outside noise interrupting them, and secluded like this, they could stay as long as they wanted without catching impatient servers' eyes hinting for them to go.

As she stepped inside, however, and saw no windows in the long, narrow room, Marianne got slightly claustrophobic. Like everything else in the place, the walls were paneled in wood. *Good luck getting out of this room if a fire ever breaks out,* she thought.

Nora was already inside, sitting at the far end. She, too, had brought gifts, hers in what looked like homemade cloth bags, tied with a pretty bow on the front, from which an instruction card—with calligraphy, layers of cardstock, inked stamps, and what looked like a Christmas tree ornament—hung. The cards alone must have taken her forever to make. And she had certainly made them herself. That was the kind of thing Nora did.

Was there *nothing* the woman couldn't do?

"How are you today, Marianne?" Nora asked with a wide smile, showing her white teeth, which were a startling contrast beside her maroon lipstick. She gestured toward the chair across from her, and Marianne walked to it.

"I'm doing very well, thanks." Marianne put her basket next to the table and shrugged out of her coat, which she draped over the back of her chair, then sat down. "How's your mother?"

"Oh, about the same," Nora said with a wistful smile. "Old age is really hard to get used to. Mother thinks she can do so much more than she really can. She'd be liable to drive if I let her."

Marianne shook her head in sympathy. "My grandfather was the same way. Mom and Dad bought his car to keep him from driving it. The thing was a piece of junk—and a huge boat—but at least he wasn't on the road with a two-ton missile anymore."

A moment later Brenda and Jessie arrived together, poking their heads through the door and waving. Jessie carried a stack of oddly shaped gifts, and Brenda carried a short stack of what looked like wrapped books.

Kim arrived a moment after they took their seats, and Jessie squealed. "Look at you! You're finally *looking* really pregnant."

"Cute maternity shirt," Marianne added, nodding at the denim blouse Kim wore, which in some illogical flattering way made her look both thin *and* very pregnant at the same time. Or maybe it was just that Kim was still young, perky, and skinny except for the bump in front. "They didn't have anything like that back when I was having babies," Marianne lamented.

"Thanks, guys," Kim said, laughing. She took her seat next to Jessie, and they all looked at the menus, which had thick, brown leather covers with a P stamped into the front of each. The thick papers inside were rubber-cemented to the leather and seemed to be coming loose in half of the menus. Kim looked around at the gifts and blushed. "I didn't have time to get you anything . . ."

"Oh, heavens, presents aren't a requirement," Nora said with a dismissive wave of her hand. "Don't you worry about it."

"And I brought mine more as a thank-you for everyone helping me out," Marianne added.

"How *is* McKayla?" Jessie asked, putting her menu down.

"Better," Marianne said and felt it. "Not a hundred percent yet, but I have hope. She was furious when I brought her to counseling without telling her first. But after a few appointments, she's being more open with the therapist."

"That *is* encouraging," Jessie said.

"Yeah, it is," Marianne said. Seeing the progress was hard day to day; talking about how far McKayla had come over a period of weeks was easier. "Even better, she's snuck out only once since Thanksgiving. She's getting three D-minuses, but technically she's not failing any classes, and I haven't found any drugs since that first baggy." She shrugged. "I'm still praying that she'll come to church with us, get her grades up, dump that Jake kid once and for all, and a bunch of other things, but I'm trying to be grateful for how far she's come, even if it is just baby steps."

Scooping out the ice from her glass—even though she'd asked for plain water—Nora said, "What does Brian think of it?"

Marianne was suddenly glad she'd told him more of the situation after she'd begun taking McKayla to see Deborah. "He's worried, of course. But when I said that I think she really needs to know that he loves her, he started sending her personal e-mails almost every day. She's eating them up—even though he sneaks in scripture references and other advice. McKayla doesn't write back that often, but she checks her e-mail every morning before school."

The server arrived, and they placed their orders. Marianne opted for a steak, medium-well. With the menus gathered and the server gone, Nora clapped her hands together.

"All right. Time for *my* present to you all. I know how busy all you moms are, so I thought I'd make breakfast a little easier for you at least one morning." She handed out her big cloth bags, one to each wife. "It's my homemade pancake mix," she explained then pointed at one of the cards. "The instructions tell you how to make it—plus five or six variations on the back. Tastes better than the Lehi Roller Mills mixes, if I say so myself." She added the last while jabbing her thumb over her shoulder in the general direction of where the Roller Mills were, down the street east a mile or so. She grinned and settled back, apparently waiting for reactions.

Everyone gushed about the gorgeous bags, the cards, and how yummy the pancakes would be. It was a very thoughtful, personal gift.

"Thank you so much," Marianne said sincerely.

"My kids thank you," Jessie said. "Lately, I haven't been making breakfast at all. It's a 'grab some cereal or make your own toast' affair."

Brenda lifted her head from her glass of water and held her nose, laughing. "That's my house too!" she gasped. "When my kids are *really* lucky, I'll put some Eggos into the toaster for them. Actually, I did make pancakes a few weeks ago. I should get an award or something."

"I try to make a warm breakfast most days, but it doesn't always happen," Marianne said, almost embarrassed that she cooked as much for her kids as she did. They were older than most of the other wives' children. McKayla and Bailey were plenty big enough to make pancakes on their own on a Saturday morning. "This mix will be very nice to have on hand, Nora, so thank you. I think McKayla's getting sick of oatmeal and scrambled eggs." As she set her pancake sack next to her chair, she noticed Kim holding hers a bit awkwardly and realized that she couldn't use the mix the same way everyone else could. She didn't have a houseful of kids begging to be fed. It was just her.

Well, she can use my bath gift just as well, Marianne thought with satisfaction. *She's young and alone, so she'll appreciate a little time to relax. And without any kids around, she's more likely to use it soon.*

"Since it's gift time, I'll pass mine out," Marianne announced. "We're all under a lot of stress, right? I figure we all deserve some pampering." She pulled one of the gifts out of the basket, which lay on the floor, then pointed out each item inside, finishing with her personal bath salts. "Peach is my favorite scent to make. It's divine," she said as she passed around the presents.

"You *made* the bath salts?" Jessie asked, passing one of the gifts to Kim and then peering through the cellophane at her salts. "I'm suddenly feeling very undomestic." She picked up her odd-shaped stack from the floor. The packages clanked together with a wooden sound as she handed them around the table. The women pulled the wrapping paper off planks of wood.

Brenda was the first to read the vinyl lettering on the front. She burst out laughing. Marianne ripped off her wrapping paper, and everyone else did the same. It was a wooden sign to hang on the wall.

You just don't GET it!

A chorus of laughter rang out. "This is perfect!" Brenda declared. "I'm half-tempted to get this put onto a T-shirt."

"I want to hang this on my front door," Marianne said. "It would stop the idiots in their tracks." She giggled.

"What about making bumper stickers?" Kim said, grinning. "And if we weren't Mormon, tattoos!"

Another gale of laughter erupted at that. Marianne had a sudden image of Nora sporting a "You just don't GET it!" tattoo on her bicep, something so ludicrous that it was impossible to *not* laugh over.

Jessie chuckled, looking pleased at everyone's reaction. "I figure it's sort of become our motto," she said with a grin. "It deserved to be put in concrete form."

Brenda set her sign against her chair and reached for her stack of wrapped books. "I'm feeling even less creative and domestic than Jessie. But hey, maybe you can all read while you're in the bath, right? It's all the same book for everyone, but it's my new favorite." She double-checked the name tags before handing them out, explaining, "I got lucky enough to arrive at the store when the author was signing them," she said. "I was thrilled. I probably looked like an idiot fan, but I swear, I've read this book four times, and it gets better every time. It even won some big award last year. Okay, now open them!"

Marianne opened hers. The book had a purplish cover with a night sky and a cityscape. The inscription said something about finding your own stars. She didn't recognize the title or the author but looked forward to reading the book. Brenda read a lot, and she was extremely picky. If she said this one was good, it probably was.

Their food arrived a moment later, and no one said much else until they had all taken a few bites. Marianne cut her steak—which was tender and juicy—and asked, "So what are you all doing for Christmas?"

Quiet silence swept across the table. Marianne scolded herself. Of course no one wanted to talk about Christmas, because it would invariably lead to what it meant for their families without their husbands around. "We'll be spending it with Brian's parents," she said, trying to lighten the mood. "If the kids can't have their dad home for Christmas, then I figure maybe being with their grandma and grandpa Gardner is the next best thing."

"It'll be me and Mom," Nora said with a sad shrug. "Scott met a girl at college, so he'll be spending Christmas at her parents' house up in Idaho. Dan's family is going to his in-laws', and neither of my daughters can make the trip from out of state this time—it costs a lot to come that far, now, with gas prices the way they are—but at least I'll get a missionary mom phone call from Steven." She smiled, but it didn't reach past her mouth. "The good thing there is that with the time difference to Toronto, he won't be waking me up in the middle of the night like Dan did on Christmas when he was in Japan."

The table lapsed into silence again, the only sounds forks and knives scraping and clinking on plates. Then Kim spoke up. "I'm going to Cedar City to visit my mom. She, uh . . . wasn't all that happy to hear that I'm pregnant." She lowered her gaze, eyes glassy. "This was supposed to be my first Christmas together with Justin. Last December we weren't even engaged." She pressed the back of her hand into one eye as if warding back tears.

Jessie put an arm around her and declared, "Christmas is officially the worst part of deployment, don't you think, everyone?"

Murmurs of agreement rolled over the table. Kim sniffed and tried to smile. "Thanks, Jess." She took a deep breath. "I'm such a baby to be upset by this, when all of you guys have so much more to worry about with your kids and stuff. But it . . ."

"It stinks," Jessie filled in.

"I was going to say it sucks, but basically, yeah." Kim nodded. "The whole deployment does. And we're only four and a half months into it."

Marianne tried to think of something comforting to say, but part of her agreed with Kim: she *was* very young, and she didn't have the same problems the older women did. But then Marianne tried to imagine herself as a young newlywed—pregnant—without Brian around. *I would have panicked and run home to Mom and Dad the first week,* she realized. *Kim's a stronger girl than I would have been.*

"At least we only have to face one Christmas without our husbands," Marianne said. "Think how neat next year will be for you and Justin . . . and your baby."

The sight of a smile slowly rounding Kim's mouth made Marianne warm inside. Kim nodded. "That *will* be pretty cool. I wonder if the baby will be crawling or walking by then."

An idea occurred to Marianne, and with excitement, she leaned forward on the table. "What if we all spend next Christmas together? Sort of a wives' family reunion. We could rent out a cabin up the canyon or something. The guys would probably love to hang out together again, and it would be like a huge celebration that the deployment is *over.*"

"Can you imagine how much fun we'd have?" Brenda added.

"And how much better next Christmas will be than this one, when all our men are home safely?" Marianne added. "The five of us will have to find something else to discuss besides deployment stress, but I think we could handle it." She winked.

"I like that idea," Nora said. "Looking forward to next year's Christmas will be a great way to get through this one, don't you think, everyone?" She pulled out her planner and began jotting notes. "My home teacher owns a cabin up past Heber. I'll call him to see what he'd charge . . ."

Dear Nora, Marianne thought. The woman was always jumping in to save the day and take care of everyone and everything. Nora surprised them all further when the server returned and she insisted that she pay the entire bill.

"My Christmas gift to you all," she said, pulling out her credit card.

"But the pancake mixes—" Brenda began.

"Consider it a second gift," Nora said, handing over the card to the server. "I want to do it, so let me."

"Well, thanks," Jessie said. With a laugh, she added, "Here I was feeling guilty for getting the bigger steak because I'd have to cut down on diapers or something else in this week's budget to make up for it. Running out of diapers wouldn't have been good."

Chapter 24: Brenda
Powdered

FRIDAY, DECEMBER 18, 2009

Brenda dipped her toe into the hot water. She sighed with pleasure as she slipped into the bath, the warm water covering her like a soft, heavy blanket. The lingering aroma of Marianne's peach-scented bath salts hovered above the surface. She adjusted the inflatable bath pillow behind her head and leaned back, eyes closed in bliss.

Ah, finally, she thought. *Marianne was right. This is glorious. I should do this every week. No, several times a week.*

She could almost feel the aches and tension in her joints melting into the water. Eyes closed, she felt the corner of the tub for the gel eye mask Marianne had included in her Christmas gift. She found it and placed the cooling pack over her stressed eyes.

Good-bye wrinkles, she thought, about to drift off to sleep. *I wonder how long the boys will let me stay in here.*

Bradley was at school, and the twins were downstairs, planted in front of *Toy Story*—a show with plenty of boyish fun without the profusion of sword fighting that most of the fairy tales had. Not that she had anything against the boys playing with swords; she just knew what could happen if Mom wasn't present when they tried to kill each other. They'd jump off couches and charge as intensely as Prince Phillip fought the evil dragon or Aladdin battled the giant serpent.

For swords, they'd use anything long and narrow, whether it was wooden spoons, butter knives, or—Brenda's personal "favorite" to referee against—baseball bats. A few months before Rick left, they'd bought a few plastic swords and light sabers. A fellow customer gave them nasty looks about buying "weapons" for their kids, but that mother didn't understand. Boys *will* find a way to fight in their play. It was either get harmless plastic swords or have them gouge one another's eyeballs out with butter knives.

A hollow plastic sword doesn't leave a cut that needs eleven stitches. Baseball bats *did,* and Bradley had a scar above his right eyebrow to prove it.

So while she was in the bath, *Toy Story* would be the much safer bet than the boys' current favorite, *Peter Pan.* That one had them stabbing each other with pencil daggers, attempting leaps off countertops as they "flew," and holding large metal objects like ladles on the end of their arms when playing the part of the evil Captain Hook.

Just when Brenda felt certain her plan had worked, a quiet knock sounded, followed by the bathroom door creaking open a few inches. Brenda lifted the corner of her mask, hoping for the best. Three-year-old Josh peeked into the room.

"What do you need, handsome?" she asked in her happy mommy tone, replacing the mask and hoping against hope that he didn't have a leaking poopy diaper or anything else that would require her to leave the blessed warmth of the tub.

"I found something that belongs in here," Josh said. "In the basket of stuff you put in the tub."

"Something like these?" Brenda asked, pointing at the jar of bath salts. Maybe she'd forgotten part of Marianne's gift downstairs. *Where did the loofa go?* She lifted the corner of the mask again to see what he was holding, but Josh was now so close to the tub, she couldn't see it. "What is it?"

"It'll help you feel better, Mommy." With a speed that defied his three years, Josh upended a fabric sack and dumped most of its contents into the tub.

A sack with designs of snowmen and snowflakes. Like the one Nora had sewn and filled with her homemade pancake mix.

"Oh! Ah! No! Stop!" Each syllable was screamed at a high pitch.

Josh's brown eyes grew wide at his mother's shrieks, his hand holding the half-empty sack frozen over the tub. Brenda scrambled to her feet, a thin, peach-scented pancake batter dripping off her skin. Powdery chunks clung to her legs.

"Go! Get out of here!" she cried. She nearly slipped, stomping out of the tub as she frantically searched for a towel. Josh got the use of his body. His chubby arms pumped as he ran out of the bathroom, sprinkling a white trail of pancake mix behind him. The sight made her change her tactic.

"No, Josh, stop! Get back here!" Brenda grabbed a towel and wrapped it around herself then raced after him and the powdery trail. She didn't want to think about how difficult it would be to get pancake mix out of the carpet. The vacuum was unlikely to get it all, and any water would turn it into batter.

Terrific.

Somehow Josh managed to get all the way to the kitchen, where he hid, cowering under the table. *Sheer terror over his mother's crazy behavior. Poor kid.* At least if he spilled any more, it would be on the linoleum.

From the top step, she saw the sack upended on the bottom stair. It was empty, with a pile of mix under it. "Oh, no . . ."

Brenda raced down the stairs, still holding up her towel with one hand. Halfway down, a shocking pain shot through her foot. "Ow!" On reflex, she switched feet, only to get the same agony in that one. "Ah!"

She stumbled down the last two stairs—stepping on several more sharp objects in the process—and tripped, landing in a heap, arms first, at the base.

Stupid Legos. She glared at the colorful plastic building blocks in cheerful red, blue, and yellow, scattered all over the stairs. She pushed a strand of wet hair from her face. *Those things are deadly.* It didn't matter how many times she'd enforced the "Legos stay in your room" rule; Bradley still managed to spread them to all corners of the house.

She was vaguely aware of a cold breeze and a sudden drop in temperature. Slowly, dreading what she suspected, she turned her head. The front door stood open. Tyler held the knob with one hand and drank from his sippy cup with the other.

And in the open doorway stood Kim, somewhat stunned.

Their eyes met, and Kim burst out laughing. She came in and shut the door. Brenda got to her knees, wrapped the towel around herself, and stood up. She cleared her throat, tucking the end of the towel under a fold to hold it in place.

"I, uh, was taking a bath," she said, smoothing her wet hair awkwardly and knowing there was no way to regain any shred of dignity.

Kim pressed her lips together. She nodded, seeming to be in control, and said, "I wanted to bring by my Christmas gift, since I didn't have it with me at lunch this week." She held out a canister of hot cocoa with a green bow on top.

"Thanks," Brenda said, still feeling . . . exposed.

"Looks like you've had quite the adventure here." Kim chuckled in spite of herself.

Brenda wiped pancake batter from her arm and smeared it on the towel. She pointed to Kim's protruding belly. "Watch out. This is a preview of coming attractions."

Chapter 25: Kim
Good Will Toward Mom

"Are you sure?" Jessie asked over the phone.

Kim threw her toiletry bag into the suitcase and sighed. "I'm sure," she said, but she wasn't. She'd prefer to stay with Jessie for Christmas but knew that her mother would never forgive her if she didn't come home for the holiday. As it was, she was cutting it close by not getting there until lunchtime on Christmas Eve. Mom had wanted her there for a week. Why wouldn't her daughter race down south to be with family when her husband was deployed? But Kim couldn't handle being there that long.

"Your mom already knows, right?" Jessie asked.

Neither had to clarify what she meant. "I told her last month." Kim tossed a couple pairs of socks into the suitcase and pulled some maternity jeans from the bottom drawer.

Truth was, she had used her diagnosis of placenta previa as a good way to tell her mother she was expecting *and* to get out of coming down for Thanksgiving, even though she was technically off bed rest.

Gee, darn. I'm stuck in Provo. Shucks. Can't come down for Turkey Day. Sorry. Hate it when that happens.

But since then the placenta had moved completely. She hadn't bled in weeks and was no longer considered anywhere near high risk. Eleanor had even given her the green light to travel. Kim no longer had an excuse to avoid her family—or to avoid helping with any housework or cooking.

"Well, my door is open even if you change your mind last minute," Jessie said over the phone. "The kids would love having someone else to jump on, and I'd like the company. We could rent some goofy movie that's only funny when you're tired and with friends, like *Better Off Dead*."

"Like what?" Kim sat on her bed to stare at her closet and pick out a few shirts, but now her thoughts went to Jessie's voice. What kind of comedy would be called *Better Off Dead*? Sounded like a reality show about suicidal people.

"It's probably before your time," Jessie said. "I keep forgetting that I'm a geezer. Trust me—you'd love it. It starred John Cusack before he was Mr. Cool Actor Dude. It shows him with Q-tips up his nose." Jessie laughed aloud, and Kim couldn't help but chuckle too. Q-tips stuck in a nose sounded like something her brother Jeff would do.

"Thanks, but I'd really better go home," Kim said. "Mom's still annoyed that I didn't go down for Thanksgiving."

"Well, call me if you need anything, all right?"

"I will," Kim said and found herself meaning it.

Within the hour she pulled out and headed south on I-15. The hollow feeling of dread didn't start until she'd passed Payson and was gradually leaving behind the cities of the Wasatch Front and entering the scrubby, desolate—and ugly—landscape of central Utah. Even with the rolling mountains covered in white, the barren land was a reminder that she did, in fact, live in a desert.

The farther south she drove, the less like Christmas the landscape looked. Banks of snow melted into slush and then dry pavement. Half an hour out from Cedar City, she turned off the heater. It was like moving into a different world and leaving the old one behind.

The drive felt longer than it usually did. But then, Kim had never taken the trip six months pregnant. Her feet were swollen, her lower back and hips ached, and the stupid heartburn was still bugging her. She kept a Tums bottle in the cup holder for easy access, though they didn't seem to do much. But at least they made her feel like she was doing *something* about the pain.

Cacti and red-stone cliffs sprang up on the sides of the freeway. She couldn't help but imagine early pioneers trying to navigate the sharp hills and rocky paths that led south. Some women might have even been expecting. Or maybe they gave birth out here in the brutal heat. She should be grateful that she lived in a day with hospitals and cars and medical technology and air conditioning.

She rolled her eyes at herself. That kind of expression of gratitude was something Sister Ward, her old Laurel advisor, would have said. Kim herself never really cared much about church. Sure, she went. That's what good girls did. And she believed in all the important things. It was the activity part she didn't care for.

But all the other girls were so excited about making their lists of what they'd look for in a husband and gluing them into their journals. They loved piecing together entire quilts by hand for Laurel projects. Learning how to bake bread. All that feminine stuff had seemed so stupid to her at the time.

But those times seemed frighteningly recent. And some of those skills didn't seem quite so silly anymore. She'd like to know how to make a blanket for her baby. To bake some bread for Justin when he got home from work. But she'd never been girly-girly. She'd never wanted to think about the future, let alone about fulfilling her "divine role" as a mother.

I'm still a young woman, she thought. *Why in the heck did I think I was old enough to be a wife? I'm sure not old enough to be a decent mom!*

She blew a raspberry at the windshield as if showing the world that she really didn't care. As if, through the wind, her mother could get the gist of it.

But then she glanced at her belly and quickly back to the gray road flying past her wheels. She *did* care. She had to, because this baby didn't have anyone else. At least, not until Justin got home.

"Poor kid," she said aloud. "You're in for a tough one. And now I take you to a place where your grandmother is going to call me stupid for letting you come into the world."

She gripped the steering wheel hard. Anger suddenly coursed through her body. Her mother *would* say those things; Kim had no doubt about it. Her mother was a Ph.D. and a true-blue feminist. Kim's being barefoot and pregnant was probably her worst nightmare.

But how *dare* her mother say such things in front of a baby, born or not. How dare she decide when a life should enter the world. What right did she have to judge? Maybe this baby was supposed to come down now, in this way.

"She'd better love you as much as she loves Ashlyn," Kim grumbled. Her jaw clenched as she thought of how doting her mother had been with her first granddaughter—who happened to live all of forty-five minutes to the south in Washington. No way would this baby get that kind of attention when it lived several hours away, even if it were a girl.

Which it wasn't. What were the chances her mother would coo and coddle a boring boy who couldn't be dressed up in frills like a real-live doll?

The road grew blurry, and she had to wipe her eyes dry to regain focus. She didn't think her mother intended to be so unfair in her affections. She probably wasn't aware of how out of balance it all was. But the fact remained that Kim's older sister Jana was Mom's favorite. So it was natural that her daughter was also Grandma's favorite. And Lori . . . well, she had been spoiled her entire life. Even when she started acting like Marianne's McKayla, she apparently never did anything wrong. The slightest achievement—yea, Lori read a book!—warranted a family celebration. Okay, that was a slight exaggeration. But not much of one. Lori came in second with Mom's affections, while Kim remained dead last.

The reality remained that Kim was the black sheep of the family, the one everyone wished would "just try."

"You have so much *potential,*" they'd say. Even Jana and Lori.

Kim made a face. *Potential* was such an ugly word. It meant whatever she *wasn't* and *might never be.* It meant whatever you were lacking. It meant you weren't enough.

"Well, baby," she said. "I don't know about you, but I'm starving. Grandma will have a bunch of crappy food for us like scary Jell-O salad, but I say we stop off at this little Mexican joint now. I think we could both use a burrito."

She pulled off the freeway next to a fake miniature lighthouse—an odd landmark for a desert. It belonged to a restaurant or something, but to her it always meant that she was almost home. On some trips, the sight made her happy. Today it made her stomach tighten.

"You know where I want to go before we head home in two days?" she asked the baby. In answer, she got two sharp kicks right in front. "I want to show you where your daddy and I were married. It's not that far away. Less than an hour from here. That'll make the drive back to Provo a little longer, but it'll be worth it; the temple down in St. George is gorgeous."

She pulled into a parking space at a tiny Mexican restaurant, a spot that she'd forgotten was there until the craving for salsa hit her. As she pulled out the key, she looked through the windshield in the direction of St. George.

"I've done okay," Kim said. "I was married in the temple. That's saying something, right?" She placed her hand over her stomach. A small, round something poked up and down, up and down. A fist? A knee? A heel? She had no idea and couldn't tell. But she smiled.

"That was something Sister Ward wanted for all of us. I did it. And I didn't even do it for her or for Mom or Dad. I did it for me and for Justin. So maybe I'm not all bad." With a sigh, she got out of the car and slid her purse strap over her shoulder. She slammed the door shut hard, wishing she could get credit for the few things she did right.

Another glance at her belly. "You know, baby, maybe you're one of them."

* * *

Kim ate her burrito faster than she thought she could—and more of it than she expected—but was sure she'd pay for it later with more serious heartburn. It was worth it, she decided, as she started the car, but before driving off, she hesitated and gazed southward again, toward St. George. She glanced to the right, where her parents' house lay, then into her rearview mirror, as if she could see Jessie's home to the north.

Decision made, she killed the engine and reached for her cell phone, knowing she had three calls to make. First to Eleanor, who could give her some medical excuse for not going home for Christmas, after all. Then to Mom to apologize for not coming—but not mentioning that she was sitting ten minutes away and was about to turn around. And finally to Jessie to take her up on the offer to spend Christmas with someone who understood, cared, and wouldn't judge her.

Six minutes later, she'd made all the calls—the one to her mother taking four and a half of them. Kim had to cut that one off because it could have gone on for an hour. As she turned the car key again, she brushed away the shadow of guilt her mother had cast over their conversation.

I want to spend Christmas where I can be happy and be me, she thought.

She pulled out of the parking lot and headed back to the freeway entrance. Jessie knew not to expect her until late; Kim had decided to visit the St. George Temple before driving back. It wouldn't be open for a session at that hour on Christmas Eve, but she'd be able to walk the grounds and the visitors' center and maybe take in the movie playing there.

As she sped along the on-ramp, she talked to her baby again. "I'll show you where Daddy and I were standing for my favorite wedding picture," she said. "You've got an awesome dad, kid."

Maybe seeing the temple grounds again would help her feel some of the peace she'd been lacking lately, plus some of the love she and Justin shared there not so long ago. She thought of other spots on the grounds and inside the visitors' center, like the model of pioneer-era St. George, and the photographs of the temple when it was under construction. The brass cannon barrel used as a pile driver on the foundation.

If she remembered the story right, the Saints had filled the thing with lead, hoisted it up on a big pulley with ropes pulled by horses, then let it fall to drive volcanic rock into the boggy soil. They did that over and over until the cannon bounced a certain number of times and they knew the ground was firm enough.

That's what I feel like right now, she thought. *Like I'm getting pounded into the ground by a pile driver, over and over again.*

But then she couldn't help one half of her mouth from curving upward. Look what came of *that* pummeling—a gorgeous temple. Something good might come from what she was going through with Justin gone. Some things already had, like getting a stronger testimony of prayer, like growing up and maturing in ways she didn't know she could. Like finding dear, true friends even if they were much older than she ever would have thought her closest friends could or would be.

She pressed the accelerator harder, eager to get there and see the bright white building standing against the rust-orange cliffs.

Wait until Justin comes home, she thought. He'd have a wife he hardly recognized—better, stronger, wiser.

She imagined her personal brass cannon, hoisted into the air and ready to release again.

Bring it on.

Chapter 26: Jessie
Joyful

Jessie woke up around seven when Joey cried for her from his crib. Since Alex and Becca were still sound asleep after a late night playing with their aunt Kim—and Kim herself looked worn out—Jessie returned to her room to wait for the Christmas morning mayhem to begin. She nursed Joey then picked up a book to read while he played with a board book next to her.

"Mama?" Alex's tired face appeared around the doorway. "Is it Christmas?"

"Sure is," Jessie said with a grin. "Why don't you go see if Santa came? Then come back and tell me."

Alex clapped her hands and raced to the front room. Jessie waited a minute, but Alex didn't come back. She hitched Joey onto her hip and followed in her pajamas. She found Alex standing before the tree with its lights sparkling off the red and gold balls and stacks of wrapped presents beneath. Her mouth hung open, and her eyes looked as big as half dollars.

Jessie grinned. "Looks like he came."

Alex nodded mutely, still staring in awe. Jessie put a hand on Alex's shoulder and leaned down. "Go wake up your little sister so you can open your presents."

The words broke the spell, and Alex raced down the hall. A second later, Kim appeared from the family room, rubbing her eyes and yawning.

"Sorry to wake you," Jessie said. "I know we were up late." *Late* being relative. The kids went to bed around nine, after which Jessie and Kim watched *Better Off Dead* and then talked for an hour. In Jessie's college days, *late* meant two or three o'clock in the morning. At thirty-three, anything past ten thirty qualified.

The girls trotted back to the living room a minute later, Alex nearly dragging Becca by the hand. "It's presents!" she cried. "Hurry, Becca!"

Jessie sat the baby on the floor and grabbed the camcorder to catch the magic so she could e-mail the morning's fun to Tim. She'd be sure to get Kim on tape for Justin's sake. Kim and Jessie helped the kids find their own presents—a relatively simple matter, since instead of writing names on them, "Santa" had wrapped each kid's loot in paper that fit their personality. Alex had Barbie wrapping paper. Becca's was Dora, and Joey got Pooh Bear. Had Tim been home, he'd probably have insisted on something more manly, like Spider-Man, even though Joey wasn't old enough to know what a super hero was.

The camera caught all the excitement, from Joey enjoying the wrapping paper more than his new building blocks and Little People to Becca's baby doll set and Alex's excitement over uncovering a box of dress-ups. The kids took turns showing the camera their presents and telling Daddy why they were so cool.

The kids ripped through the unwrapping process and soon moved on to unpacking their toys from the boxes. Jessie set the camera aside to help them. Kim was unwinding one of about eighty-five wires holding Becca's doll and its accessories prisoner when her cell phone rang. Instinctively, both women froze and looked at one another with hopeful expressions. Jessie held out her arm to take the box, and Kim shoved it toward her as she stood and hurried to her purse by the front door.

"It'd better not be my mom," Kim said, digging through her purse. When she saw the caller ID, she did a little hop and a, "Yes!" She settled on the love seat to talk to Justin, her face glowing with happiness.

Jessie quickly picked up the camera and taped it. This was Kim and Justin's first married Christmas; there should be some record of it. Kim laughed and giggled as if she were flirting with a teenage boy instead of her husband. She talked about how she'd spent the night with Jessie instead of with her parents. How the pregnancy was going—and she was "totally showing" now.

It was sweet. Kim unconsciously rubbed her belly as she spoke about their baby. Watching her gave Jessie a little ache in the chest. It reminded her of what she and Tim used to have. Or at least what she'd *thought* she'd married. She couldn't remember the last time they'd flirted or she'd felt a flush in her cheeks, her heart racing at the prospect of talking to Tim. Most of the time, their conversations gave her a twinge of dread that she'd say the wrong thing or upset him unintentionally. What she'd seen as "moody" during their courtship had morphed into a temper problem.

After a few minutes—when the kids started begging for their toys—she quietly turned off the camera and returned to opening up the boxes and unwinding wires. Kim and Justin talked for a good half hour. Jessie had the kids settled with toys as she picked up the mountains of trash and then set to making muffins for breakfast, all the while waiting for her own phone to ring.

It had better ring, she thought as she roughly stirred the lemon poppy-seed mix. If Tim didn't call today of all days, she'd be livid. He obviously had access to a phone, because Justin did. But just as strongly, she wished the call were—happily—over.

She spooned the batter into the baking cups, sliding the pan into the oven as Kim hung up and trotted into the kitchen. She beamed.

"Good call?" Jessie said, trying to smile broadly.

"Yeah," Kim said, blushing again and not offering more than that. "They got to be at the base for all of Christmas Day."

"That's great," Jessie said, and she felt a swoop of relief. If something bad were to happen to any of the boys during Christmas, the day would be ruined forever—for all of them. But they were all at the base, safe and sound. Their Christmas Day was also nearly over. The time zone thing still took getting used to. Tim had already *had* his Christmas, had already opened the cards and gifts from the kids— assuming he didn't open the packages when they first arrived—and he'd be eating dinner soon.

"Man, Justin's so dang awesome, you know that?" Kim said, sitting on a barstool. "I'm so lucky that I snagged him. He had girls chasing after him when he got off his mission. But I won." She grinned like the Cheshire Cat. "Ugh, but I can't *wait* until he gets home."

"Yeah," Jessie said with a supportive nod. She grabbed a dishcloth and wiped some batter that spilled onto the counter. "Sounds like you have a keeper."

"This is going to sound totally soap-opera cheesy," Kim said, leaning against the counter. "But there are times I love him so much it *hurts*. Know what I mean?"

Jessie turned to the sink to rinse out the dishcloth. As the water ran, she considered. What Kim meant probably wasn't *quite* what Jessie had experienced. But yes, she knew what it felt like to love someone so much it hurt. To not be able to stop caring for someone when they hurt you. To wish so badly you didn't care, so they weren't capable of wounding you like that anymore. To pray that things would be happy and like they used to be—or how you dreamed they *should* be. To see glimmers of hope in that direction when Tim showed affection or did something sweet for her as a surprise. Then to have the hope come crashing down to reality again when he still flew off the handle over dumb things. Telling her she had no right to be angry over something that was big to her—but he was obviously ticked off by something ridiculously minor like a loaf of bread left out that got dry.

"You okay?" Kim asked, her eyebrows drawing together in concern.

Jessie turned off the water, which had been running so hot her hands were pink. She wrung out the rag and spread it on the edge of the sink to dry. "Yeah, I know what it's like," she said vaguely, avoiding Kim's last words. "But Justin's leave is coming up soon, right?"

Biting her lip with excitement, Kim nodded. "He arrives January fifth. I swear, I know it's almost here, but I can't *wait.*"

Tim's two-week leave wasn't until March, and Jessie was terrified for it. "You guys will have so much fun," she said, keeping her voice light. She glanced at the timer on the oven. The muffins still had almost fifteen minutes to go. "Let's send our guys the video I just took," she said, waving Kim toward the office where the computer was.

She paused as they passed the living room to be sure the kids were okay. Becca was burping her doll, and Alex wore nearly every dress-up in the entire box, including what looked like four skirts, a boa, several plastic necklaces, and heels. She was prancing around the room with her lips in a pout and a toy purse over her arm.

When Alex caught sight of Jessie, she picked up her new Play-Doh set. "Mom! Open this now!"

Jessie scooped up Joey, who was gumming a wire that had been left on the floor. "Not so fast, buddy," she said, taking it away. She settled him in his high chair with a couple of blocks and a handful of Cheerios then pried open the Play-Doh box and got the ice cream shop inside set up. By then, the timer went off, and Jessie had to delay sending the videos again to get everyone's muffins cut up and buttered.

Little Becca bounced in her booster seat and shouted, "Nolk! Nolk!"

Jessie obliged, filling her sippy cup with milk. She got Joey a bottle of formula, which he happily grabbed, tilted into his mouth, and sucked on merrily. Alex had her nose in the fridge, and Jessie knew what she was grabbing. "No, you don't," she said, snagging the pitcher of orange juice before it created a reservoir on the floor. "Let me pour you some. And take off your new dress-ups first. You don't want to get stains on them." When Alex protested, Jessie held the cup of juice out of reach and tilted her head. "Excuse me? No whining. Take them off now. You can put them back on after breakfast."

Alex groaned and stomped out the room but came back a minute later having obeyed. She climbed onto her chair, where she was suddenly happy again, munching on muffins and drinking down juice.

With everyone happy, Jessie turned back to Kim. "All right. *Now* let's go send the videos."

But Kim stood there, staring at the kids around the kitchen table, shell-shocked.

Jessie looked around, confused. "Um, Kim? You okay?"

"Yeah," Kim said weakly. Her hand went to her belly. "You're so good at that."

"At . . . what?" Jessie had no idea what Kim was talking about.

"Being a mom. You were doing tons of things at once, and you've got *three* kids, and you understood what Becca said even when it didn't sound like anything, and *how* do you know what to do? Every time I see you with them, I'm amazed." She blinked, breaking the stare, and looked at Jessie for an answer.

"It comes with the territory," Jessie said, putting her arm around Kim. "You figure it out one day at a time. And most people don't get three all at once."

"Yeah, I guess," Kim said. "But it's scary, you know?"

"I know," Jessie said. "But you'll do great."

They got to the computer, where Jessie took the card from the camera to upload the videos. The phone rang. Jessie jumped and stared at it.

Kim squealed. "I bet it's Tim!"

Jessie hoped Kim didn't notice her hand shaking as she answered. "Hello?"

"Hey, babe. Merry Christmas."

"Hi, honey," she said, smiling at Kim. Jessie lifted her feet onto the office chair and hugged her knees to her chest. "How was your Christmas?"

Kim mouthed something and excused herself. Jessie nodded and waved as she left, immediately grateful; she wasn't sure how this call would go, and she didn't want to have an audience for it.

"Pretty good," Tim said. "Someone handed out Santa hats for everyone, so we're all wearing them today. There's been lots of sugar from care packages. Thanks for the books. They look awesome."

"You're welcome," she said, relieved. She knew Tim loved reading and missed not having enough books out there, but she was always nervous about which titles to send.

"And the picture of you . . . wow. *You* look awesome."

In spite of herself, Jessie smiled. "You're sweet."

"No, you're *hot,*" Tim insisted. "That picture is killing me, you know that, right?"

Jessie's eyes went wide. He was serious. She hadn't thought much about the picture, just figured she should send something of everyone in the family. She'd had her next-door neighbor take a couple of shots of her in front of the garage door. Of course, she *was* two pants sizes down from the last time Tim had seen her.

"Thanks for sending those cards and pictures," she said, deflecting the compliment. "The kids loved them." His praise felt foreign, and she wasn't sure how to respond—whether to enjoy it or resist it. She was losing weight for herself, not for him. But the attention still felt good.

Tim's handmade Christmas cards were part of that week's family home evening. Jessie figured the kids would actually pay attention to pictures of Daddy in the desert better when there weren't bright-colored toys to distract them.

"Glad they like them," Tim said.

"Oh, and I'll send you a video of the kids unwrapping their presents in a few minutes."

"That'd be great." Tim paused. "I miss you, babe. I always knew you were a great mom and a great wife, but not having you around—and having to deal with a bunch of dirty guys all the time—I see what I'm missing, you know?"

"Thanks," Jessie said quietly.

"How are you doing, really?" he asked. "Colonel Lambert tells us how hard this whole thing is on you wives—but you seem to be doing okay."

He had an odd edge to his voice, as if the fact that she was surviving fine without him was a problem. Of course it sort of *was*.

"If it weren't for the other wives, I'd be having a much harder time of it," Jessie said. "Really, they're my lifeline."

"Glad to hear it," Tim said. "And hey, less than three months, and I'll be there for leave."

"Wow. Less than three months." Jessie tried to sound excited. Her mouth went dry.

"Hey, are you okay?" Tim asked.

Jessie hurriedly answered. "I'm fine. It's so good to hear your voice. Do you want to talk to the kids?" She hopped off the chair and hurried to the kitchen. "Daddy's on the phone! Here, Alex, you tell him all about what Santa left you."

Alex snatched the phone, tucked it under her chubby chin, and started gushing. "Oh, Daddy! I got some Play-Doh that has pink and purple in it. And dress-ups with *high heels*! And a Barbie. And lots of candy in my stocking, like *three* candy canes! One is filled with M&Ms!"

She jabbered on, and Jessie felt guilty for being relieved that the phone wasn't against her ear anymore. What a bizarre Christmas. On one hand, it felt *wrong* for Tim to be gone, to not see the kids' eyes light up when they saw their presents. But at the same time, he wasn't there to get annoyed with the mess or to snap at one of the kids for whatever. Or to be annoyed that all she made for breakfast was muffins from a mix.

He should be here. He thought she looked great. He missed her.

She wanted him here . . . but only the *happy* version of Tim. The loving one. The one she didn't see all that often without the angry one showing up shortly behind. The one on the other end of the phone right now. She genuinely missed *that* Tim.

She raised her eyes to the ceiling to ward off the emotion threatening to build. She didn't want to sound upset when the phone came back to her. Kim came over and gave her a hug. Jessie returned it, making the tears squeeze out of her eyes.

"I can't imagine how tough today must be for you," Kim whispered. "You guys have been together longer and have kids and everything. But don't worry. He'll be back next Christmas. It'll be okay."

Jessie nodded and pulled back. "You're right—it will be." She wiped at her cheeks and smiled. "Next year."

Chapter 27: Marianne
Trouble

Justin arrived the day before for his two-week leave, so Kim wasn't at lunch that day. They had a feeling they wouldn't see much of her for the next little while, and not a soul begrudged her one minute with him. If anything, Marianne envied Kim. What she wouldn't do for a night in Brian's arms again. Another five weeks, and he'd be home. She could last that long.

"Mother's not doing well today," Nora said, standing from her chair at Training Table. Likely that's why she ordered only a side salad, Marianne figured—less to eat, quicker to leave. "I'd better get back to her."

"I hope it's nothing serious," Marianne said.

"Oh, we'll be fine," Nora assured everyone at the table. "You call if any of you need something, all right?"

"We will," Marianne promised, and the other wives chorused the same sentiment. "Although I doubt Kim will need anything."

They all laughed at that, but before Nora stepped away, she put a hand on Marianne's shoulder. "How's McKayla?"

They hadn't quite gotten to that topic in the short time they'd been together today. Marianne tilted her head back and forth. "A little better, I think. It's hard to tell. Some weeks it's one step forward, two steps back, and other weeks, we actually make some progress. But she's going to therapy regularly now, and I think she'll pass all her classes this semester, after all." She smiled grimly. "That's the best I can hope for right now."

"Let me know if I can do anything to help," Nora said, squeezing her shoulder.

Marianne patted her hand. "Thanks. I will."

They waved as Nora headed out through the wooden double doors toward the parking lot. But then Marianne wondered aloud, "I hope *she's* doing all right."

"You mean Nora?" Jessie played with the brown cord of the fake phone used to order the food. "I think she's fine. I swear, she looks like she leads a charmed life."

"Maybe," Marianne said doubtfully, "but I wonder if she'd tell us even if she were going through something difficult." Her cell phone rang then, blaring Pink's song "Trouble."

Jessie laughed. "Love your ring tone," she said, dipping the tip of a forkful of chef salad into her dressing on the side.

"It was Brian's idea," Marianne said with a laugh. "And the song fits. I swear, 'Trouble' is Kevin's middle name lately." She fished inside her purse and pulled out the phone. "Uh-oh," she said, glancing at the caller ID. "It's the school."

Maybe Kevin had left his homework sheet on the table again. She hoped he hadn't fallen off the jungle gym and broken his arm like he did last year. More likely, he was feeling "icky" and wanted to be checked out. Again. She braced herself to be strong, remembering the deployment counselor's advice that maintaining a regular schedule would be best for her kids, that the stress of deployment could manifest itself in stomach pains and nausea.

But keeping a steady schedule seemed to be taking a very long time to work. Kevin had just stopped wetting the bed at night, something he'd outgrown a year ago but had started up again after Brian left. She punched the TALK button and answered. "Hello?"

"Mom?" came Kevin's voice. "I don't feel good. Can you come get me?"

Marianne looked at her watch and came up with a strategy. "Isn't it almost time for your art class? You love art. Why don't you try to last through that, and then if you're still feeling sick, you can call me, and I'll come get you." She was betting that he'd get so distracted experimenting with clay that by the time art class was over, he'd be feeling fine and would manage to get through his last class of the day, PE.

"How does that sound?" She smiled at the other wives, whose conversation had stilled as they listened with concern to her end of the call.

"But this time my stomach *really* hurts," Kevin said. "*Bad.* I didn't even go out to first recess."

Marianne's brow drew together. Not go out to recess? Kevin would rather face a room of angry rattlesnakes than miss recess. When he broke his arm falling off the jungle gym, he didn't even tell his teacher that he was hurt until the bell rang for the class to line up.

"Can I talk to Mrs. James for second?"

"Okay," he said, sounding dejected, as if he might die if he weren't picked up right away.

As she waited for the teacher, Marianne searched the purse for her key chain, somehow knowing that she'd be leaving soon. She pulled out crumpled receipts, half a crayon, a sore throat lozenge, and some lip gloss before locating the purple rabbit foot key chain Brian had given her for luck during the deployment.

Mrs. James got on the line. "Mrs. Gardner?"

"Hi. How's Kevin doing?" Marianne asked. "He sounds worse than usual, but if it's nothing but nerves again, I'd hate to check him out of school and prolong the problem."

"I think you'd better come get him this time," Mrs. James said. "He feels feverish. Any time I try to get him to move—for his reading group or even for recess—he shakes his head and holds his stomach. He's usually so cooperative—and talkative. I haven't had to shush him once today."

That alone said volumes. *Kevin* not loud and disruptive? Something had to be wrong.

"I thought maybe it was one of those things that would resolve itself," Mrs. James went on, "but he's not getting better."

"I'll be right there," Marianne said, worry squeezing her middle. "I'm in Provo right now, so it'll take me a few minutes, but I'm on my way." She hung up. "Sorry guys," she said, standing. "I have to go. See you next week? Where are we set for next time?"

"Olive Garden," Jessie said. "It's time for breadstick heaven. The new one in American Fork, so it's right by you."

"Unless you need anything before that," Brenda added. "Be sure to let us know how your little guy is doing, all right?"

"I will," Marianne said with a smile. What a great group of women these were—so willing to make sure they all had what they needed. "I'll send an e-mail report to everyone," she said, tucking her chair under the table. "Bye."

She went down the short staircase to the exit, where she pushed open the wooden doors. Jostling her keys nervously in one hand, she hurried to her car. She had been to the school to check Kevin out several times before for illness and injuries besides the broken arm. There were also the stitches in his forehead from the time he fell off the school's retaining wall and smacked into the concrete. And the time he twisted his ankle after jumping ten feet from the top of some monkey bars. Once he was sent home with what turned out to be the obscure Fifth Disease, something she'd never encountered with either of the girls. And he'd come home several times in the last few months with stomach pains until she clued in that they were just from anxiety.

But as she got into her car and drove to the school this time, her stomach balled into a knot. Kevin hadn't sounded like himself. And if Mrs. James was concerned, then Marianne probably should be too. At a red light, she pulled out her phone again and called home to leave a message for the girls so that after school they'd know where she was—and to stay home. The family rule was that if they got home and Mom wasn't there, they had to call her cell. But lately, she didn't know if McKayla would follow that.

When she reached the school, Marianne didn't bother going to the office for them to call Kevin in. She headed straight for the new addition to the school where Mrs. James's class was and glanced at her watch. The kids would line up to switch to art class any minute. She headed down the long hallway with colorful tile designs on the floor. She went past several classrooms until she reached Kevin's. He sat at his desk, backpack and coat already on. He was pale, and his eyes were vacant. He was slumped forward, his arms wrapped tightly around his middle.

Oblivious to the stares from the other students, Marianne scurried to her son's side. When he saw her, his eyes welled up with tears of relief. "Mom."

"Oh, sweetie. I came as fast as I could," Marianne said, pulling him close. He winced. Marianne pulled back. Even that movement hurt? And he was very hot. "Can you walk, or do you want me to carry you?"

"Carry me," he said, looking so much like the little baby he used to be. It broke her heart.

"I'll try to be gentle," she said, picking up her growing nine-year-old. At the movement, he held his breath and pressed his eyes closed. But once she held him firmly, he rested his head against her shoulder.

"It hurts, Mommy," he whimpered.

"I know," she said. She pressed her lips together. He hadn't called her *Mommy* in years. She waved to the teacher and left. A brief stop at the main office got him checked out for the day, after which Marianne drove straight to the emergency room. It was either that or her regular urgent care clinic, and something inside told her to go to the emergency room first—they were on the same street anyway.

They sat in the stiff, plastic chairs for what felt like hours, Kevin miserable and sitting on her lap for comfort. They were finally taken back to the examination area and shown to a room off the hall. The bed was pushed up against the wall, and as they entered, Kevin clung to Marianne, reluctant to be put onto such a spacious and sterile-looking mattress, so Marianne stayed close and held his hand.

Bailey called from home to see how much longer they'd be. McKayla hadn't arrived yet. Not knowing how long she'd be there, Marianne called Nora to see if someone could watch out for her girls and get them some dinner.

"There are four of us who can pitch in, you know," Nora said. "I'm glad you called. I'll make sure your girls are both accounted for and fed."

Marianne gushed her thanks. *What a relief to have good friends I can count on,* she thought, hanging up. *Now if only I can get this little guy home soon.*

As she hung up, she heard sirens blare in the distance. A few minutes later, people rushed past the door, doctors barking orders and nurses hurrying about, flushed, as they complied. Kevin breathed in sharply and squeezed Marianne's hand.

"I'm scared." His eyes were wide as saucers.

Marianne bit her lip and looked around, as if she'd be able to find help to calm her son. She wished for a nurse to talk him through this. A thought dawned on her. Of course. Kevin had a crush on the one nurse Marianne knew personally.

"Hey, remember my friend Jessie?"

A tentative smile crossed his face, and he blushed. "Yeah." Already his attention was taken away from the commotion, and his death grip had loosened somewhat. This would work.

"Did you know that she's a nurse?"

"She is? Cool," Kevin said. "She works in a hospital? Like this?"

"She doesn't work right now, but she knows all about this kind of stuff." Marianne pulled out her cell phone and waved it in front of him. "Do you want me to call her? She can tell you what to expect and what all these gadgets are." She waved at that monitors, computers, and some other equipment attached to the walls, some of which she could guess the purpose of and others she had no idea about.

Kevin nodded. "Yeah."

Marianne dialed and explained the situation to Jessie.

"Poor thing," Jessie said. "Sure, I'll talk to him."

Marianne handed over the phone, grateful for the second time in about an hour for being able to call on one of the wives for help.

They talked for a good five minutes. Kevin described items in the room—the blood pressure cuff, some valve-looking things sticking out of the wall, the way the bed moved up and down, and so on, then he listened to her explanations of each one. He got a little quieter when he asked, "What do you think the doctor's going to do to me? Will I get a shot or something?"

Marianne braced herself as he listened to the answer. He might not get a shot, but she wouldn't be at all surprised if he got some blood drawn, which would be *worse* than a shot. Kevin hated needles almost as much as missing recess.

But somehow Jessie calmed his nerves from the other side of the line. Kevin even laughed before hanging up and handing over the phone. "This isn't so bad," he said, looking around the room and nodding.

"Glad to hear it," Marianne said, patting his leg.

He got bored and asked to play with her cell phone. After playing a game of Sudoku, he took pictures of the walls and his arm. Every so often he grimaced and held his stomach. But suddenly he grew somber. He flipped the phone closed and stared at his lap. "Mom?"

"Do you need something? Are you cold?" She reached to unfold a thin, white blanket at the bottom of the bed.

"No. It's just that . . . what if I'm so sick . . . that I die?"

"Oh, honey, you aren't going to die," Marianne said, her throat tight.

"But what if I *did?*" He looked over at her with a youthful wisdom in his eyes. "It would be sad, but I'd be in heaven, right? And I'd still be your son forever?"

Tears pricked Marianne's eyes. "That's right," she managed. "You'll always be mine, forever and ever, because Daddy and I were sealed in the temple."

Kevin nodded thoughtfully. "I'm glad. Because you know what else?"

"What?" Marianne said, grateful that her son understood some basic gospel concepts, like eternal families.

"You know how some soldiers die?"

Marianne nearly choked. "Yes," she said, trying to keep emotion from her voice. She wouldn't lie to her son about the dangers his father faced in Afghanistan, but she didn't want to dwell on them and worry him either. "What about it?"

"Well, I'm glad we're a forever family, because if Daddy dies, it's still okay, because he'll still be my dad. Forever and ever."

Marianne nodded, unable to speak for a second. She squeezed his hand and leaned forward to kiss his hairline. She cleared her throat. "That's exactly right."

When he busied himself again with a Pac-Man-style game on her cell phone, she wiped her eyes, suddenly hating the fact that Brian was in another dangerous area right now and wouldn't be in contact with her again for at least another couple of days.

Not that that would stop her from checking her e-mail a hundred times between now and then.

A doctor came through the door. Marianne scooted closer to the foot of the bed to give him room. "Hi there. I'm Dr. Brown," he said, scanning Kevin's chart. "So, your tummy's been hurting you, has it?"

Kevin nodded, apparently losing his voice to shyness.

"How about you lean back for me on the bed there?" Dr. Brown said. "Let's see what we have." Kevin complied, and Dr. Brown probed his belly.

"Ow! Oh, that hurts," Kevin said, his hands splaying on the sheet. Marianne flinched, wishing she could reach him, but she sat helpless at the foot of the bed. She put her hand on his leg instead.

Dr. Brown nodded and sat on a rolling stool. "How long have you been hurting?"

Kevin shrugged. "Two or three days, but it's a lot worse now."

Two or three days?

"This is the first I've heard of it," Marianne said but then remembered Kevin lying around after school, watching television instead of making snow forts in the backyard or torturing his sisters. He hadn't said he was hurting; she thought he was tired.

Maybe he kept quiet so I wouldn't worry, she thought. That would be like him. "I didn't know you were hurting, buddy."

Dr. Brown set the chart on the base of the bed and clapped his hands. "Could you get off the bed for me?" Kevin eased off the bed, sucking air between his teeth as he put his weight on his feet. "Good. Now show me how high you can jump."

Kevin tried but didn't do more than a pathetic attempt at a hop before doubling over. Dr. Brown didn't look at all surprised. He nodded and made a note on the chart. Marianne helped her son back onto the bed.

"I'll order some blood work to confirm," he said. "But it looks to me like he's got appendicitis. We'll probably need to take it out tonight."

Chapter 28: Marianne
Undone

"Thanks, Nora," Marianne said at the door. "I don't know what I would have done the last few days without you."

"You're welcome." Nora leaned in, giving her a hug. "I'm glad I could help out. That's what the wives are for. Besides, your girls are so sweet, I enjoyed every minute of it."

"Oh really." Marianne gave her a look of disbelief. "Even McKayla?"

Nora shrugged. "Even McKayla. She's been a delight to talk to."

"Good," Marianne said. She was grateful that McKayla hadn't pulled any of her *really* stupid stunts this week. If she'd run away or something while Marianne had been at the hospital, she didn't know *how* she would have handled it all.

"Mother hasn't been doing that well," Nora said. "So it's good for me to get a home healthcare nurse periodically so I can get out."

Marianne nodded, feeling guilty that Nora's "night out" consisted of tending someone else's kids. Whenever Nora mentioned her mother, Marianne didn't know quite what to say. Nora had been so secretive about her mother's condition. At times, it sounded very serious, with important doctor appointments and medications and tests. Yet at others times, Nora made it sound like her mother was simply getting on in years.

"Thanks for coordinating with everyone," Marianne went on. She still could hardly believe how, within moments of knowing about Kevin's operation, Nora had e-mailed all the wives for their upcoming schedules and arranged for an entire week of caring for Marianne's girls. She'd done it all between the wives, Marianne's local family, visiting teachers, and a few other neighbors. Turned out Marianne needed only four days of it, but it was so nice to know her family would be watched out for no matter how long it took. Jessie had even taken the girls to church today—which made Kevin ragingly jealous, because *he* would have loved to sit next to Jessie during sacrament meeting, and instead, he was cooped up in a "stupid hospital bed."

"Helping is what we're here for," Nora said, stepping down from the porch.

"It feels like we wives are always on the receiving end, and you're the one always helping out," Marianne said. "Let me know if I can ever do anything for you in return. Please."

Nora paused a second as if considering the idea, but she didn't accept the offer. "You go get some sleep now. It's late. You need it."

"I will," Marianne promised. "As soon as I check my e-mail."

With a laugh, Nora took her keys out of her purse. "Of course. I'll be doing that when I get home too." After a wave, she carefully made her way along the walkway, which was covered with a two-inch blanket of snow from the evening's storm.

Marianne closed the door and clicked the dead bolt into place then leaned against the wall. It had been an exhausting several days juggling life between home and the hospital, trying hard to spend some time with McKayla and Bailey when she *was* home. If it hadn't been for the help she got from the ward, her parents, and the other wives, the girls would have survived on nothing but peanut butter sandwiches.

She took a deep breath and headed for the staircase. She'd check on the kids again—especially Kevin, to be sure he was asleep and not in any pain—before taking a nice, hot, *long* bath and letting the fatigue and tension seep out of her body. Every inch of her felt wrung out like an old rag. But first—e-mail. She glanced at the clock above the kitchen window. Almost eleven.

That meant it was about nine thirty in the morning in Afghanistan. If Brian wasn't still on that mission, he might have Internet access . . .

Knowing that the chances were unlikely, she headed downstairs to the computer in the family room anyway. She'd be unable to sleep without checking, to be absolutely sure she hadn't missed a message.

She probably went to the computer a hundred times every day—fifty in the morning hours before Brian retired for the night his time, and as many times in the evening before bed, when *he'd* just woken up in Afghanistan. If Brian hadn't been able to write something, then she'd still write an e-mail telling him that Kevin was home, safe and sound.

As she sat down, Marianne combed her fingers through her hair and yawned then clicked on *send/receive*. Four messages arrived. Two were spam. One was from Brenda, and the other was from Kevin's teacher. Marianne tried not to let disappointment get the better of her. After Brian's last—and necessarily cryptic—message about the upcoming mission, she knew he probably wasn't anywhere near a computer with an Internet connection right now, so it was silly to get her hopes up.

All the same, she hadn't heard from him in four days. And after spending those days in the hospital with Kevin—well, seeing a loving message from her husband would have been a nice way to end a difficult week.

She deleted the spam and opened Mrs. James's message, which turned out to be a sweet query as to Kevin's health and a hope that he was feeling well and would return to class soon. Marianne didn't reply, deciding that first she'd let Kevin see it in the morning. He could help her compose a response.

She clicked on Brenda's message addressed to all the wives. It was probably about this week's lunch, since it was her turn to pick the restaurant. Maybe she'd changed her mind from the Olive Garden. Instead, the message was about something else altogether.

Hey, Ladies—

Have any of you heard from your husbands today? I'm guessing we're in another communication blackout, but I couldn't find anything about a battle or casualty on any of the online news wires. I swear, this is the worst part of deployment—the worry. Let me know when you guys hear so we can know all our men are accounted for, and I can stop freaking out.

Brenda

The all-too-familiar knot in the stomach appeared in Marianne's middle. A communication blackout—if that's what it was—*could* mean nothing. It might be nothing more than a precaution like it had been several other times in the last five months. Still, she felt a sinking feeling in her middle.

It might mean something much worse—what every family at home dreaded: a U.S. casualty. A communication blackout would explain not hearing from Brian even if his mission was over. The thought of a blackout always brought a thud of worry to her stomach.

Closing her eyes, she mentally offered a little prayer, hoping the blackout didn't mean anything. If it *wasn't* a precaution—and even if she received an e-mail from Brian in the next few minutes saying he was fine—it meant that a family somewhere had lost their son, their husband, their father. The few times these things had happened always made her heart ache, even as she felt relief that the soldier wasn't hers.

She wrote an e-mail to Brian about the week. It was briefer than usual, because her lids were heavy, and she could hardly type she was so tired. She sent it.

As she stood, she heard a knock on the front door. Nora had forgotten her casserole dish—something so unlike her. She'd probably come back for it. Marianne jogged up the short flight of steps and grabbed the dish from the counter before hurrying to the door. Through the sheers on the bay window, she could barely make out the image of a vehicle. It wasn't Nora's Taurus. Marianne set the dish on the floor by the couch and cautiously opened the door.

Two men dressed in full Army uniform stood before her. The older of the two had gray hair and bore a silver star on his uniform—a brigadier general. Her eyes passed over the rank of the younger one, instead seeing the gold leaf indicating he was a major, then landing on the gold cross he also wore. He was a chaplain. Marianne's hands flew to her face. Her body suddenly felt hollow.

The presence of these men could mean only one thing.

No. No. No!

Violent images of gunfire, shrapnel, and exploding vehicles filled her mind—Brian getting hit because he *was* six inches to the left this time. Of him collapsing inside the Humvee or maybe falling out to the ground, suffering, bleeding. A torrent of tears appeared from nowhere and flooded down her cheeks.

"No," she said aloud, shaking her head. "No. Please, no." As if they could somehow not say the bad news and make it not exist.

The younger of the soldiers, the chaplain, looked uncomfortably at the other. He took a small step forward and said, "Mrs. Gardner?"

Somehow Marianne managed a nod and what sounded like a squeak of confirmation.

"Mrs. Gardner, we regret having to be the bearers of bad news. But . . . Major Gardner was killed earlier today."

The moment she'd seen them in their perfectly pressed uniforms standing on her front step, she knew what they were going to say.

Why did hearing the words seem to stop her heart? And why did they have to be so impersonal, using only his rank and last name?

Not Major Gardner. Brian. Brian was killed. He's Brian. My Brian. Was Brian.

Her knees threatened to buckle. She pressed two fingers to her forehead. "Um . . . what?" She knew what they'd said—had known what they were going to say—but those were the only sounds she could get her mouth to make.

Brian *wasn't* dead. They had to be wrong. They *had* to. A wife should know somehow in her heart that her husband no longer lived, shouldn't she?

The soldiers glanced at one another. One nodded sharply to the other, and the second lowered his eyes. He reluctantly repeated the message. It hurt as much the second time.

"I . . ." She couldn't speak as her eyes darted from one soldier to the other. Emotions swirled inside her, making it hard to think. It was as if there were two of her, one that was sobbing with pain inside, and one of her that stood aloof, refusing to comprehend what they'd said.

It wasn't real. It wasn't. Brian *would* be coming home. His two-week leave would be in February, overlapping with Valentine's Day. They'd spend a couple of nights, just the two of them, at a hotel, and then they'd visit Disneyland with the kids.

And after that . . .

Brian is dead.

She imagined a flag-draped coffin and had to grip the doorjamb to not fall over. "What . . . how did it happen?" Her voice came out like a squeak.

"We haven't been informed of the circumstances yet," the general said. He tilted his head in concern, likely because Marianne looked ready to pass out. Her face was cold, and she had trouble breathing.

She murmured, "Thank you for coming." Her voice sounded strangely disembodied. Her lungs felt unable to get enough air; her chest seemed to be collapsing.

The soldiers repeated their condolences and said that she would be contacted soon with further details—things like when "the remains" would be returned to U.S. soil.

"Perhaps we should stay with you for a few minutes," the chaplain said, stepping forward.

"No." The word came out sharp. She lifted her head and shook it firmly, swallowed, and gripped the doorframe. If she saw their uniforms much longer, she'd collapse on the threshold right then and there. "Thank you, but no."

"Is there anyone you'd like us to call?"

Her mind went immediately to the one person she'd always relied on in emergencies—Brian. She choked and shook her head. "No. Please go. Thank you for coming. Good night." She moved to close the door. They made quick, formal nods and turned to walk down the porch.

She locked the door and stumbled to the love seat. Dropping to the cushions, she stared at the carpet. Her mind was stuck, repeating the same ideas like a vinyl record hitting a scratch. Brian couldn't be dead. There had to be a mistake. He *couldn't* be dead. It's not real. He's still alive. Breathing. No way would someone with such life in him be dead.

Maybe there's still a chance that there was a mistake . . .

Through the fog of disbelief, the meaning of the soldiers' message pierced through. Brian was killed. He would never again lie beside her at night. Their children would never see his smile again or feel his hug. He'd cheered at his last soccer game. He would never watch their children grow up.

And I'll be alone. For the rest of my life. There would be no celebratory homecoming with a banner and balloons this summer. Marianne tried to breathe, but the air wouldn't come at first. She inhaled in sharp, painful spurts. Sobs built up, slowly at first, then more powerfully, until they wracked her frame and cut through the denial.

Pulling a throw pillow into her lap, she curled her knees up to her face and wept into the cushion, feeling as if a black void were encircling her. The threads of hope and strength she had clung to for months were suddenly snapped. Gone.

She punched the pillow and screamed into it. Last time Brian was in mortal danger, she'd known. She'd *known*. And she'd prayed him to safety. Why hadn't she been warned this time? Why couldn't she have gathered her children into a circle and called down a heavenly shield of protection a second time? Why once, but not this time? Maybe the prompting did come, but she didn't hear it because she was so caught up with Kevin's surgery or McKayla's problems. Or maybe it hadn't come at all. If not, why not?

Her fingers pushed through her hair and held on as if the pain would somehow take away the agony growing in her heart. She choked on another sob as she lifted her head from the pillow. Her gaze landed on her cell phone lying on the armrest of the couch. With shaky fingers, she picked it up and dialed Nora's cell. As it rang, Marianne leaned her forehead against the now-damp pillow.

The way Nora answered showed that she'd seen the caller ID. "Hey, there. I forgot my pan at your place, didn't I? Sorry. I'm so distracted lately."

"It's not that," Marianne said, her voice strained and cracked. "Oh, Nora . . . could you come back? Please?"

"Of course. Is something wrong with Kevin?" Now Nora's voice was abrupt, filled with concern.

"Please hurry," Marianne said.

"I'm turning around right now."

"Thanks," Marianne said, knowing she'd need a shoulder to cry on more than ever before. "But Nora?"

"Yes?"

"It's not Kevin. It's Brian."

Chapter 29: Marianne
After

Marianne rocked back and forth on the couch, arms tightly wrapped around her middle. She made a foreign sound—a strange, high-pitched keening coming from her throat. Her eyes darted to the top of the stairs, where the kids' rooms were. One hand whipped up and covered her mouth to muffle the sound so they wouldn't wake up. The kids couldn't know. Not yet. Not until their mother was under control and could break the news the right way.

Whatever that was.

A soft knock rapped on the front door, and for a brief instant, Marianne stared at it with tension gripping in her chest, as if the soldiers had come back. But then she began breathing again, reminding herself that even if they had returned, what news could they possibly give that would make it worse?

"Marianne?" A voice called from the other side. "It's me, Nora."

With a sob of relief, Marianne crossed to the door. She pulled it open, the weight feeling three times heavier than usual, and threw herself into Nora's arms. "He's gone. He's . . . he's gone."

"I know," Nora said. She managed to squeeze into the house and close the door against the winter chill. Then she wrapped her arms around Marianne, and the two women stood there in the entryway, crying together.

"I knew it could happen. We all knew," Marianne said, her voice coming in jerky spurts. "But deep down, I always thought he'd come home to me. And to our kids." Emotion built up again, and she covered her face with her hands then buried them into Nora's shoulder again.

"I know," Nora said again, holding her tight with one arm and cradling Marianne's head with the other. "I'm so sorry."

After a few minutes, Nora led Marianne to the couch. They held hands as she rambled on, spilling her emotions in an incoherent river. Nora didn't try to offer advice, for which Marianne was thankful. There would be a time for that soon. For now, she needed to weep. She wiped at her cheeks and pushed her hair out of her face, still unable to comprehend what had happened. It didn't feel real, and part of her still tried to deny it. Brian would be coming home for leave next month. He *would.*

Marianne was intensely grateful that Nora was here—Nora, who had so much experience with deployment.

And yet. Marianne looked up at Nora's pained eyes and realized that three deployments notwithstanding, her friend had no personal experience with *this*—with losing her soldier. Marianne would have to be alone in this grief.

Nora pulled out her cell phone and made a call to the woman who was staying at the house with her mother, asking if she could stay the night. Then the two of them sat in the living room, lit only by the glow of street lamps spilling in through the sheers on the bay window. Bare branches from the tree outside waved their skeletal arms in silhouette on the wall. Marianne shuddered and wrapped her hands around her head.

"I don't want morning to come," she said weakly. Her body felt a paradoxical combination of absolute emptiness and agony filling every square inch of her insides.

"Come here," Nora said, opening her arms. Marianne lifted herself and leaned again into Nora's embrace. It felt so much like her mother's that Marianne sobbed anew. "Let it out," Nora said. "Don't think about tomorrow; just let it out right now."

They sat there for who knew how long. She must have cried herself to sleep, because the next thing she knew, she was opening her eyes—swollen and stinging from crying. The purple-black of night had yielded to an ugly, yellow-gray of morning. An annoying bird was chirping cheerfully from somewhere.

It's January. It's too cold for birds, Marianne thought glumly, irritated at the high-pitched screech that might, under normal circumstances, sound happy to someone. *Stupid things should go away and leave me in peace.*

Gingerly, she sat up, feeling tight muscles up and down her back and a nasty crick in her neck. For a minute, Marianne felt disoriented. Why was she on the couch? An afghan was spread across her. She looked across the room to the other couch. Nora slept there by the window, head propped against a decorative pillow and a hand under one cheek. She must have put the afghan over Marianne.

Because she'd come back. Because Brian was dead. The memory cut through the drowsiness like a bolt, and she sat upright, breathless.

The chirping noise stopped abruptly, and she realized it wasn't an actual bird at all but McKayla's stupid alarm clock. She'd be coming out of her room any minute to take a shower and get ready for school.

Brian's gone. Marianne tried to get herself to grasp it. She had to tell McKayla soon, because she couldn't very well go to school today. But something in her head kept saying that Brian *couldn't* be gone. It was a mistake. The Army must have misidentified the body or assumed he was dead, but he was now getting medical care, and they'd let her know of the mistake very soon, or . . .

She pushed the afghan aside and went downstairs to the computer. If Brian was all right, if the communication blackout was over, she'd have a message. If not . . . maybe she could believe. She'd left the computer on last night, so it took only a moment to click a button and know that she'd gotten nothing from Afghanistan overnight.

Her throat constricted, and she looked up at the ceiling toward the girls' room. *We lost our daddy,* she thought, face crumpling into her hands. *How can I tell them?*

Details about his death would be forthcoming, the chaplain had said. But she wanted them now. Her imagination was going overtime. Facts. She wanted the dry, hard facts. She searched all the news wires, looking for answers.

Was it an IED? Was it on the way to or from a delivery? Was it an RPG like the one that had almost killed Brian before? Was it—heaven forbid—friendly fire? *What happened?*

Would she be able to see Brian's body, his face? Or would he be too disfigured for his wife and children to look on him one last time?

She found nothing online. It was still too soon, she figured. Her fingers raked through her tousled hair, and she stood up with a groan. McKayla would be down in a few minutes. Time to get moving.

She went upstairs and looked around the kitchen in a bit of a daze. The kids would need a nice breakfast this morning of all mornings. This wasn't a time to let them get by on Trix or Eggos. *Pancakes,* she decided, pulling out the griddle from a lower cupboard. With the plug halfway into the wall, her eyes pricked. This was the perfect time to use the Christmas gift Nora had given her.

She pushed the plug into the outlet all the way before heading to the pantry and finding the red and gold bag on the right side of the top shelf. As she stirred the batter, the shower turned off upstairs, and a glance at the stove clock confirmed that the morning routine was on schedule. Bailey's alarm would go off any minute so she could get ready for junior high. Kevin's elementary school track started an hour after that, so he was used to waking up later than his sisters. His alarm wouldn't be going off today, not after he just got home from the hospital. His teacher already knew not to expect him.

She scooped out the batter onto the griddle, and the pancakes sizzled, wafting a delicious aroma through the room. It wasn't at all tempting to Marianne's sour stomach; all she could think of was how to tell the kids. Should she tell the girls first? They were older. Kevin might need to be told in a different way. Then again, he'd probably resent not finding out when his sisters did, who needed to know right away, before they tried heading out the door for school.

Noises of shifting came from the living room, and a moment later, Nora appeared around the corner. She smiled at the sight of her Christmas present. "A good time to use it," she said, nodding at the colorful bag. She wiped some smeared makeup from under her eye.

Marianne tried to smile back, but it turned into more of a grimace. "I thought so." She shrugged. "Of course, after today, they may hate the memory of pancakes altogether."

Tears welled up again, and she covered her eyes with the back of her hand. "Stop it, stop it, stop it!" she told herself. "I've got to get a grip." Last night she'd totally fallen apart, and she was awfully close to doing it again. Her kids needed a mom right now. She pressed against the bridge of her nose, hard, as if that would stop the tears.

Nora crossed to her and gently lowered the hand. She looked Marianne in the eyes and said, "Not now. This is a time when the rules can be broken."

Marianne's brow drew together. "What, seeing a mom have a nervous breakdown is now a good thing?"

"No," Nora said. "But if they don't see you crying, they won't have permission to do it, either. Let yourself cry around them. They need to grieve. You all do."

That made sense, and yet . . .

Marianne took the spatula and flipped all eight pancakes on the griddle. The bathroom door opened, and McKayla came out. She went into her room, saying, "Bathroom's yours," to her sister as she slammed the door shut. Marianne started at the sound then evened out her breath. The slightest thing made her jumpy.

"You've been so generous with your advice this whole deployment," Marianne said, staring at the browned sides of the pancakes and avoiding Nora's face. "But . . . well, how do you know how to deal with . . . with this?" After a pause, she turned and lifted her eyes to Nora's. They were glistening.

"I don't, exactly. But my best friend lost her husband in Desert Storm. I watched it and lived it with her nearly twenty years ago. And there have been others. I didn't lose Russell, for which I'm grateful, but I've seen more than I have wanted to about becoming a widow in the military." She lifted a finger to her eye and took away a tear. "Would you like me to let everyone know?"

Marianne knew she meant the wives, not her children. She nodded gratefully. "Yes, please. That's three phone calls I'd rather not have to make." And suffer through.

All of the wives would want to be with her, express their condolences, hear about every minute of it. Maybe soon she'd be able to talk about it, but not yet. For now, having Nora take care of it was a load off her shoulders. She almost asked Nora to call Brian's parents but realized the military would have done that already.

"I'll call all the wives," Nora said. "Now I'll get out of here so you can have some time alone with your kids. Should I call the schools or any carpools or your bishop or . . ." Her voice trailed off expectantly.

"Yes. Good idea," Marianne said. "I just can't think clearly right now." She'd *thought* plenty since waking up but not about logistics like these. Calling the school and bishop hadn't occurred to her. Of course they'd all need to know right away. She'd need to tell her parents. Nora shouldn't be the one to do that. Marianne wiped her hands on a dish-cloth and headed for the cabinet where she kept a pad of blue sticky notes. She wrote down the numbers of the high school, the junior high, Bailey's carpool mom for the week, and lastly the bishop. She cringed at that one, because while she knew he'd need to be told— and her family would need help—she didn't want the entire ward descending on her home right away.

She held the slip out, but as Nora reached for the little square, Marianne didn't release it at first. They locked eyes. "How do I tell our kids?" Her voice was pleading.

Helplessness filled Nora's face. She shook her head. "I don't know."

"Thanks for coming." She pulled her friend into a big hug. "And for staying with me all night."

"I'm glad I could," Nora said, patting her back. "I need to check on Mother and relieve the nurse. But I'll be back soon. Don't you worry about dinner or anything, all right?"

"All right," Marianne said as they pulled apart. She walked Nora to the front door. As she closed it, McKayla came down the stairs. Her hair was still wet, but she was dressed and had on her makeup.

"Who was that?" McKayla asked over her shoulder as she headed for the kitchen. "Weird for someone to show up so early in the morning." Her step paused, and then she whipped around, her face suddenly pale. "Mom . . ." Her voice had a layer of fear in it.

It was Nora, not soldiers. Marianne tried to say the words, but they didn't come out. Did it matter that it was Nora who had left? It *had* been soldiers a few hours ago. The answer to McKayla's real question was the same.

"Mom?" McKayla's voice went up a level, and her eyes went wide, shooting toward the door. "That wasn't . . . was it . . . ?" She took a breath and then said, "Is Dad . . ."

Marianne swallowed, wanting to clamp her mouth shut. McKayla shouldn't find out now, in this way. This wasn't like the day Marianne's father died and she cried and cried and told the kids right away. They hardly knew their grandfather, so while the kids were sad, it hadn't knocked their world off its axis.

Their dad's death would destroy them.

"Mom?" McKayla's voice raised in pitch, and Marianne panicked, not knowing what to say.

Later. She had to find a way to tell McKayla later. When the family was gathered around and she was armed with General Authority quotes about the resurrection and eternal families. At the very least, Bailey and Kevin needed to be there.

But in spite of herself, tears welled up in her eyes. She lowered her gaze, biting her lip in a vain attempt to hold back the tears. Her face said enough. McKayla's eyes went wide. Her arm reached back, looking for support. She pulled out a kitchen chair and fell into it.

"No. No . . ." McKayla kept shaking her head, wet chunks of hair undulating back and forth.

Chapter 30: Nora
Support

As far as Nora was concerned, there was no way they could cancel lunch *this* week of all weeks. She was pleasantly surprised that even with Justin home, Kim had come—it was as if they all knew how much Marianne needed them right now. Justin came along too; he and his wife were practically attached at the hip during his leave. When he first walked in, Nora could hardly believe how *young* he was. But Russell was probably about that age when he joined up. And she wasn't too much older than Kim when they married.

"It's nice to meet all of you," Justin said, shaking hands around the table. "You've become Kim's family while I'm gone. I'm so glad she's had you all during the pregnancy."

"We all adore Kim," Nora said.

They placed their orders, and after a little small talk, the server brought their salads and breadsticks. As they dished up salad, Jessie said, "I'm surprised Marianne wanted to have lunch this week." As planned, they were at the American Fork Olive Garden, minutes from Marianne's house. Even so, she was the last one to show up, and she was twenty minutes late already, which wasn't like her.

One clue to how upside down her life had suddenly become. No one blamed her a bit.

"She needs to be with us more today than ever before, I think," Nora said. "She needs to know we're still here for her."

"But what do we say?" Kim asked, leaning forward in her seat and holding Justin's hand tightly on the tabletop. Nora wondered if Kim would let go enough for the two of them to actually eat. "Do we act all normal and pretend everything is fine? Do we let her know how sad we are and talk about Brian—or would that make it worse?"

Nora felt the other wives' gaze. They'd looked to her many times for advice and counsel. And she'd given it as many times. This situation wasn't something she knew how to handle. She'd seen plenty of soldier deaths during their time in the military, but every widow she'd known had reacted differently. She'd seen the gamut—intense depression, the family carrying on quite functionally, a full-blown nervous break-down. One widow had come completely unraveled, ending up with shopping and plastic surgery addictions. There were no clear-cut rules for how to handle it.

"Let's follow her lead," Nora finally said. "We shouldn't pretend it hasn't happened. That would only create an elephant in the room. But we should be able to tell if she wants to talk about it . . . or not. Our job right now is to support her any way we can."

"Agreed," Jessie said.

"Hi, guys," Marianne said, coming around the corner. The server leading the way nodded toward the table. Marianne paused when her eyes landed on Justin. She smiled widely as if seeing an old friend. "Justin? It's so good to meet you." They shook hands.

"I'm sorry for your loss," Justin said.

"Thank you."

Before the server could leave, Marianne quickly ordered the fettuc-cini alfredo then sighed and sat down. She smiled weakly so it didn't go past the edges of her lips to any other part of her face. Violet ringed her eyes, which were half-closed, as if she lacked the strength to open them all the way.

Brenda broke the suddenly uncomfortable feeling at the table with, "How are you feeling?"

Marianne swallowed and took a deep breath. "I'm *not* feeling, yet." The look in her eyes sent a pang to Nora's heart, and she reached over for Marianne, who said, "I hurt so much that I'm numb." Her voice had a questioning quality in it, as if the emotions didn't make sense even to her. She searched Nora's face for an answer.

She didn't have one. After a beat, she said quietly, "When's the funeral?"

"The twentieth. He'll . . . his *body* will be in Annapolis tomorrow. I hear they do a really great job making soldiers look . . . *good.*" She tried smiling again, as if that were positive news. She lowered her eyes. "So it'll be an open casket. I'm glad. The kids need to be able to see their dad one last time. Three different news stations have called for interviews, and I think they're all showing up to the funeral, too." A shudder went through her at that. "I wish this could all be private, but I guess you can't have a military burial without the community wanting to know about the fallen soldier, right?" She smiled halfheartedly.

The server arrived with Marianne's plate for salad along with everyone else's main dish orders.

"So what else is planned?" Nora asked after the server left, trying to veer the conversation away from the media.

Marianne broke a breadstick in half and breathed out heavily. "Well, his dad will dedicate the grave. I've asked the bishop to speak. Brian's older brother will do the life sketch. My mother-in-law wants me to sing, but I . . . I just can't."

"It's ridiculous for her to ask that of you," Nora said with a firm shake of her head. "You're in charge of the funeral, anyway."

"Exactly, so I won't do it," Marianne said. "It's hard to tell her no, because I've never been her favorite daughter-in-law. She always wished Brian had married someone else, so for years I've bent over backward to please her. It's tough to disappoint her yet again this way."

She took a bite of breadstick. Everyone lapsed into quiet, eating their meals. After a moment she spoke again in a quieter voice. "This is going to sound totally bizarre, but I keep having this feeling that everything's okay, even though I'm still in a really dark place right now. I can't see the light at the end of the tunnel. Not at all. And the kids are taking it really rough—especially McKayla."

Jessie had been reaching for the salad tongs, but her hand froze midair. "Do you want to talk about it?"

Marianne shrugged. "There's not much to say. She's refusing to go to counseling anymore. She needs it more now than before, of course, but she won't go."

"Oh, no," Brenda said, putting down her fork and leaning across the table.

Marianne sighed and pressed on. "In spite of it all, something keeps telling me that it'll work out, that the darkness won't last forever. I have no idea *how* that'll happen, but somehow I have to hang on to the idea that we'll be okay and that this is some part of a greater plan."

"Do you mean *McKayla* or *Brian* as part of a greater plan?" Brenda asked skeptically.

"Brian," Marianne clarified. She folded her cloth napkin in half and half again. "I don't get it, and I don't *like* it, but even though I spend hours crying every day, there's something that keeps telling me this is what was supposed to happen."

"So . . . your husband was supposed to die?" Brenda asked with a tone of disbelief. Nora shot her a look, and Brenda sighed then picked up her fork again and swirled her spaghetti as she softened her words. "You have a better perspective than I would. I don't think I'd be handling it so well."

A sharp laugh came from Marianne. "I'm hardly 'handling' it. It happened on Sunday, and every day I've been a sobbing mess."

Marianne had used the words "it happened."

"Brian died" was glaringly absent, Nora noticed. She couldn't blame her.

"I'm nowhere *near* over it. Maybe it's everyone's prayers or something—I know the entire ward is praying for us, and so is all our family. Something's holding me together so I don't shatter."

Nora nodded, thinking she understood. As the server returned for Marianne's order, Nora lapsed into quiet thought. For some time she'd been considering releasing her stranglehold on the "mother hen" label of the group and letting the other wives help *her* for a change. Marianne's words from Sunday night still rang in her ears.

It feels like we wives are always on the receiving end, and you're the one always helping out, Marianne had said. *Let me know if I can ever do anything for you in return. Please.*

At last week's lunch, Nora thought about telling the wives about her mother's imminent death. Then, when Marianne had made that plea this weekend, Nora had almost come out and told Marianne about the cancer, that her mother had only a couple weeks left. But her pride got in the way, and she hadn't said a word.

Now she was glad she'd kept it to herself; Major Gardner's death gave the wives plenty to worry about. They didn't need to find out that the "mother" of their group had her own life-changing event about to take place. She'd keep it to herself a little longer.

She'd also send a note to Russell demanding that he stay at the base from here on. Being a colonel should offer a few perks, and one of them should be not turning your wife into a widow.

Chapter 31: Jessie
Burial

Today should have been lunch day. But even though all the wives were gathered in the same place, it wasn't over restaurant food.

A good-sized crowd had assembled at the cemetery. Jessie stood close to Brenda, Kim, and Nora on one end of the gathering. Justin stood up front in his uniform, and Marianne sat with her three children on the front row of seats with blue velvet slipcovers. They clutched blankets draped over their laps to help keep out the biting winter cold. Next to Marianne's family sat a couple that had to be Brian's parents.

In the rows behind them, other relatives were seated, including Brian's and Marianne's siblings. Brian's younger brother, Rich, looked so much like the pictures Jessie had seen of Brian that she kept staring at him.

Nothing about the situation felt real. The funeral service hadn't either. Rich had given Brian's life sketch. It had been an eerie experience hearing highlights of a life from a man who looked so much like the picture of Major Gardner sitting beside the podium.

How could they discuss the life—and death—of a man who'd scarcely reached his prime? Jessie had never before attended a funeral that wasn't for someone who was at least eighty—people who'd died of "causes incident to age." Those services were sad, but they were also celebrations of lives well lived. Those memorials had children, grandchildren, and often great-grandchildren all remembering their loved one who had *lived.*

Brian Gardner hadn't finished living.

Yet as unreal as the moment felt, every bit of the *pain* was vivid.

Jessie couldn't help but analyze the faces of Major Gardner's family as they watched the seven-man honor guard carry the casket across the cemetery, the snow crunching beneath their boots. Brian's mother was perfectly pressed and proper-looking, but the expression on her face read like she'd been trampled by horses. His father's face was unreadable.

Marianne sat stoic, looking almost peaceful. The reality of what Brian's death meant would have to come crashing down soon, Jessie figured. Marianne would be able to put on a strong face for now—but for how long?

In the background, seven men in uniform stood in a straight line. A deep voice called, "Present arms!"

As one, the men lifted their weapons into position. On verbal cues, they shot into the sky, once, twice, three times, seven shiny rifles in unison. The shots boomed and echoed off the mountains in a twenty-one gun salute.

As the vibration of the last shots faded, the bugler put his instrument to his lips. The first melancholy note of "Taps" sounded, bringing tears to Jessie's eyes. On the second phrase, a single note broke for the briefest second, sounding like a strained sob, then corrected itself and kept going through the sad melody played over the fallen.

While the bugle continued, the honor guard removed one of the two flags covering the casket. In quiet solemnity, the men began folding the first one. As they did so, a thundering sound boomed, and Jessie looked up at the pale, bluish white sky to see military planes and a helicopter flying overhead.

With both flags folded, the soldiers handed one to General Wilcox. He walked to Brian's mother's side, knelt before her, and presented it. "On behalf of a grateful nation."

Mrs. Gardner accepted the flag from his outstretched hands, acknowledging the offering with a nod, tears streaming down her cheeks.

When General Morton presented the second flag to Marianne, saying the same words, "On behalf of a grateful nation," Jessie clamped her eyes shut and tried to breathe through the surge of emotion before opening them again.

"Thank you," Marianne said, holding the flag close. Bailey and Kevin both reached around her and put their hands on the flag. Jessie imagined Alex and Becca doing the same thing with their chubby fingers, of Joey on her lap, not understanding what was happening— never remembering his father. The pictures in her mind weren't real, at least, not yet, but they could be.

Don't take him, Lord. Please.

The generals stepped forward and placed their personalized coins on the coffin. They bore each general's own design, and receiving such a coin at any time during service was a moment to remember. Having two soldiers with that rank place theirs on Brian's casket had poignant meaning.

Twelve-year-old Bailey's cheeks were tear-streaked; her chin trembled every few seconds. Her nose was bright red from the cold, and a tissue wiped at a continuous stream of tears. Kevin, looking grown-up with a new haircut and suit, buried his face in his mother's coat sleeve. His shoulders shook.

Then there was McKayla. She sat with a straight back, face pale and lifeless, like a marble statue. She stared at the cherrywood casket as if she saw right through it, as if it weren't there.

For now, Jessie envied McKayla's apparent lack of feeling. It would be so much easier to be numb than to feel this emotional pain so exquisitely that it made her physically ache all over. Until today, she hadn't felt the pain of deployment like the others; she paid for that emptiness now in droves.

Although she'd never met Brian, she felt like she knew him, that he was family. His death drove home the reality of what Tim was facing— and what could happen to her at any time. How could she have ever been glad to have him gone? Guilt seeped into her pores. She didn't want Tim gone anymore. She wanted him home, safe. In some awful place of her heart, she'd even considered what it would be like to lose him and figured that if it happened, sure, she'd cry, but she'd survive. She'd get over it.

Standing here in the cemetery, she knew that wasn't true. *I want Tim home. Safe. Now.*

With the military honors complete, Brian's father stood to dedicate the grave. He covered one leather-gloved hand with the other and bowed his head as he prayed over his son's final resting place—an act no father should have to do. By the time the crowd murmured "amen," there wasn't a dry eye. Jessie glanced over at Kim, who was gazing at Justin, tears in her eyes. Sending Justin back over there after his leave would be doubly hard.

After the bishop made a few closing remarks, the crowd began moving toward their cars, making hushed noises as they spoke.

The wives didn't move. Jessie stared at the coffin and whispered, "I can't believe one of ours is gone."

Brenda reached an arm around her shoulder in a gesture of comfort. "Me neither," she said reverently. "I think I've been kidding myself all along that they're only helping out. That since they're not in battle, they're safe . . ."

When Brenda's voice trailed off, Kim tried to finish the thought. "I don't think any of us believed that one of *ours* would really be . . ." But she couldn't finish either.

"And another still could." Nora clamped her eyes shut and lowered her chin.

The four of them turned toward one another in a group embrace as despair, anguish, and worry flowed through them all. It felt wrong for Marianne not to be part of the circle, but they were close by, "mourning with those that mourn" in the most vivid, real way possible.

They were likely the only ones here who had an inkling of what Marianne was going through. No one else did, not really. Any military spouses and family members who'd attended had the best idea. Jessie hoped their presence would be a comfort to Marianne. Having one another would be a comfort as each of the five women faced the grieving process and grappled with renewed worry about her own husband's future.

Additional guilt wracked Jessie's heart at how little she'd cared before. She felt as if she should be the one with the flag in her arms, and not only because she'd been so emotionally distant from Tim. *It should have been me.*

In the time since Major Gardner was killed, more information had been released about how it happened. Tim had been in the tower of the Humvee when they were hit by an RPG. There was no question that it had been aimed at Tim, the one with the weapon to fire back. But the grenade veered off course and blew up in front of the vehicle, killing Brian, who got the brunt of the explosion. Tim broke an arm and got a bit scraped up but was fine. So instead of Jessie sitting in the velvet-covered chairs with her husband in the casket, it was Marianne.

It might still be me, Jessie thought with an ice-cold finger of fear running down her back. The deployment was only half over. Their men—she thought of all of them as "ours"—were literally at war. Somehow people tended to forget that the situation in Iraq wasn't the only one, that the U.S. Army in Afghanistan wasn't merely babysitting a skirmish.

It was war.

She got that now. The worry she'd seen in the eyes of Brenda and the others was hers, now that her false sense of security had been blown apart.

The small crowd thinned more, but the four wives on the side waited for a proper moment to approach Marianne. She hugged her in-laws, her siblings, her parents. The wives didn't have long to wait; in a few minutes, Marianne turned, searching the faces for them, and holding the flag in one arm, she held the other out to them.

As one, they rushed forward and enveloped her in a crushing embrace. Tears and sobs broke out from the group. After a moment, Marianne pulled back. She wiped her hands across her face, leaving it shining with moisture. Nora and Brenda stood in the center, arms wrapped around one another. Kim had a hand on Marianne's shoulder, and Jessie did the same on the other side, completing the circle.

"I'll be okay, guys," Marianne said. She held the flag tightly to her chest and stroked the stars. Her hand went to her heart, and she choked on a sob. "I feel it in here. He's okay. So I'll be okay too . . . someday. He finished his job here before I finished mine."

At some point, Marianne would crack and fall apart, Jessie figured. They'd need to be there for her when that happened, when the reality—the finality—of the situation hit.

"I'll see you at the chapel, okay?" Marianne said, releasing their hands. "Thanks for coming."

"Of course we came," Nora said, and the others chorused the same.

Marianne nodded then turned to her children. Kim went to Justin, who had his hand outstretched. The other three women headed down the hill toward Nora's car, which they'd ridden in together to the cemetery. On the way, they overheard a woman talking to her husband as they left the gravesite.

"This is why I don't want Mark to enter the service. I don't want Julie to be a military spouse. What a horrible life. Who would *do* that intentionally?"

Jessie's jaw clenched, and her step paused. Brenda and Nora stopped too. By the looks on their faces—expressions of hurt and shock—they'd heard the same words. At least Kim and Justin were out of earshot. The woman's voice held a patronizing tone, as if someone who wanted to represent their country by joining a branch of the military was nothing but a moron.

"They don't understand," Nora said under her breath, taking Brenda's and Jessie's hands tightly, as if trying to calm them. But her voice cracked, and her eyes flamed, belying her tone. "All they see is the pain. They don't understand."

They all nodded, because each of their husbands had that burning desire to serve their country this way.

"Honestly, I don't always get what drives Rick," Brenda said. "But I know the military is important to him. So I support him." She glared at the woman's retreating form. "And he's *not* stupid. No matter what happens, I'm proud of my soldier. I'm proud of all of them."

"We all are," Nora said. "As well we should be."

Chapter 32: Brenda
Anticipation

"Tim's leave is coming up, isn't it?" Brenda asked as she and Jessie left the cultural hall after the funeral luncheon.

"In a couple of months—end of March, first part of April," Jessie said as she pushed the first of the double doors open.

"Wasn't Brian's supposed to be before that?" Brenda whispered, as if Marianne, who was still in the cultural hall, could hear them.

They paused between the double doors. "Yeah," Jessie said soberly. "Next month, I think."

They went through the second set of doors, and as they walked to their cars, Brenda wished she knew what Jessie was thinking. She had to be excited for Tim to come home, even though leave was a paltry two weeks long. Brenda herself could hardly wait for Rick's turn to come home in mid-April. It might overlap with Easter and the kids' spring break. It would be perfect timing.

And yet she worried, too. She glanced at Jessie, who wore a stiff face. Was she worried about Tim's upcoming leave in the same way she was—wondering how Rick had changed, what he'd be like?

Halfway across the parking lot, Brenda said, "Tim and Rick have seen a lot." Her voice was vague.

"They sure have," Jessie said, pausing as she fished in her purse for her keys. "Has Rick told you much about it?"

Brenda shook her head. "He won't. He says he's seen a lot of things he can't talk about . . . yet. But a few months ago, he promised to tell me everything. Someday. Just not yet. I wonder if he'll ever really be able to."

Jessie nodded thoughtfully. "I imagine it'll take all of the guys some time before they're ready to talk about what they've seen—if they ever reach that point."

They stopped beside Jessie's minivan, and Brenda hitched her purse higher on her shoulder. "I worry. You know, about the whole posttraumatic stress disorder thing? It shouldn't be much of a problem during leave—at least, I hope not—but what about when they come home this fall?"

Jessie nodded in silence, as if she'd thought of the same thing.

"What if Rick has flashbacks or gets violent or retreats into a shell and won't talk to me? I want him back more than anything, but at the same time, I'm really scared about what it'll be like when he's home for good."

Jessie fiddled with her keys, not looking at Brenda. "I'm nervous about that too. I mean, of course it'll be a relief. But I keep hearing horror stories about the reentry process. Did you go to the workshop about it?"

"Oh, you bet I did." Brenda's eyes widened at the memory. The workshop included one nightmare scenario after another. It was almost enough to make you have a nervous breakdown as you waited for the sky to fall. She'd left with such a bizarre combination of emotions—wanting Rick home so badly but at the same time so scared for it that she half wanted him to stay in Afghanistan indefinitely so nothing *worse* happened.

She breathed in deeply and stared at the clouds—odd wispy ones that looked like pieces of hair floating in water. "You know one thing that's weird? I'm scared that Rick won't tell me about all the things he's been through. But I'm almost as scared that he *will*. I don't want him to withdraw and put up a wall, but at the same time . . . honestly, I don't know that I can handle hearing all of it." She waved away the thought. "I mean, I know they're dealing with the actual Taliban and all that, but it's still surreal to me. I sort of try to forget that part."

She shuddered. Last Sunday a sister in the ward had sat next to her during Relief Society and probed into how Rick was doing—then asked questions like how many people he'd personally killed.

Fortunately, she didn't know the answer. Since he wasn't in battle situations, the number could be zero. Or not. She hoped she'd never know for sure.

Inevitably, people would see Rick differently when he came home. Some might see him as a patriotic hero. Others might see him as a murderer. The weight of that knowledge was heavy on her shoulders— and she wasn't the one pulling the trigger.

"We'll deal with whatever aftermath we have to when they get home," Jessie said. She took a deep breath. "I'm nervous about post-traumatic stress too. That could be . . . scary." She nodded back at the chapel. "But anything we face is better than losing them."

"You're right," Brenda said. "I'll take all the reentry scary stuff if it means Rick is still alive."

She and Jessie said their good-byes, and Brenda headed for her car. When she got in, she leaned against the headrest and closed her eyes, forcing herself to relax and breathe deeply. She'd gone back to taking the same antidepressants she'd had after the twins. The medication was helping. Of course it didn't take away the stress, but at least she no longer felt as if her spirit were going through a meat grinder all the time.

As she opened her eyes, she caught sight of Nora leaving the church and walking to her car. She was always put together, but today she wore her fancier Sunday clothes and looked as if she'd walked out of a fashion magazine, as if she had a professional makeup artist and hairstylist at home.

How much you want to bet that Nora's never had to take antidepressants? Brenda thought dismally. *But hey, I'm doing what I need to do to survive.*

Brenda sighed and turned the key.

Chapter 33: Nora
Lingering

Monday, January 25, 2010

It's been six hours, Nora thought, looking away from the clock above the pantry door. Her mother had slept that long, straight through. Nora felt guilty for being grateful for each minute. Over the last several days, her mother had grown increasingly irritable—yes, it *was* possible—criticizing and accusing her daughter of messing up the medications.

Once she yelled out, "You're trying to poison me—I just know it. Nancy would never do that."

At the time, it was all Nora could do not to make a snide remark about how her little sister, Nancy, had always been Mother's favorite. Even in her delusions, Nancy was still preferred—forget the fact that it was Nora, not Nancy, who'd taken her in during her last months.

Another time it was, "You *want* me to die, don't you?"

Do I? Nora thought as she sat at the table. *Do I want her to die? I want this to be over. But I don't want to lose my mother. And I can't have both.* She set down the hot cocoa mug and dropped her forehead into her hands. Rubbing her scalp, she sighed and closed her eyes. *I love my mother, but how much longer can either of us go on like this?* She rarely left the house anymore, taking quick trips to the grocery store. Somehow she managed to make it to the lunches, with help from a neighbor friend and Sherry, the hospice nurse. Lunch was her one sanity-saver. She didn't often go for the entire three-hour block of church because her mother couldn't go that long without her. She attended sacrament meeting or Relief Society if it was her week to teach, and skipped out on the rest.

But six hours was six hours. She should check on Mother. Reluctantly, Nora stood, leaving the chair askew instead of pushing it back under the table. *Mother will never know,* she thought, giving the chair a disdainful glance, then looking over the kitchen, which had gotten rather cluttered over the last few days.

Mother won't see this, either, she thought, half grateful, half grief-stricken. Her mother wouldn't be around much longer. Sherry said Mother was showing many typical signs of someone in their last days. She was unlikely to ever leave her room—or her bed—alive.

Nora would give a lot to be able to call someone and talk out her frustrations. When Russell was gone during Desert Storm, she had her own group of young wives for support. The group now was different, and she had to keep reminding herself of that. The other four leaned on one another exactly the way Nora had leaned on her friends nearly twenty years ago. She had to keep a distance to provide the nurturing and guidance they needed.

I could use some nurturing and guidance of my own about now, she thought, rubbing her eyes as she headed down the hall. Again she wondered if she'd made the right decision not to tell the wives about her mother's condition. They'd want to help out of the goodness of their hearts; she knew that. But they were already so overburdened that she couldn't bear to put more on their shoulders.

There was another reason she didn't want to speak up. What would they think of her if she let them know how weak and frail she felt? Her advice and aid wouldn't mean nearly as much coming from a tired-out old woman instead of a put-together, strong one.

Nora peered into the room. The portable commode stood a few feet away from the bed. They hadn't removed it even though her mother no longer had the strength to get up and now relied on a catheter.

She seemed to sleep peacefully, lying on her back in exactly the same position she'd been in when she fell asleep after her last morphine pill. Nora knew they lasted about four hours, but her mother almost always fought taking another—she wouldn't even agree to a morphine pump. Her irritability increased with her pain, and it was a relief when Nora managed to get her to swallow the pills.

Her mother's breath came slow and shallow, and Nora counted silently between each one. Sometimes she got all the way to fifteen before the next. Knowing she'd better shift her mother so the bed sores wouldn't get any worse, Nora went to the side of the bed. She tucked her hands under her mother's back, but at the touch, Mother sat bolt upright and gasped. Nora started and stepped away. Her mother stared straight ahead, body trembling. She took short, rapid breaths.

"Sorry, Mother. I—I didn't mean to wake you." With hands on her mother's shoulders, Nora tried to ease her down to the pillow. "Here. Get some rest."

Weakly, her mother tried to wrench away and turned glaring eyes at her daughter. "Don't touch me, you viper!"

Nora pulled back as if slapped. *It's just the pain,* she reminded herself. *It's the pain speaking.* Sherry had warned her that sometimes people get this way when death was imminent.

"It's all right, Mother," Nora said gently, smiling. "I'm trying to help."

She didn't seem to be listening. "I—I—I can't breathe," she said, with barely enough air to make her voice heard. Her hands felt around the blanket as if searching for something to help. One hand went to her chest. "Can't . . . breathe. I hurt." Her eyes changed from glaring to pleading.

"I'll get you some help, Mother," Nora promised, touching her mother's hand. "Right now." With a queasy feeling in her stomach, she snatched the cordless phone from the nightstand and dialed Sherry's number. "Please come. And hurry," she said as soon as the nurse answered. "She can't breathe."

"Can she get any air at all?" Sherry asked.

"A little," Nora said, clinging to the phone.

"What's her color like?"

"Pale," Nora said, eyeing her mother and taking her hand in a comforting gesture. Her mother clung to her. "And cold."

"What about her lips? Are they blue?"

Nora leaned over and peered at her mother's face again. With relief, she straightened. "No. They're pale but definitely pink."

"Good. I'm on my way," Sherry said. "If she wants more morphine, give it to her. It's a bronchodilator as well as a painkiller, so it'll make it easier for her to breathe."

"How much?" Nora asked, releasing her mother's hand. She fumbled through the prescriptions, water bottle, tissue box, and other items on the nightstand to find the morphine. She wondered if her mother could swallow a pill in this state.

"As much as she wants," Sherry said. "Because of the stage she's at, her latest doctor's orders don't have a limit. More than normal won't hurt anything."

"Thanks." Nora had known that—somewhere in the back of her mind. But at tense moments like this, her brain stopped functioning. "Please . . . hurry." She hung up and struggled to open the prescription bottle.

Finally victorious, she tapped out a pill into her palm and handed it to her mother. "Here's some medicine," she said, reaching for the bottle of water. "Sherry says it'll help you breathe." She expected her mother to fight the pill, insisting that she didn't want to fill her body with chemicals—the same rant Nora usually heard several times every day.

Instead, her mother snatched the pill. She tossed her head backward and swallowed it without water then gasped, "More."

"All . . . right," Nora said, surprised. She shook another pill onto her palm and handed over the tablet. This time her mother took the water to wash it down.

"Another." Her mother's voice was raspy.

Sherry said she could have as much as she wanted, Nora thought, but still she hesitated. Could she kill her mother with too much morphine? Then again, what difference would it make at this point, if it meant she'd die in peace? "Okay, Mom. *One* more."

"Two," her mother snapped.

She can have as much as she wants, Nora repeated in her mind. She nodded silently and handed over the pills. She prayed her mother wouldn't ask for more—yet she almost wondered if even more would help her breathe better.

After swallowing the pills—four in all—her mother shifted in bed restlessly, still struggling for air and probably with pain as well. "Why did you do this to me?" She glowered. "All I ever did was love you, and this is how you treat me?"

Nora had already screwed the bottle cap back on. She paused and looked up. *She's delusional,* she thought, but aloud she couldn't help ask, "What did *I* do?"

"You're happy I'm dying, aren't you?" She turned to look right at Nora, clouded eyes flashing. "I won't let you take my husband, you floozy. 'Flo the Floozy.' That's what you are. Get lost." She jerked her head upward in a dismissing gesture.

She's hallucinating. Nora tried to calm herself. "It's me, Nora. Your daughter. I'm not Flo." *Who's Flo, anyway?*

Her mother's eyes narrowed. She struggled again for breath, then said, "Leave my husband alone, you home wrecker."

Being called names—even mistakenly—hurt. Her own mother didn't recognize her. The realization cut. Nora took the water bottle from Mother's clenched hand and cleared her throat. "The medicine will take effect soon, I'm sure."

"It'd better," her mother spat.

Nora sat on a chair beside the bed and checked her watch, wondering how much longer it would take until Sherry arrived. Who was Flo? Had she ever made advances on Nora's father? Every so often, Mother called out something caustic. Then she closed her eyes for a few minutes before opening them and again laying into Nora—or Flo. Or Virginia or Bertie, two more women her mother apparently despised, whoever they were.

"Who's that man standing behind you?" she suddenly demanded, crinkling open an eye.

Nora looked around, knowing full well they were alone. "I don't know, Mother," she said wearily, not having the energy to argue. "Why don't you ask him?"

"Who are you?" her mother snapped at the corner. Her face softened. "Oh. In that case, it's nice to meet you. It's not time quite yet, is it?"

In spite of herself, Nora looked at the corner. Of course she saw no one. Maybe her mother *wasn't* hallucinating this time—maybe she was seeing someone on the other side who'd come to take her home. But if that was the case, why wasn't she seeing a loved one who'd already passed on, like her mother or her husband? Why a stranger?

Her mother's face relaxed, and she leaned back against her pillow. She blinked lazily, eyes still trained on the corner as if she were listening to someone talk. She responded with nods and "m-hmms" but gradually drifted off.

By the time Sherry pulled into the driveway, her mother was unresponsive. Nora figured it was the level of morphine in her system; of course she was sleeping. She answered the door and led Sherry toward the bedroom but paused outside.

"Mom's dying now, isn't she?" Nora asked.

"Might be," Sherry conceded. "It's always hard to tell when it's the end. Could be that this was just an asthma attack."

Mother had never had an asthma attack before. Nora shrugged off the issue and, with a nod, led the way into the bedroom. Her mother was pallid, her wrinkled skin waxy. Sherry checked all the vitals then straightened. "How long was she conscious after you called me?"

"Until a few minutes ago," Nora said. "Why?"

Sherry put the stethoscope around her neck and looked at her patient. "I could be wrong, but this doesn't look like she's napping. I think she's slipped into a coma."

Nora's eyes darted to her mother and then back to Sherry. "Coma? Did I give her too much morphine?"

"No. Morphine doesn't cause comas. If anything, it helped her relax enough to let the coma happen naturally. And . . ." Sherry seemed unwilling to say the rest. "I doubt she'll be coming out of it."

Nora didn't register what she'd said at first. She blinked. "What?"

"I don't think she'll wake up," Sherry repeated.

Nora stared at her mother's weak form on the bed, looking so small and frail. But . . . they hadn't said good-bye yet. She'd imagined the sweet scene between mother and daughter where they expressed tender love and forgiveness, completing all that "unfinished business" you always hear about.

What about all those stories where people wouldn't let themselves die without finding closure? Mother couldn't go without making things right. She couldn't go after their last conversation of delusional accusations.

"*Could* she wake up before the end?" Nora asked, still clinging to the idea that maybe, just maybe, she wouldn't be robbed of her moment.

"It's possible," Sherry said, but her voice made it sound unlikely.

She stayed at the house for another hour but let mother and daughter have some privacy. Nora wasn't sure she *wanted* the time alone, the two of them, not when her mother couldn't hear or understand what was said to her. Even so, she sat by the bed and held her mother's cool, limp hand.

Mother's gray curls were matted on one side of her head, and her face muscles relaxed so her jaw hung loose. *Mom would be horrified to know she looked like that right now.* A tiny smile worked its way onto her lips. *And she'd see her behavior from a few minutes ago as shockingly disgraceful.*

Sad how so much of what her mother experienced and felt was based on appearances. Who cared if her hair wasn't perfect right now? Who cared if she started drooling on herself or if she talked to her daughter as if Nora *were* a floozy?

I bet what I saw a few minutes ago was part of who she really is underneath all the pretense, Nora thought with a sudden realization. Her mother must have seen Flo and those other ladies as threats, women beneath her but who made her feel insecure. Never once in her life had her mother been able to voice those opinions until every mask she wore in public fell in the face of cancer, pain, and medication.

"I wear a lot of masks myself, Mother," Nora said. "You taught me to."

She looked around the room, suddenly hating the carpet, the paint job, the designer furniture. Who cared what a guest bedroom looked like? Who was she trying to impress? She hadn't gotten it decorated like this after Scott left for college because this was the kind of look *she* liked. She'd picked the sage-green color scheme because the lady at the design center said it was fashionable. Other people would think it looked good. But Nora hated it. The colors looked like mold growing and spreading.

Like mother, like daughter, she thought wistfully. How many other masks did she personally wear, and how easy—or hard—would it be to take some of them off?

Who am *I under all of them?* If she had to pick out colors all by herself to create a room to please no one but herself, what would they be? She had no idea. Her first thought would be about other houses she'd seen—maybe ones she'd seen in the latest Parade of Homes tour—and what had looked good in them. Or she'd ask for other people's opinions on what was "right" or fashionable.

How sad. I should drop a few layers and discover who I am underneath.

Nora glanced at her mother, and a small smile curved her lips. *This* was a piece of unfinished business for herself. She might not get to have a real talk with her mother again, but at least she'd gained something from the experience. A final gift.

Chapter 34: Jessie
SOS

Jessie made an appointment for Alex's kindergarten physical and shots and hung up. A few months ago when she took the kids in for flu shots, it took three adults to hold Alex down enough to get the needle in—and she shrieked the entire time as if someone were ripping off her leg. Getting several shots this time around would *not* be fun.

As Jessie jotted the date and time on the calendar, the phone rang again. A glance at the caller ID said it was Marianne. The first thought was that maybe tomorrow's lunch needed to be rescheduled. Or maybe she needed a favor done because she was still dealing with Brian's death.

She turned on the phone and put it to her ear. "Hey, Marianne. What's up? Do you need anything?"

"Um . . . yeah. I could use some of your nursing expertise." Her voice seemed shaky, unsure.

"Is someone hurt?" Jessie had worked the mother-baby clinic with Eleanor for so many years that she felt most comfortable with her skills in that department. Sure, she was trained in first-aid type stuff, but it wasn't her forte.

"Um . . . how much Lortab elixir would be an overdose? Is it bad to take that on top of Phenergan with codeine?"

Jessie's eyes popped open. "Who's taking those?"

"McKayla. I think she took some of Kevin's medication. The Phenergan is from Kevin's surgery, and the Lortab was left over from when he broke his arm last year. She emptied both bottles."

Jessie began pacing. The tension in Marianne's voice went right through the phone line. "Where is she? How does she look?"

"She's on her bed, sleeping. She looks okay, but I can't wake her up. I didn't want to panic and call 911 or anything if it's nothing to worry about."

Closing her eyes, Jessie breathed out slowly to calm herself. A teenage girl downing two bottles of liquid pain medication was *always* something to worry about, even if it didn't kill her. "How big were the bottles?"

"Just normal size—about the size of a cough medicine bottle."

"How's her breathing? Deep or shallow?"

"Normal. Like she's sleeping."

"Good." Sounded like Marianne was right there in the room with McKayla. "How does she feel? Is she warm? Cold? Clammy?" As she spoke, Jessie slipped on her shoes and grabbed her purse. On the way out, she'd call her mom to see if she could drop the kids off with her on the way.

"She's a little cold and clammy." Marianne's voice was breathless. "Should I call 911?"

"Call poison control first." With the phone held between her chin and her shoulder, Jessie shoved shoes onto the girls' feet and prayed that Joey didn't need a diaper change. "Have the medicine bottles with you so you can read off exactly what she took and how much. They'll tell you what to do. Do you have any ipecac? It's okay to induce vomiting with pain meds, and it might be a good idea to use it if you have any."

"I don't think I do," Marianne said. "But I'll check. And I'll call poison control now. Thanks, Jess."

"No problem. I'm on my way. If you end up going to the hospital, call me on my cell, and I'll meet you there." She spoke fast, her heart beating quickly. Ten years from now, this could be Alex. What would it be like to find *her* unresponsive after an apparent suicide attempt?

"Thanks," Marianne said again. The one word was enough. Jessie knew there wasn't much she could do to help, regardless of how good—or bad—McKayla was doing. But being there as a friend and an RN might be a comfort, even if Jessie was used to dealing with newborns instead of sixteen-year-olds overdosed on pain medication.

In a matter of minutes, Jessie had the crew buckled up and heading for her mother's house. Her mother didn't answer. All four of the other wives were on speed dial, so she held down number two to reach Nora. The answering machine clicked on, and as Colonel Lambert's voice droned on about leaving a message, she hung up and tried Brenda, knowing that Kim, who was the only other option, wouldn't be home from work yet. It would take her longer to drive down to Spanish Fork and then backtrack to American Fork, but it was her best option. She gunned the car southward before anyone answered. Brenda told her to bring the kids right over and to keep her updated on the situation.

Twenty minutes later, the kids were happily eating spaghetti and garlic bread at Brenda's kitchen table, and Jessie was back on the freeway, racing north to Marianne's house. No ambulance was out front, and Marianne hadn't called to say they were en route to the hospital. Good signs.

With her minivan parked in front of the house, Jessie hopped out and raced to the front door.

Bailey answered, her face pale and drawn. "Mom's in our room." She pointed upstairs and opened the door more so Jessie could come in. "Is she going to be okay?"

Jessie wanted to bolt inside, but she pulled back. "I think so," she said, wanting it to be the truth. She didn't *think* that McKayla could have downed a lethal dose of either medication. If poison control had been overly concerned, she'd be in the back of an ambulance right now. But that didn't mean she wouldn't be very sick—or that she wouldn't try again.

Nodding, Bailey closed the door behind Jessie and followed her up the stairs. Kevin stood in the hallway outside, forehead crinkled in worry. His eyes darted to the room and back.

"It'll be okay," Jessie said, putting a hand on his shoulder. "Why don't you and your sister go downstairs and watch TV or something?"

He nodded mutely and headed for the stairs. Bailey hesitated for a minute before doing the same. Jessie found Marianne in the girls' room, sitting on the bed and holding McKayla's hand with her left and the phone to her ear with her right. Her face relaxed with relief when she laid eyes on Jessie. She confirmed something on the phone and then hung up. When she put it on the bed, her hand trembled.

Jessie went straight to McKayla. Her eyes were partially closed as if she'd been woken up and she was trying to fall back asleep. Her mouth hung open. Jessie lifted her lids and peered into her eyes. The pupils were tiny. Not uncommon with those kinds of drugs.

"What did poison control say?" Jessie asked as she took the vitals she could without any equipment. She had a bag with a stethoscope, blood pressure cuff, and other items under her bed at home and wished she'd thought to dig it out and bring it.

"I'm supposed to watch her, try to wake her up. Her symptoms aren't serious enough for an ER visit, they said, but they told me what to look for in case she gets worse—and I do need to take her in."

Standing between Marianne and her daughter, Jessie nodded and rotated McKayla's arm so she could take a pulse. She wore a long sweater, so Jessie had to push the sleeves up. Sticking out from her wrist were angry lines of red. Startled, Jessie gripped McKayla's hand and pushed the sleeve higher, up to her elbow. The entire forearm was covered with deep cuts. Some had newly formed scabs; others were healing into a pearly pink. She snatched McKayla's other arm and forced the sleeve up on it. That arm had matching cuts and scratches. They were *not* from the family cat.

McKayla was cutting herself, and by the looks of it, she'd been doing it for a long time. And recently, judging by how many scars there were and the ages of them. Taking a little too much Lortab was the least of McKayla's problems right now. But how to explain that? Feeling Marianne's gaze on her back, Jessie eased the sweater cuffs back down, then pulled the chair out from the desk between the girls' beds and sat on it.

Her teeth worried her lip for a few seconds until Marianne burst out, "Should we take her in?"

Jessie couldn't rip her gaze from McKayla's arms. Did Marianne really not know what McKayla was doing to herself? "Yeah," she said with a nod. "She needs to be admitted to the psych ward."

Marianne's eyebrows drew together. "But why? She gets migraines sometimes. Of course she shouldn't have taken Kevin's prescriptions, but she was probably just trying to find some relief. Migraines can be pretty intense. Wait—do you mean you think she was trying to . . ."

Jessie pinched the bridge of her nose; newborns were so much easier to handle than this. This was definitely an attempted suicide, for starters, but there were other issues as well. She didn't know a lot about cutting, but she knew enough to understand that McKayla almost certainly had issues that her counselor didn't know about or at least hadn't been able to help her with. And that the girl had a long road ahead of her if she would ever get beyond the need to hurt herself like this.

Not having any better way to explain, Jessie stood and took McKayla's arm again. She groaned and tried to pull away, but her weak effort was futile. "Look," Jessie told Marianne. She pushed the sleeve back again and held out the forearm. McKayla grunted in displeasure and tried pulling it back down. Apparently, she was growing more conscious. That was a good sign for now.

"A lot of these are fresh. She could have done it other places, too, like on her stomach or her chest or . . ." She paused and caught her breath, letting McKayla's arm drop. "This makes me think she *was* trying to end her life. People who cut hate themselves for some reason. It's an attempt to override guilt and other emotions. The physical pain drowns out their feelings so they can cope. For some people, it's a way to punish themselves."

Marianne's face drained. A hand went to her lips, and she dropped to McKayla's side again, taking one hand between both of hers and kissing the tips of the fingers. "I didn't realize . . ."

"Let's take her in," Jessie said. "She needs professional help."

Nodding blankly, Marianne looked around, trying to figure out where to start. She found McKayla's sneakers by her closet and fumbled with the laces.

"Let me," Jessie said, taking them and helping to put them on McKayla's feet.

"I tried . . ." Marianne's voice was small.

"I know," Jessie said. "You did everything you could. This isn't your fault."

"I took her to therapy," Marianne said, still talking as if she were bordering on being a zombie. "If Brian were here, maybe he'd have done better."

Jessie whipped around from tying McKayla's shoe. "Now don't you dare go thinking that. You've got to be here for McKayla, and blaming yourself will do her no good. So stop it." She sounded as if she were scolding her own daughter, but it seemed to work.

Marianne nodded wearily. "You're right."

"Let's go." Jessie pulled McKayla to a sitting position and patted her cheeks. "McKayla? Wake up. We have to go."

She groaned and tried to lie down again. "I'm sick."

"I know you are," Jessie said brightly. "Let's go get a doctor to help you feel better."

"I don' wanna doctor," McKayla slurred, head lolling back and forth—probably the best shake she could manage. But at least she was talking and was somewhat responsive.

Jessie put her arm around McKayla's waist and helped her to her feet. "Come on. Let's go."

On the way to the car, Jessie asked if Marianne would prefer that she stay with Bailey and Kevin or come along to the hospital. Marianne looked confused, as if she wasn't sure which she wanted.

"I'd better drive you. Bailey and Kevin are old enough to hold down the fort alone for a few hours."

"I can drive," Marianne protested as she got McKayla buckled in.

"I don't think so," Jessie said, holding the sliding door open. "I'll drive. You sit back here with McKayla."

It didn't take much to convince Marianne. "That's probably best."

After she climbed in, Jessie slid the door shut and let out a breath. She wouldn't be leaving Marianne's side for several hours. If Brian couldn't be here, she deserved to have someone else nearby for support.

As she turned the key, Marianne called from the bench behind her. "Jess?"

"Yeah?" Jessie looked at Marianne in the rearview mirror. She was cradling McKayla in her arms.

"Thank you."

"Anytime."

Chapter 35: Nora
Faces

It was two days since Mother had slipped into a coma; still she held on but grew weaker by the day—sometimes by the hour.

Yesterday Nora had ignored a phone call from Jessie and another from Brenda. But she couldn't help them. Not now. She had been about to tell the wives that she wouldn't be coming to lunch—not providing a reason, of course. She simply couldn't leave her mother's side. She could have gotten Sherry to come, but what if her mother had passed during the hour or so she was gone? Nora wouldn't be able to forgive herself for that. And she'd always wonder if her mother had woken up at the end, if they'd have been able to have some kind of good-bye after all.

Besides, Nora simply could *not* face the wives right now—she'd have to press a blouse, do her hair—*wash* her hair, for that matter—plus spend time on makeup and nails.

So much for dropping masks.

Beyond the physical appearances, Nora wouldn't be able to face them with her regular big smile and confident bearing. They still didn't know that her mother's condition was terminal.

And Nora had to maintain her role as the "mother" of their group.

She sat down to send Marianne an e-mail to excuse herself but first found a message from Jessie saying that Marianne's daughter was in the hospital. It rallied the wives back into "help" mode like they'd been not too long before, when Kevin had gone through his surgery and Brian had been killed. Nora swallowed a bitter taste in her mouth. With Kevin, *she* had been the one planning the schedule for help among the wives.

This must be what Jessie and Brenda were calling about yesterday, she thought, feeling guilty that she'd really dropped the "mother hen" ball. Apparently it had already been passed on to someone else. But even so, she couldn't reply to the message and volunteer to help. Not now.

She left a blank e-mail open, unsure what to say, and went back to her mother's room. This time she'd been gone only a couple of minutes. Nora peered in. Mother was still asleep.

Nora sat down again and took up her vigil. After several minutes, she picked up a novel she'd used to pass the time and read a few chapters. Still no change. Mother slept on. Nora stretched her back, stiff from sitting in Mother's room for so many hours over the last couple of days and nights.

The doorbell rang. Instinctively, Nora put her bookmark into the novel and left it on the nightstand before heading down the hall to answer. On the way she paused by the hall mirror. She leaned in, not happy with the blue bags under her eyes and her flat, disheveled hair. Of course the doorbell had to ring *now*. She didn't have to open the door. She could pretend she hadn't heard the bell or that she wasn't home.

Take off a mask.

She didn't have to keep up appearances for *everyone*. If there was ever a time to *not* look like Mrs. America, this was it, she told herself. She'd been caring for her dying mother around the clock, for crying out loud. Lately she was lucky if she managed to brush her teeth, let alone get out of her pajamas during the day.

But did she really need to start removing the masks *now*?

The thought made her sigh, but it nagged at her.

Fine!

A moment later she opened the door to find a cheerleader in the ward who was going around with one of those infernal high school fund raisers. But Nora ordered a candle anyway, handing over the check with a smile before closing the door. The girl hadn't batted an eye at Nora's appearance. Either she was very kind or utterly unobservant.

Passing the mirror on the way back, Nora averted her eyes, not wanting to see her disheveled reflection again. She covered her mouth in a yawn as she walked. When she reached the bedroom door, she instantly sensed that something had changed. She held her breath and looked around the room, letting her gaze settle everywhere else first—the drapes, the abandoned commode, the nightstand, the prescription bottles. The novel. The bed.

Quietly, Nora took one, two, three steps inside then paused. Her mother's chest didn't move. Another three steps, and Nora reached out a hand, resting it on her mother's chest. No breath.

No heartbeat.

Nora closed her eyes and inhaled. She held her breath and waited, counting the seconds. Still no heartbeat. Finally, Nora's lips released a stuttered breath, and she opened her eyes. Mother even looked different now. Her jaw hung open, her entire body lay limp. Lifeless. A shell of what she'd once been.

Mother was gone. Nora's knees went weak; she dropped to the chair.

"You couldn't even let me see you die, could you?" she whispered, fighting the web of emotions vying for dominance. Her mother had to maintain one more mask right at the end—had to wait until her daughter was out of the room to make her exit. Nora lifted her mother's gnarled hand and held it for several minutes as she tried to sort through the thoughts and emotions swirling through her mind.

Her eyes remained dry; shouldn't she be crying? Instead, her chest felt hollow. Mother's death wasn't the sweet, reverent moment she'd hoped for. Instead, she felt an emptiness with a bit of relief—and guilt for that part.

She should call Sherry to let her know it had happened. A doctor would need to come and pronounce her mother dead. Funeral arrangements would need to be taken care of. She should call the Relief Society president about that. And the bishop.

The wives. I should tell them.

They'd shower Nora with compassion and love; she had no doubt of that. But they would also want to step in and help, as she constantly did for them. But McKayla was in the hospital. The wives were already in crisis mode. They couldn't handle one more thing, not after Brian's death and now McKayla. She'd handle this one on her own.

Nora shook her head and sniffed. "Mother of the group" was a mask she couldn't drop, not *quite* yet.

Chapter 36: Marianne
Uncovering Guilt

Sitting in a chair at the base of McKayla's hospital bed, Marianne stared out the window. The winter sky was gray and flat, the clouds covering everything, making the world feel enrobed in gloom. A hand rested on her daughter's foot, making at least one small contact between them.

As usual, guns and explosions crossed her mind, and with it the usual worry. It was almost a reflexive, instinctual anxiety she'd come to live with since last summer. But on its heels came an unexpected feeling of relief washing over her. Brian wasn't in danger anymore. Never again would she have to obsess over whether he was in the line of fire or about to be ambushed. She knew *exactly* where he was. And while it wasn't where she preferred him to be, her deployment anxiety was, by definition, over. Gone were the days of feeling attached to the computer, hanging on every e-mail or waiting for the phone to ring. No more fear of a ringing doorbell and who might be on the other side. Her worst fears about that had already come true.

It was an ironic cup of comfort in an otherwise bitter circumstance.

Without realizing it at first, she began rubbing her thumb along McKayla's foot through the thin blanket—a foot only half a size smaller than her own. Marianne looked over at it then traced her eyes along McKayla's resting form. She was nearly a woman now.

How did her chubby, giggly baby girl grow up so fast? Yet if something didn't change—and McKayla succeeded in her attempts— she might not have much of a future as a woman. She might not go to college or get married or have children. A shudder went down Marianne's spine, and she looked away, back to the bleak window scene.

"Mom?"

Marianne snapped her head to face her daughter. How long had she been awake? "Did you get a good nap?" she asked, putting on a smile. She hoped it looked real, but her face felt as if it had been through a taffy puller.

"I slept okay," McKayla said, shrugging a shoulder.

"Your lunch should be here soon," Marianne said. Even she could hear in her voice that she was trying too hard to be cheerful, but she didn't know how else to behave. She stood up and went to the head of the bed. "If you're hungry, I can go find a nurse and see how long it'll be—"

"Not hungry." McKayla didn't look at her mother. Instead, she picked nervously at the long, thin scabs on her forearms. Marianne watched with worry. If there was anything her daughter could use to cut herself with in the room, she'd probably find it. She was under close observation, but what if she still managed to hurt herself? Picking at the scabs and making herself bleed again wasn't much better than making new cuts. Or was it? And if she didn't stop, would the doctor decide she needed to be restrained?

Marianne put a hand over McKayla's, stopping the action. "Please. Don't."

"They itch, okay?" McKayla groaned and rolled the other away. She folded her arms defensively. "Freak, Mom. Lay off already."

"Sorry." Marianne pulled her hand away and sat back down.

If Brian were here, he'd know how to get through to her.

She winced at the thought. It was true. Brian could always get his little girl to open up. But if he were home, Marianne and McKayla wouldn't be in the hospital together. Brian would have managed to head off her problems before they ever got to this point.

"I'm sorry your dad isn't here," Marianne said. Might as well tell McKayla how she felt. It might open up a dialogue. "I know you could talk to Dad about anything. I'm . . . I'm not so good at that stuff. But I'm trying."

McKayla caught her breath and made a strangled noise, covering her face with both hands.

"What is it? Are you all right?" Marianne flew to her feet, ready to find a doctor. Was McKayla injured? In pain? But McKayla wasn't hurt, not physically. She was crying. Sobbing.

"It's okay," Marianne said, daring to reach out and brush some of her daughter's hair from her face. "I love you. I'll do anything I can. Tell me how."

"It's *not* okay," McKayla said between sobs. Her breath staccatoed, catching a few times and lapsing into another cry. She shook her head wildly. "It's my fault." Her fingers pulled at her hair. Marianne had to force herself to not say anything.

What was she talking about? *What* was her fault? Marianne tilted her head, trying to follow. She stroked McKayla's arm. "What do you mean?"

"Dad. It's my fault he's dead."

Confusion swirled around the room. How in the world could McKayla even consider herself responsible for a death that happened a world away? Were the medications making her thinking foggy? She wasn't making sense, and Marianne wondered if she should call in a doctor to hear this.

"Why would you blame yourself for that?" she asked tentatively. They had to get to the bottom of this nightmare. This was the most McKayla had been willing to speak to her mother in months; Marianne took advantage of the moment.

No answer came for several seconds. McKayla cried into her pillow, moaning with the pain. Marianne didn't interrupt or press the question but still hoped to get an answer. Somehow this was a clue to the entire mess. She was sure of it.

Finally McKayla turned her head, glanced at her mother, and sniffed. "I . . . I didn't come down to pray for him."

Again, Marianne had to search to figure out her meaning. The family had gathered plenty of times in prayer. McKayla was usually there, but sure, there were a few times she'd refused to come down for their morning or nighttime family prayers. She didn't think *that* had any bearing on Brian's fate, did she?

A lightbulb went on. "You mean last fall?" Marianne asked quietly.

McKayla nodded miserably. Turning toward Marianne, her face crumpled into a look of torment.

It was the time she'd felt that burning urgency to pray, right then, with everyone for Brian. It was the day he'd been inches from death. It was also the first time McKayla hadn't come down for a family prayer. The following week at family home evening, Marianne had told them about what had happened, how their father had been spared. How she believed their prayers that day had helped protect him.

Did she think that one prayer on one day would impact her father's life months later?

"Oh, honey." Marianne pulled her daughter close and held her tight. McKayla burst into another round of tears, and this time Marianne cried too, wetting her daughter's hair.

"Maybe . . . if I'd come down and prayed too . . . maybe he'd have been protected longer. He'd still be alive. Either God answers prayers, or He doesn't. If more people pray, then their faith makes a difference, right? So if fewer people pray, there *has* to be less of a difference. Either God's not real, and our prayers make no difference, or I killed Dad."

Her burden of guilt spilled throughout the room, leaving Marianne stunned and overwhelmed. Before this, she'd spent hour upon hour wondering how McKayla could possibly hate herself enough to begin cutting and even attempting suicide, which she'd admitted to. Her behavior had been unhealthy and risky, and Marianne had assumed that's what McKayla had hated herself for—abandoning the values she'd been raised with.

But McKayla's self-loathing went deeper than that. Marianne had done some reading up about cutting and learned that some people used it to punish themselves for things they believed they had done wrong. As illogical as it was, McKayla must think she might as well have pulled a trigger to kill her own father. If that painfully twisted idea of prayer and faith—or blame—wasn't enough to burden anyone, Marianne didn't know what was.

No wonder she's self-destructive. But what can I do to help her? Never, not even during the deployment, had Marianne felt *this* helpless. She was right next to her daughter and still could do nothing. If only she could take her thoughts, her feelings, her beliefs, and upload them into her daughter's mind and heart. If only there were a way to *make* her see and believe the truth—that God did love her, that He did answer prayers and that she was in no way responsible for her father's death.

"Dad was supposed to die when he did." Marianne found herself saying the words, slowly and distinctly. As they left her mouth, they surprised her. Before today, she'd certainly *felt* that Brian's death was part of a bigger plan, but saying it now, in this way, in this context, was different. "Look at me, Kay," she said, using an old nickname from years past.

McKayla raised her chin, eyes pleading, asking for redemption but clearly not expecting any.

Taking her daughter's face between her hands, Marianne looked her square in the eyes. "You had nothing to do with Dad's death. I didn't feel the same need to pray on the day he died as I felt in October. I don't know why—maybe there was something he was supposed to do in the extra few months he had. We may never know why he was saved once and not the second time. But no matter the reason, it had *nothing* to do with you."

McKayla lowered her gaze and closed her eyes. A new round of tears squeezed out between her lids. She didn't argue or debate or pull away. So Marianne went on. "I love you. Dad loved you. He *still* loves you. And he's looking down on both of us right now from where he's supposed to be. I don't know why he's up there and not down here. But he is." Her fingers wiped at her daughter's wet cheeks.

"So . . . you don't blame me?" McKayla asked.

Marianne shook her head. "Of course I don't. What happened to Dad had nothing to do with you. *Nothing.*"

"Thanks, Mom." McKayla's voice was mouse-quiet; it was hard to tell whether she believed Marianne. Even if she did, she'd still need months of counseling and probably medication as well to get through this murky, confusing place she was in.

Coming together as mother and daughter for this moment was one tiny step in a very long road.

"Do you believe me?" Marianne asked.

Sniffling, more under control now, McKayla shrugged one shoulder. "Maybe."

Marianne half wanted to jump and cheer—or at least record the moment. This might be the only time her teen didn't contradict or say her mother was outright wrong. Instead she leaned a little closer and said, "So hey—no more of this trying to get over to the spirit world to see your dad again, okay?"

"That's not why I did it," McKayla said drearily, looking up through her lashes.

"Oh, I know," Marianne said. This was a touchy topic, and she'd hoped levity might help make her point. She tried again. "The thing is, I can promise that if you show your face in the spirit world *before* you're supposed to be there—as in, anytime in the next few decades— so help him, your dad will be *so* ticked off." She couldn't help but laugh through her tears at that.

McKayla smiled wanly, nodding in agreement. Then her chin tightened into a ball, and her eyes pulled down at the corners with a new round of tears. "Mom, I was so *mad* at him for going away. But I . . . I still should have prayed for him."

"I'm sure he's forgiven you," Marianne said, wiping at her daughter's tears and releasing her face. "And you have to forgive yourself for something you did on impulse on one night of your life. A few minutes of your life shouldn't define you. We all make mistakes."

"No. It's more than that one night," McKayla said with a heavy shake of her head. "I mean, it was *mostly* that night, but I was so mad I stopped praying for him at all, even in my personal prayers. I . . . I stopped saying *any*. I knew I'd feel like I had to pray for him if I said even one. So I didn't. Sometimes when I did come down for family prayer, I didn't really pray with you. I wouldn't do it anywhere—not in seminary or Sunday school, either. Nowhere. It's been . . ." She lifted her eyes to the ceiling, counting. "Three months since I've said a single prayer."

Marianne had the urge to suggest they pray right then as mother and daughter, and she'd even offer to be the mouthpiece. But something held her back. McKayla hadn't shared so much with her in ages. Trying to offer any kind of help might look like she was slapping on a Band-Aid rather than being the listening ear that the doctor said McKayla needed right now. Another thought came to her, so she voiced it.

"I've probably been praying enough for both of us the last four months. And a lot my prayers have been asking for help . . . for you."

McKayla's eyes squinted. "Really?" she asked, clearly not believing.

"Really. Actually, I've been praying for you every day for a lot longer than that. Somewhere around, oh, sixteen years." Marianne smiled. "It's something we moms do. Some days the prayers for our kids are more general, and sometimes—like the last few months, when I've been worried about you—they're more specific. But I've never stopped loving you or praying for you . . ." She pressed her lips together until the crest of emotion waned and she could speak again. "And praying you'd make decisions that would make you happy."

A look of incomprehension still covered McKayla's face. "But . . . I've been a pain in the neck."

One side of Marianne's mouth pulled up. "I haven't been that easy to live with either, I'm betting."

"Well, no," McKayla conceded.

"And I hope you still loved me through my crazy mom stuff."

"Yeah. Of course." McKayla rolled her eyes. "Sure, I was ticked at you half the time. Sometimes I thought I hated you. But deep down, of course I always *loved* you. I mean, duh, you're my mom."

Marianne leaned forward and kissed her daughter on the forehead, something she used to do when McKayla was in grade school. She didn't pull away. Instead, she burrowed closer into her mother's embrace. "You're my treasure, Kay. And you deserve every happiness and success. I want Dad to watch from heaven and *beam* over what you're becoming, what you're doing with your life."

A pause. Then in a timid voice, "Help me?"

"I'll try," Marianne promised. "But will you let the doctors help too? And let in a tiny bit of the churchy stuff as well? That's the only way Dad can help anymore, where he is."

McKayla pulled back and scratched her nose. "I'll try."

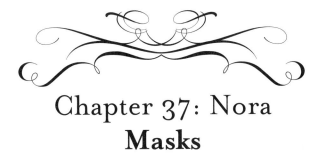

Chapter 37: Nora
Masks

The house had noise again, and lots of it. It wasn't made by small children but by Nora's children, all grown up—four of the five, at least. Steven was unable to return from his mission for his grandmother's funeral, but all the others were there. Dan, the oldest, had come with his wife, Heidi, but they'd left their kids at home in Arizona. Scott was home from USU, and Nora's two daughters had both flown in—on her dime—without their husbands.

Wearing her navy silk dress and the pearls Russell gave her for their twentieth anniversary, Nora bustled about the kitchen, getting dinner for everyone. Tomorrow morning was the funeral. There was no point in holding a formal viewing tonight, because so few people in Utah knew her mother. She'd be buried in Salt Lake next to her husband, who had wanted to be buried in the family's old pioneer plot.

Nora was glad; going up to Washington State for the funeral would have been costly and complicated, and fewer of the kids would have made it. She checked the rolls baking in the oven, set the timer for three more minutes, and turned to cutting up vegetables for a salad. The kids—everyone but her daughter-in-law Heidi, who was at her side helping to prepare the meal—sat around the table, chatting.

The situation felt almost normal; Nora kept expecting to hear grandkids shouting from the basement. Far worse for her heart, she half expected to see Russell coming into the kitchen with his charcoal-gray suit and the paisley tie she loved, wearing his brilliant smile with those dear crow's feet. She closed her eyes to ward back tears.

"Powerful onion," she said in excuse, moving away from where Heidi was chopping a red one for the salad. She hoped her daughter-in-law wouldn't comment on the fact that red onions had almost no fumes.

Missing Russell is what kept her on the verge of tears this week. She was still too numb to really think about what her mother's death meant or to register much emotion about it. She'd been too stressed out, first caring for her mother and then so busy handling everything that led up to the funeral to let it all sink in. When everyone went home and the house was empty again, the sadness—and the reality—would arrive.

Nora wondered if at that point she'd start feeling the deployment more than she had. Focusing on Mother and the other wives had been a good way to *not* focus on how much she missed Russell, how three deployments was too many. Maybe when the hubbub of the funeral was over and silence descended on the house, she'd wish she could still hear Mother's criticisms to keep the ache of missing Russell at bay. Or would the quiet be a blessed relief?

The doorbell rang, and the conversation at the table quieted as everyone looked to the door.

"Who in the world . . ." Nora wiped her hands on a dishcloth, removed her apron, and headed for the entryway, patting her hair as she went to be sure it was in place.

When the door swung open, Nora instinctively tensed, her knees locking and her hand gripping the door handle. But she also put on a bright—if fake—smile. "Well, hello, Nancy! What a pleasant surprise."

Her younger sister gave Nora a look that said she doubted that, and then she stepped into the house.

A little warning would have been nice, Nora thought.

A cloud of expensive perfume entered with Nancy. "Of course I made it," she said airily. Then, waving her fingers at Nora, she added, "That's such a pretty dress you have on."

"Thank you." Surprised, Nora smoothed the skirt. It *was* pretty.

Fingering a large diamond-looking pendant that hung from a silver chain, Nancy walked past and added, "I had a dress a lot like it when that was the style."

Nora stood there, door still open, knob in her hand, stunned. She shouldn't have been. Nancy had always acted this way, but even though they were middle-aged women now, Nora still didn't know if her little sister was genuinely oblivious to how she came across or if she was really trying to be mean.

"I had no idea how bad off Mom was. You really should have let me help care for her," Nancy said, turning around as she took in the living room. Nora winced under the scrutiny. She'd had an interior designer put it together, so she shouldn't have been nervous, but Nancy was too much like their mother; she could find fault in anything. Except herself.

The scene felt as if her mother had come back to life to criticize and belittle again. Nora thought of the masks she'd decided to let come off. But no *way* could she let them down in front of Nancy, Mother's little clone. Later.

Suddenly glad she wore Russell's *real* pearl necklace and earrings, Nora gritted her teeth and closed the door. In spite of what she'd implied, Nancy wouldn't have helped with Mother; they both knew that. Nora had tried to arrange something along those lines, and Nancy had conveniently never returned her calls.

It simply looked right for her to make the offer after the fact. Nancy never had been one to inconvenience herself for anyone. Which might explain her three divorces and completely messed-up only child, Brent. Nora wanted to ask where he was—maybe open the door again and peer out to Nancy's car to see if he was out there—but didn't dare. What if he was coming to the funeral? He might show up high on his latest drug and cause a scene. Or maybe he was in a treatment center—again. Nancy would be embarrassed if that was the case, so Nora didn't ask. Her sister might have no qualms about insulting jabs, but Nora never stooped to that level.

Nancy waved a hand around the room's warm, chocolate-brown walls. "You know, I thought about painting my living room this dark but then decided it would be too dreary."

Doing all she could to ignore her sister—acerbic or simply idiotic, Nora wished she knew—she said, "Come on in," and walked toward the kitchen. "We're about to eat. You're welcome to join us."

As if on cue, the timer for the rolls went off. Nora strode into the kitchen and grabbed the mitts, heading for the oven in a beeline and calling to the table as she passed. "Hey, everyone. Aunt Nancy is here."

Nora removed the rolls from the oven, the heat wafting over her face like a sauna. After removing the tray, she let the oven door slam shut a tad too hard then loaded up a bowl full of rolls. "Salad done?" she asked Heidi.

"Yep. I think we're all ready to eat," Heidi said, taking the bowl of rolls from Nora and carrying it to the table.

Nora squeezed another place setting onto the table. As the conversation settled down, Nora asked Dan to give a blessing on the food. Dinner was a relatively quiet affair, whether from the somber nature of the reason they were gathered or because Aunt Nancy had effectively quashed everyone else's enthusiasm for talking, it was hard to tell. When they finished, Nancy started cleaning up, and Nora had to stop herself from telling her not to help. Of course her sister could—should—help. It was good manners. And it was, well, helpful. But Nora couldn't keep from thinking how Nancy was surely analyzing the kitchen and determining how much better it would be if she refinished the cabinets or arranged the cupboards differently or—heaven forbid—notice that there were crumbs in the silverware drawer.

Russell, if you were here, I'd be able to laugh this off with you tonight. She scrubbed at a pot a bit harder than necessary. *The darned notebook will have to do.*

* * *

That night, the kids went downstairs to watch some DVD that Nora had no interest in. Every so often, someone came up to dish themselves some ice cream or deposit used dessert dishes. She considered going down anyway to avoid having to talk to Nancy, who was now setting up shop in Scott's old room.

No, Mother's room.

Why did having Nancy in there feel so wrong? It was as if that room should remain vacant for a time out of respect. But it hadn't ever really belonged to Mother, Nora reminded herself. And with all the rooms downstairs taken, and Dan and Heidi needing privacy in the only other one upstairs, it was really the only room suitable to put Nancy in.

Nora sat on the couch across from the fireplace, which she'd turned on to take the nip out of the air, and read a book. Every page or so, her eyes drifted to the cupboard holding her venting notebooks, but invariably, each time, she returned her gaze to the page. Writing in them was out of the question while Nancy was still up.

As Nora turned the page—not entirely sure what she was reading, because her mind had a hard time focusing—she heard footsteps in the hall. For a flash, she thought it was Mother coming from her room to ask for something.

Mother is gone, she reminded herself. Then why did the same negative cloud fill the house? Because Nancy was practically Mother incarnate.

Nora looked over as her sister entered the room and sat on the other leg of the L-shaped sectional.

"Oh, I love leather," Nancy said, running her hand along the armrest.

"Me too," Nora said absently without looking up.

"But with the color this pale, isn't it hard to keep clean?"

Nora let the book flop to her lap. She couldn't win. The paint in the other room was too dark; the couch in here was too light. "It's not too bad," Nora said with a wan smile. "With the kids grown up and moved out, it's not like I have a lot of sticky hands around to mess things up anymore."

"Of course," Nancy said with a bob of her head. But she licked her finger and—presumably—tried rubbing some dirt off the couch.

Nora looked away, her tongue pressed to the roof of her mouth to keep herself from screaming. She tried to read, but her eyes tracked the same words over and over without comprehension.

"My goodness. What does it take?" Nancy asked with a tone of exasperation.

"What?" Nora looked up, startled, with no idea what Nancy was talking about.

"Why do you hate me so much?"

Nora lowered the book to her lap, lips parted but with no idea what to say. She floundered, knowing by her voice that Nancy was emotional. Somehow Nora couldn't get herself to feel much sympathy. "Hate you? I don't *hate* you."

"Could have fooled me," Nancy said with a lift of her chin.

"What are you talking about?" Nora asked. "I've never hated you in all my life. If anything, *you've* looked down on *me*. I've tried to be the sister you wanted, but I've never been enough. Not for you, not for Mom. Apparently, I can't even wear a dress that's in style or pick the right couch. I don't know why I bother." She closed the book and slapped it onto the cushion beside her. She stared at the gas flames, horrified that she'd said so much. She could almost sense a mask—a big, thick one—falling off her face and hear it shattering on the floor into pieces like a terra-cotta bowl.

"You don't—you don't think I was *criticizing* you, do you?" Eyes wide, Nancy looked stricken. A hand went to her chest, fingers splayed. "I wouldn't intentionally do something like that."

Nora's level gaze turned to her sister. "Sure you wouldn't."

"I'm so sorry if that's how it came across."

"That's how it *always* comes across."

The sisters stared at one another for several seconds. Nora finally broke the connection and turned away, arms folded. Forget being the peacemaker, the mature one. She didn't care anymore. Let her little sister think she was a miserable excuse for a sibling.

When Nancy spoke, her voice had a quiet tremor in it. "I didn't think my opinion ever mattered to you. I'm just your silly little sister."

Nora raised one eyebrow in disbelief, saying nothing.

"You were the big sister, the one with all the answers," Nancy said. Color rushed into her face, and she leaned forward. "You were the one who graduated with high honors and made Mom and Dad *so proud*. What did I ever do? Sure, I passed all my classes, but I was normal. Average. And I was always proud of having you as my big sister. Can you honestly say you were ever . . . *ever* . . . proud of having me as your little sister?"

The question hung in the air. Nancy lowered her head to her hands and sniffed. Nora felt disoriented, as if the room had spun around. Nancy? Proud of *her*? Since when? Why would she care if Nora was or wasn't proud of her?

"Have you?" Nancy asked again, this time not lifting her face.

The answer that leapt to mind was no, of course not. What did Nancy ever do to make Nora proud of her? Nothing. She'd made a mess of her life since high school with all her marriages—and divorces—and her sad excuse for a son.

But their parents had never seen it that way. Nancy looked the part, Nora figured. And that's what mattered more to Mother than a 4.0 or any honors she could bring home. The first time Nora got a mani-pedi and dyed her hair, her mother practically threw a party.

That was the day Nora put on her first real mask.

She couldn't say any of that to Nancy, not after laying into her already. Mask or no mask, Nora didn't want to be cruel.

And then a moment from when they were young crystallized in Nora's mind. Nancy had found a kitten drenched in mud, shivering and meowing miserably. She carried it home, gently washed it in warm water, and nursed it back to health. She even used a cleaned-out container of Elmer's glue as a milk bottle. The kitten lay in Nancy's arms and drank the milk drop by drop as if Nancy were its mother. She'd been all of nine years old at the time. Nancy had looked up from the bottle and smiled, joy lighting her eyes.

"I'm going to be a vet someday," she announced, looking at the kitten and rubbing the fur between its ears.

"You'll make a great vet," Nora had answered.

Now, more than forty years later, she looked up at her little sister and could honestly say, "Yes, I have been proud of you."

Nancy pulled back an inch, obviously surprised.

"But to be honest," Nora went on, before Nancy responded, "I'm tired of making sure every hair is in place for you and Mom. She's gone now. I'm too old and too worn out to worry about it anymore for your sake. I'm done pretending."

"Pretending?" Nancy seemed lost in the conversation.

Nora looked into Nancy's eyes, which had thin, curved eyebrows framing them. Many a time Nora had wondered if her own eyebrows were plucked enough for Nancy's taste, and for the first time in her life, she allowed herself to think that it was *Nancy's* eyebrows that weren't perfect. They were rather overplucked, in her opinion. But with that realization came a second one. Eyebrows didn't matter. Not anymore.

"Pretending I'm something I'm not. I'm too old for that kind of thing, and I've been doing it most of my life." She stood up and looked over the kitchen on the other side of the room, where the kids' abandoned dessert dishes were still scattered about the counter. "You know what? I'm going to leave those out overnight. *I* don't care if I have to pick them up in the morning, so why should I bother putting them away for someone else's sake?"

Nancy seemed truly perplexed, as if she had no idea how the conversation had gone from the color of the couch to their mother and now to dessert dishes. She turned around in her seat and looked over the table. "But you have the funeral in the morning. Won't it be nicer to wake up to a clean house?"

It was as if she were reciting from their mother's personal creed.

"Not today," Nora said. She planted her hands on her hips as if facing a lion. "Almost every night for over thirty years, I've cleaned up the kitchen until it shined because that's what was expected of me. No more." There were those few days after Russell left when she hadn't cleaned it up, and each time, she'd felt guilty for leaving stuff out even though no one but her ever saw the clutter.

Tonight she'd leave out the mess and *celebrate* it.

"So . . . you won't be cleaning the kitchen anymore?" Nancy still didn't get it.

"Oh, no, I'll clean it," Nora said, enjoying the scandalized look on Nancy's face. "When *I* want to, not when people say I should. Most of the time, I'm sure that will still be at night, and I'll wake up to a sparkling room. But if I decide I want to do it another time instead . . . I will."

Nancy looked at the table, at Nora, and at the kitchen messes again. "This has something to do with us, doesn't it?" She gestured between the two of them.

Nora crossed the distance and sat down beside Nancy. "It means that if you think my paint is too dark, my dress is out of style, my kitchen is too messy, or whatever, that it won't bother me anymore. I'm done worrying about your approval."

"I don't understand," Nancy said, her brow furrowed. "Why on earth would *you* need *my* approval?"

"I don't. But I thought I did." Nora sighed. "Okay. Here's the deal. You criticize me a lot, Nancy. Whether you mean to or not, I don't know, but that's how it sounds—as if I don't project the right image."

"Image always was big with Mom," Nancy said thoughtfully. She picked at a seam in the couch.

"And that's what I'm tired of. I'll still do my hair and clean the house, but if someone finds out that I didn't vacuum on Friday, I won't care. It takes too much effort."

This new mindset would be so freeing; Nora would still take care of herself and her home, but because she *wanted* to, not because of what people might think if she didn't. The end result might be the same, but the motivation behind it made all the difference.

They lapsed into a silence—a comfortable one, for once. Nancy scooted closer, and they held hands. Nora noticed how similar their hands were—they both had long, thin fingers. A lot like their mother's.

She looked up and found Nancy scrutinizing her eyebrows. "Do you wax or pluck?" Nancy suddenly asked. "Because I think my eyebrow girl is taking off too much. You have eyebrows to die for."

Nora burst out laughing so hard she put a hand to her face and tried to hold back tears. Chuckling and trying to catch her breath, she managed, "Pluck."

Another mask was gone, thoroughly crushed. Nora felt lighter but wondered how many more masks hid her true self.

No matter, she thought. *The biggest and heaviest of them is gone now.* It felt good.

Chapter 38: Brenda
Revelation

WEDNESDAY, FEBRUARY 3, 2010

Sitting at a stoplight on University Avenue, Brenda eyed the clock on the dashboard. At this rate, she'd be right on time or maybe a couple minutes early for the weekly wives lunch—although "weekly" was becoming relative. They'd missed a couple of weeks, first because of the funeral and then because of McKayla's hospitalization. The other wives seemed eager to get together and release their stresses.

Brenda wasn't. Maybe it was because the last two weeks had been so stressful on all the wives—although she would have thought that would make her want to go more. Maybe it was the depressing winter weather—the dingy slush made even the snow turn a dismal brown. Whatever the reason, Brenda felt too tired to get herself all dolled up and go to lunch. But she was still going.

Josh and Tyler were at a neighbor's house, thrilled as usual with the chance to play with friends. At breakfast, Bradley had complained of a sore throat. He had no temperature, so she sent him to school anyway. *I can't deal with a sick kid right now,* she thought, hoping against hope that he wouldn't call her cell from school and ask to be checked out.

When the light turned green, she moved forward, only a few blocks away from Brick Oven now, and she wondered if she should call Nora's cell and cancel—give some excuse for not coming and instead head home, where she could take a long bath in peace and quiet, neither of which she got much of with three rambunctious boys running around the place.

She thought back to the infamous pancake mix fiasco, when she had landed at the base of the stairs, au naturel. Now that it was more than a month in the past, she could laugh about it. Sort of.

I could go home and take a bath. It might be my only chance for a while to have a nice soak without getting interrupted, she thought, pulling into the right turn lane that would take her down 800 North toward the restaurant. She could always go past the parking lot and turn right then head back south toward Spanish Fork and that nice, hot bath . . .

But no. She'd come this far. She was hungry, and she loved Brick Oven's lasagna. Plus, she'd spent more than half an hour on her hair and makeup. She'd even worn earrings and a cute pair of boots in an attempt to look pulled together and *normal* for once. Ever since the funeral, Brenda had found that harder to do—to behave and look normal. For the first time since Rick left, she didn't *want* to go to lunch.

Eating out with all the other wives, who seemed so on top of everything all the time, would kill her. Even Marianne, who had more excuse than any of them to be frumpy and falling apart, looked clean and pressed every time Brenda had seen her in the last two weeks. As Brenda had brought in dinners and run errands, she'd seen Marianne a lot.

Meanwhile, Brenda was the one with clothes so nondescript that they could have been from a dozen years ago. Some of them really were that old.

Which was why, as much as she liked Nora, Brenda had always made a point ever since their first lunch of *not* sitting by her and her French-manicured nails and department-store clothing. One of Nora's shoes probably cost more than many of Brenda's entire outfits. She did a mental tally on today's outfit. The jeans from D.I. cost four dollars. Her blouse was a hand-me-down from a friend, so zero dollars there. The earrings were a pair she'd gotten as a gift several years ago. And the boots she loved were all of twenty-one dollars at Target. Twenty-five bucks for her entire outfit. Yep. One of Nora's shoes could easily cost more than that. The contrast between the two of them made Brenda look like a pathetic mouse.

She remembered the one time she'd been inside Nora's house—when Nora forgot her purse at a lunch back in November and

Brenda had dropped it off afterward. It was no surprise to see that the interior decorating was high-end and stunning, and of course the entire place was immaculate. Then again, keeping the carpet free of crushed crackers, action figures, and tiny Lego pieces wasn't hard to do when you had no toddler coming racing through the house in a whirlwind, dirtying everything you cleaned forty seconds ago.

None of her rationalizations made Brenda feel better. She had a sneaking suspicion that Nora had kept a perfect house even when all five of her kids were little. Surely none of them had ever dumped pancake mix over their bathing mother.

What would those homemade pancakes have tasted like all cooked up? Nora's children most likely knew. She probably never served her kids cold cereal, instead making them a nice, hot breakfast every morning—after coiffing her hair and putting on her makeup before they even opened their little eyes. Bet they didn't even know what their mother looked like without makeup.

With a sharp twist of her wrist, Brenda turned into a parking stall and killed the engine, feeling angrier and more resentful toward Nora the more she thought about it. *I'm trying my best, for crying out loud,* she thought, getting out of the car and slamming the door hard then marching to the concrete walkway. She hadn't told any of the wives that she was on antidepressants. If one of *them* admitted to taking medication, she would, but otherwise, she'd keep her lips sealed on that one. No reason to be any *more* of an obvious wreck.

At the door, she paused and took a deep breath, willing herself to calm down and try to be pleasant. *I look nice for once,* she thought in an attempt to reassure herself. *I won't give the others a reason to think I'm completely falling apart.*

The fact that she was this close to losing her mind made it even worse. She wasn't like Marianne—she didn't just lose her husband. None of her kids were suicidal or undergoing surgery or any of the other things Marianne or the others were dealing with.

And *she* couldn't manage three little kids?

She yanked on the handle and went inside, stepping onto the cobblestone floor. After pulling open the second set of doors, she gave a cursory scan of the benches lining the waiting area then, and not seeing any of the wives there yet, headed to the hostess podium. "I need a table for five," she told the girl—probably a BYU student in her freshman year, by the looks of her. She seemed peppy, cute, young . . . carefree.

Someday you'll enter the real world. Instead of popping the girl's balloon of innocence, Brenda smiled. "The name is Penelope."

It was the name they always gave for the party. It was Jessie's idea—Penelope was the faithful waiting wife of Odysseus, who left her alone for years to fight in the Trojan War. Not the typical deployment situation, but it worked, and it was easy to remember.

The girl didn't even have to glance at her list. "Oh, I've already got you down. Looks like two of you are here. As soon as one or two more arrive, I can seat you."

"Thanks," Brenda said, brow furrowing. Maybe whoever else had arrived first had gone to the restroom. She turned around and paid more attention to the half dozen people on the benches. When she reached the one by the vintage barber chair, she almost choked on a gasp.

Nora sat there wearing . . . *what in the world?* . . . an old pair of gray sweats with a hole in one knee. A pair of beat-up, dingy sneakers adorned her feet. Her ears, neck, and wrists were bare of jewelry, making her face look odd, since it usually had something flashy flanking it. Nora raised her eyes to Brenda's, eyes that were hardly recognizable without their usual dark eye shadow, liner, and mascara. They looked . . . blank.

Nora's pale lips curved into what could barely be called a smile. "Hi," she said with a little wave.

Stunned, Brenda just stood there, not sure what to say or how to react. If *she* were to come looking like that, she wouldn't want anyone to prod into why she looked like she'd had a collision with a truck. Then again, sometimes she *had* come to lunch looking only a notch or two more put together than this.

But *Nora*? This was such a drastic change from the norm that *not* mentioning it would be like ignoring a second nose on her face.

"I . . . thought I was the first one here," Brenda said, crossing to the bench and sitting by her. Nora nodded but didn't say anything. Brenda tried again. "Are you feeling all right? You look a little . . . pale."

At that, Nora chuckled silently. "I suppose I am pale without makeup." She ran her fingers through her hair and sighed. "I didn't have the energy to pretend today."

Pretend? Brenda, glancing at her new pink suede boots, knew exactly what Nora meant. She'd put them on to pretend all was well. That was also the reason she wore some perfume and a thin coat of pink lipstick. It was all an effort to camouflage her crumbling interior.

Nora pretended sometimes too?

"It was either stay home and look like this . . ." Nora held out her arms. "Or see you girls . . . and look like this." She shrugged. "I opted to see you all and enjoy some conversation and good food. I hope you guys won't care that I'm a bit rumpled."

This is a little more than a wrinkled shirt, Brenda thought, torn between satisfaction at seeing an icon look human—imperfect—after all, and worry at what had caused the sudden transformation. "Are you really . . . all right?"

Nora didn't answer right away, instead staring at the smooth stones in the floor. Her eyes welled up, and she wiped at one of them then looked at the tear resting in a big drop on her finger. "I'm all right. Sort of," she said at last, wiping the moisture on her sweats. She looked over and smiled weakly. "Remember how my mother came to live with me for a while?"

"Yes," Brenda said. "From Seattle, right?"

"Right," Nora said with a nod, eying the stones. "What I didn't tell you girls is *why* she came." She raised her eyes to Brenda's. "It was to spend her last days with me. She died last week. That's why I missed lunch."

"Oh, Nora, I'm so sorry," Brenda said, pulling her friend into a hug. The two of them had rarely touched like this before, but it felt natural. For once Brenda didn't have any awkward feeling of inferiority beside this woman, who was so much more mature, elegant, knowledgeable, and sophisticated . . . they were merely two women mourning together.

A minute later, they pulled apart, both wiping at their eyes. "When is the funeral?" Brenda asked.

"Last Saturday," Nora said sheepishly.

"But . . . why didn't you tell us?" Brenda asked. "I'm sure everyone would have wanted to come. That's what's we're here for. You've done so much for all four of us, and—"

"That's just it," Nora interrupted quietly, raising her hand.

"What?" Brenda asked, confused.

With a shrug, Nora said, "I'm the mom of the group. I didn't want to turn the tables and admit that I needed a little help too. Once my kids left, and it was me at home, alone, staring at the wall, well . . . let's say I've looked like this since Sunday morning. I couldn't even pull myself together enough to go to church."

"I'm not sure I understand," Brenda said. "Why . . . ?" She glanced at the dingy sweatshirt. They both knew what she meant— why would Nora not do herself up as usual?

Nora frowned at the floor. "I'm not perfect, Brenda. I feel like I've been living a charade. The truth is, I'm not handling this deployment all that well. Having Mom around sort of put the deployment on the back burner. It let me focus on something else for a while. But now . . . well, my house is a disaster. You should see the kitchen."

With a laugh, Brenda said, "I'd pay money to."

Nora chuckled. Then she seemed to stare off into the distance with sad eyes. "For the first time in probably ten years, I didn't get my visiting teaching done this month. On Sunday, last minute, I got a substitute to teach my Relief Society lesson because after the funeral, I couldn't get out of bed. My nails need a fill like you wouldn't believe, but . . . I don't care." She shook her head and paused in her effusion then looked hard at Brenda. "You know what? At first I was horrified at everything I've let slide. But after Mom died and a few things that have happened since, it seems *okay* to not measure up. I don't really care if I don't get all those things done right away." She closed her eyes as if someone had pulled a heavy weight off her shoulders. "And it feels *wonderful.*"

Brenda put a hand over Nora's and laughed. "You have no idea how good it feels to hear you say all that. I've spent several sleepless nights wondering why I couldn't be like you." She gave Nora a sly look. "So tell me. When your boys were little, did they make messes? Please say yes."

"Oh, they did—most certainly," Nora said, her eyes lighting up suddenly. "Like the time Dan spilled an entire bag of powdered sugar all over the kitchen floor. No matter how much you try to clean that stuff up with a broom or a vacuum, it's so fine that some residue will stay behind, and when it gets wet . . . you're walking on icing."

"Much like water and pancake mix," Brenda said ruefully. "Yours, in fact. Josh dumped a bunch on the carpet. But the first half he dumped into my bath. And onto me."

"Oh, he didn't!" Nora said, laughing, a clear, pretty sound, with no restraint.

"Oh, he did. Ask Kim when she gets here. She saw the result."

After chuckling, Nora said, "You know, I regret always wearing that mask, having put on a show for everyone all my life. I've spent decades doing it." She sighed. "I'm sorry that it made you feel like you weren't enough. The truth was, I did all that because I never felt like *I* was enough. Watching my mother die helped me realize how insecure I still was—and how useless it is to put on a show for other people's benefit. If I'm going to be happy, it has to be because *I* like me, not because someone else does."

Brenda sensed that there was much more to the story, but she didn't press. Instead, the two women sat in quiet companionship until the other wives arrived. Each of them gave Nora a double-take as Brenda had, only now Nora didn't seem so distant and was able to tell them of her mother's death and that in spite of her appearance, she was doing quite well.

"It was easier for me to be my plain-old-real self today," she told them, pushing a stray lock of hair—a stray lock!—behind her ear. "I hope you like me anyway."

We adore you, Brenda thought as the hostess approached and led them to their booth. Brenda followed close behind Nora. This time she slipped into the corner booth beside her, the woman who had served all of them over the last several months. She'd done babysitting, cooking, and errands. She'd been a listening ear for e-mails and phone calls. How she did all that with a dying mother to care for, Brenda would never know. Her constant selfless acts had made Brenda feel so inadequate.

But now . . .

Nora had arrived in beat-up sweats and no makeup. It was the most amazing gift she could have given Brenda.

As they placed their orders, Brenda couldn't keep a smile off her face. Having the new Nora beside her gave her a strange comfort. The only thing that could have made it better would have been to see the state of Nora's kitchen.

Chapter 39: Kim
Go Time

Kim had been having intense lower back pain on and off all morning at work. Every chance she got, she massaged the ache. By lunch—after assisting with a root canal, two crowns, and five fillings—she noticed that the entire front of her belly was tensing up. More Braxton Hicks, she figured. She hated those pre-labor contractions. "Fake" contractions, as she thought of them. When the first few came, she freaked out, thinking she was in preterm labor. Now she got them several times a day and had learned that they were pretty normal for the third trimester.

"Have a good lunch," Dr. Oaks said to her after their last patient of the morning left. He stood and snapped his gloves off then paused as if really seeing her for the first time this morning—which he might have been. An assistant didn't generally make a lot of eye contact with the dentist as she handed over tools and offered suction. "Are you all right?" he asked, pulling his face mask below his chin. "You look tired."

"Oh, I'm fine," Kim said with what she hoped was a pleasant smile. "I *am* a little tired, but they say that's to be expected at thirty-five weeks." She patted her belly and headed for the break room for her purse. On her way out, she paused at the glass doors, waiting for another wave of back pain to subside.

At least I get to sit most of the day, she thought, remembering some of her previous restaurant jobs that had her on her feet ten hours at a time. When the ache subsided, she headed for her car, thinking that it might be a good idea to take a little Tylenol and run home for her heating pad. That usually worked to relax back cramps when she had her period.

I haven't used the heating pad in eight months, she thought, wondering if she even knew where it was anymore. It was probably on the shelf in the bedroom closet.

As she pushed the UNLOCK button on her key fob, she felt a whoosh of moist warmth between her legs. Confused—and not a little embarrassed—she wondered if she had somehow lost control of her bladder. But as she stared at the puddle in the asphalt, the reality of what had happened struck her.

My water broke. These aren't cramps—they're contractions.

She clenched the keys in her fist. A rush of panic—and the beginning of another contraction—went through her. She leaned one hand against the car window, the other gripping her stomach.

The pain was suddenly much worse than it had been even a few minutes ago; having her water break must have intensified it. Her breath came in short spurts. The pain lessened and then disappeared, and she inhaled sharply then began pacing between her Corolla and the truck two spots over.

I'm in labor. I'm in labor. I'm in labor. The thought kept thrumming in her mind.

I don't dare drive to the hospital. What if the pain's so bad I crash? And I need to pack a bag. Man, I thought I still had weeks to do this! First babies aren't supposed to come early. Think—think.

A list of what-ifs ran through her mind, and she tried to stop them, much like how she'd deliberately pushed out thoughts of what would happen when it was time for the baby to be born. Unlike many women, even though she was uncomfortable being so large, she had no desire to get the baby out.

Not yet. Not alone.

When thinking about the baby, she had always jumped ahead to the *after* part, when she was holding it, caring for it. *I don't want to face the labor and delivery part,* she thought, a terrible fear gripping her chest.

Like Marianne said, women through the centuries have gone through this, she reminded herself. All the other wives in the group had done it—several times each.

There was just one she wanted to talk to right now—Jessie.

Hands shaking, she unlocked the car and opened the door to her red Corolla. She grabbed a blanket from the back and put it on the driver's seat so it wouldn't get too wet from her soaked scrubs then sat down and locked the door. She fumbled for her cell phone, dropping it onto the floor. She had to reach down awkwardly around her belly to get it securely in hand before she dialed.

Jessie answered after two rings. "Hey, Kim," she said cheerfully. "What's up?"

"Um . . ." How should she say this? *Plain and straightforward,* Kim decided, *even if I sound like a baby myself.*

"My water broke, and I think I'm in labor. Can you . . . can you come help me?"

"Of course I can help," Jessie said. "Where are you?"

"I'm at work, in the parking lot—sort of behind the Super Target in Orem," Kim said. "I don't dare drive myself, and the contractions are getting harder, and . . ." Her resolve crumbled, and tears welled up. She covered her eyes with a hand. "Oh, Jessie, I'm so scared."

"It'll be all right, Kim," Jessie said, her voice a combination of soothing and practical. "How far apart are the contractions?"

Timing them hadn't occurred to Kim, since the fact that they *were* contractions hadn't occurred to her until a moment ago. She made her best guess. "Less than ten minutes, I think. I'm not sure."

"Okay, good," Jessie said, her voice nurse-professional and clipped. "Then you're not too close. No fears of a freeway baby. I'm on my way." Keys jingled in the background, and Jessie muttered, "Where are my shoes?" under her breath.

Tears streamed down Kim's face. She gave Jessie directions to the dental office then added, "Please hurry."

"Everything will be fine," Jessie said, her voice softer now. "Just hold on. You're strong. I'll be right there. Wait for me in your car."

"I will," Jessie promised.

"Thanks." She hung up and leaned back in the seat. If only she knew what was going to happen, what to expect. The unknown loomed like a shadowy, scary giant hiding around a corner. She hated needles and cringed at the thought of having an IV. Or worse, a C-section. What if Eleanor was wrong? What if she still had placenta previa? The last ultrasound was months ago. Could the placenta have moved back down? Then she'd *definitely* end up with a C-section—or lose the baby. For the first time, that thought was horrifying. And the fact that it was horrifying was comforting. She cared about her baby.

But what if Jessie didn't come in time and she had to deliver the baby herself? What if the baby died? What if the pain would be more than Kim could bear?

Women die *in childbirth,* she thought. *My own grandmother died giving birth to my aunt.* The advances in medical technology of the last fifty years didn't calm her irrational thoughts. Instead, she felt as if she were a wire being pulled taut and ready to break.

And alone. She felt so alone. Her mother had plans to drive up from Cedar City in a few weeks to help her out, but no one thought she'd be needed this early. Even if Kim called right now, her mom couldn't arrive for several hours. The baby might be here by then. And when it came down to it, Kim didn't really want her mother with her in the delivery room. Having her around for two weeks to help after the birth would be strain enough on their already rocky relationship.

But Jessie. Jessie would be here soon. Jessie, who had helped her get through the bleeding scare all those months ago. If she came, everything would work out. Kim closed her eyes and waited, trying to relax between contractions and pressing her head against the headrest during them, tears coursing down her cheeks. Each time she felt her stomach begin to tighten with another one, she'd glance at the clock. Six minutes apart now. Much closer together than before. And much more intense. Shockingly so. She had no idea her body was capable of this kind of power.

By the time Jessie arrived and tapped the driver-side window with her knuckle, Kim had rivulets of sweat trickling down the sides of her face. Hope and relief leapt into Kim's entire being as she opened the door.

"You okay?" Jessie asked, taking her by the shoulder and looking her over.

"I'm not sure," Kim said honestly.

"Let's get you to the hospital," Jessie said, helping her climb out of the car. Jessie leaned in and grabbed Kim's purse. "I'll call Eleanor so she knows we're coming, and she can meet us there." Together they walked to Jessie's minivan. Halfway there, Kim had to stop walking until another contraction ebbed. Jessie put down a plastic garbage sack and a blanket onto the passenger seat, both of which she pulled out from the back of the van. Seeing them was a relief to Kim. She didn't want the guilt of staining her friend's car.

A few minutes later they entered I-15, and the car ramped up speed, settling at seventy-five.

Kim managed a smile. "I don't think I've ever seen you go a mile over the speed limit."

Jessie laughed and shrugged. "There are times when even I will break the law." She raised her eyebrows. "But this better not get me a ticket."

"Heaven forbid," Kim said, laughing. "I'd hate to carry the burden of ruining your perfect record." Another contraction came on then, and she clamped her mouth and eyes shut as the pain engulfed her.

"That was only five minutes," Jessie said, her eyes flitting to the digital clock readout. She pressed the accelerator further.

"Thank you," Kim managed quietly.

Chapter 40: Jessie
Delivery

MONDAY, FEBRUARY 8, 2010, 4:40 PM

By the time Jessie pulled into a parking space at the hospital, Kim was pale with pain. Jessie held Kim's hand as she stepped out of the car. She helped her into the building, where she found Kim a wheelchair. Kim sat down, and Jessie wheeled her into the elevator.

"I'd better not deliver in here," Kim said dryly as Jessie turned her around to face the closing doors.

Jessie punched a button. "No worries—I don't think you're *quite* that close." A moment later the bell dinged, and the doors opened to the labor and delivery floor.

The next several minutes passed in a blur—nurses getting Kim settled on a bed, strapping monitors to her belly, checking her dilation, putting an identification bracelet on her wrist. Every step of the way, Jessie took care of Kim as only a nurse and friend could. She explained what each piece of equipment was for, stroked her hair and held her hand during contractions, got her ice chips, told her what to expect next. After an hour, Kim was begging for an epidural.

As they waited for the anesthesiologist to arrive, Kim gripped Jessie's hand between both of hers and cried.

"Come on, Kim. Breathe through the pain," Jessie said, sitting on a chair to be eye level. She spoke in soothing tones. "Count with me."

But Kim shook her head. "It's not a contraction this time."

Jessie looked at the paper readout from the monitor. Sure enough, Kim was probably another two minutes away from the next one.

Confused, Jessie stood and looked around. "Do you need another blanket?"

Squeezing her eyes closed, Kim said, "I need Justin."

What could she say to that? "I know," Jessie said softly, lowering to the chair again. She squeezed Kim's hand tight. "I'm sorry."

They sat there in silence, Jessie watching Kim cry. Tears sprang to Jessie's eyes, and she turned away. Images of her own deliveries flashed through her mind—Tim holding *her* hand, whispering encouraging words, getting her ice chips, racing out the door to hurry up the anesthesiologist, rubbing her feet to help her relax, calling her beautiful and strong, although she probably looked like something out of a Stephen King novel.

With her last baby, an epidural hadn't worked; Jessie had scar tissue that had grown over the nerves in her back from a sports injury. When the pain got to be too much, she held Tim's hand in both of hers like Kim did now, and she sobbed to him, "I can't do this. I can't."

Tim had leaned close so their faces nearly touched and she could smell him—not the scent of his cologne, which had worn off since that morning, but the manly smell that was Tim himself.

"I can't do this," Jessie had cried.

"Yes, you can. Look at me," Tim had said, holding her hand and making her look directly into his eyes. She gazed into them—the warm, strong eyes that used to melt her knees. In the delivery room, they gave her strength. Tim kissed her forehead then pulled back. "You can do this. You're amazing. And I'm right here. I'm not going anywhere."

She had clung to him during the next hour, using Tim's strength as her own to get through the difficult labor. He held her hand, whispered words of encouragement, counted with her through the contractions, and coached her breathing.

I'd give a lot to smell Tim again, she thought, her eyes suddenly aching as she simultaneously missed Tim and felt guilty for *not* missing him much over the last several months.

No, Tim wasn't even close to the perfect husband or father. But when it really mattered, he'd been there for her. In spades.

I'm hardly the perfect wife, she thought. She had a tendency to mope and put him on guilt trips. And the more she thought about it, the more she realized that her way of asking him to do things probably sounded like nagging.

But when it really mattered, there wasn't a single person in the world she would have wanted with her at the births of her children, holding her hand, more than she wanted Tim. There's no one else she'd want to create children with besides Tim.

Voice choked up, Jessie said, "I wish Justin were here for you instead of me." An overwhelming love for her own husband filled her heart, something that had been missing for much too long—a feeling she was ashamed to have abandoned in favor of anger, frustration, resentment. "Do you want me to call anyone else to come? What's your mom's number?" Jessie pulled out her cell phone, ready to punch it in.

Kim let out a long breath after another contraction waned then shook her head and said, "No. Not my mom. The other wives. If I can't have Justin, I want my closest friends."

"You got it," Jessie said, smiling through her own tears. She flipped open her phone and began dialing.

Chapter 41: Kim
Bonded

Nora was the last to arrive. She poked her head into the delivery room and looked about, her mouth widening into a big smile when her eyes landed on Kim. She was between contractions and able to smile a weak welcome and lift a hand in an attempt at a wave.

We're all here, Kim thought. *Now the baby can come.*

"Am I too late?" Nora asked, stepping inside the room.

"You just made it," Brenda said, looking over from the opposite side of the bed. She held one of Kim's hands while Jessie watched the monitors. Marianne stood beside Brenda with a cup of ice chips.

"She's complete," Jessie said. "They wanted her to push, but we said she had to wait a few more minutes."

"For you guys to arrive," Kim said, breathless. Her hairline was damp; labor had tired her out. At least she'd received an epidural now, so she wasn't in pain.

"I told her I'd give her five minutes, and she's down to one." Eleanor snapped her gloves onto her hands as she entered. She pulled a stool over and motioned for some nurses to break down the bottom half of the bed. "Let's get that baby here."

Kim's stomach swirled like some crazy amusement park ride. She gripped Brenda's hand tighter and found Jessie's hand on the other side. She braced herself as if getting ready for a shuttle liftoff. "Here we go."

For almost an hour of pushing, Eleanor coached and persuaded Kim, and the four wives around her boosted her with positive words and encouragement. She'd never felt more loved, more powerful as each contraction came on and she pushed with all her might. Each time the tension in her belly began to wane, she fell against the pillow and breathed heavily, eyes closed, saving what little reserves she had left.

"One more push, and I think we'll be there," Eleanor said. "Push as hard as you can with this next one."

Kim was half tempted to kick her; she'd been pushing as hard as she could every time—what did the woman *think* she was doing? But before she could get too annoyed, Marianne cried out.

"It's . . . I can see the head! It's crowning!"

An intense increase of pressure made Kim's eyes open wide, but she kept pushing. A moment later, it was all over. Eleanor held a squirming mass of arms and legs in her hands, and a deliciously loud wail erupted throughout the room.

"It's a boy," Eleanor said, grinning. "And he looks great."

Before Kim got a good look at him, the cord was cut, and a Nursery team whisked the baby to the other side of the room, where, she assumed, they were making sure he could breathe and was otherwise okay. She could barely make out the sharp little kicks of his legs next to some medical personnel, his little feet now visible, now gone, now visible again. His skin was dark pink, and he wailed in complaint—a good sign that he had pretty mature lungs in spite of his young age, she figured.

She blinked, breaking her gaze, and looked from one of her dear friends to the other. "I'm . . . I'm a mom." The words sounded bizarre and foreign coming out of her mouth. That little person on the other side of the room belonged to *her*. He was her *son*.

Suddenly she wanted him back. She shifted uneasily on the bed, trying to get a better look. "What are they doing? When can I hold him?"

Jessie stroked her arm and chuckled. "Mother bear's coming out. Better hurry over there. She's liable to jump off this bed and snatch him back."

"Ha, ha," Kim said, still watching the workers, itching to hold her baby, to make sure he was okay, to stroke his sweet head and see if he had Justin's eyes.

She turned to Jessie and replayed the words she'd said. *Holy cow, I am becoming a mother bear.* She grinned. *I'm a mom. I'm a mom.* The phrase felt good.

A little scary, but fitting. Right.

I can't wait to tell Justin.

A minute later, Eleanor was the one to bring the baby back, now wrapped in a blanket, the blood wiped off. "He'll get his first real bath in the nursery, but I think it's time he meets his mama," she said, handing over the tiny bundle.

Kim gulped, suddenly afraid of breaking her baby. "He has his daddy's nose," she said, stroking it with the back of a finger. He had wide eyes that looked around curiously, as if trying to take in this strange new world he'd been thrust into.

"Have you picked out a name?" Nora asked quietly, bringing a reverence to the moment.

"Yeah," Kim said, gazing into the perfect features of her little boy. She put her pinkie near his hand, and his fingers gripped on tight. "Justin and I thought we'd like to name him Brian." She looked at Marianne. "If that's all right with you."

The tip of Marianne's tongue pressed between her lips for a moment, trying to keep emotion from spilling out. She closed her eyes for a second then opened them, smiled, and said, "That would be an honor. Thank you."

"In that case, hey, little Brian," Kim cooed. "Welcome to the world."

Nora took Marianne's hand. Each of them took the hand of either Brenda or Jessie. As if on cue, they rested their hands on Kim's shoulder. They created a circle of sisterhood and support.

Holding her sweet little baby, Kim felt a wave of love sweep through her as she looked around the circle of women who had stood at her side, women who had lifted one another for the last six months.

At twenty-nine, Brenda was the wife closest in age to Kim but was still eight and a half years older. Nora, who was more than thirty years older than Kim, was a grandmother several times over.

But none of that mattered. When she'd been faced with the scariest moment of her life a few hours ago, Kim had turned to the friends she'd made in weekly visits around restaurant tables. She hadn't given a moment's thought to calling her best friends from high school, Hailey or Laura. At the birth of her baby, she'd wanted these four women who knew her, understood her, and loved her anyway.

"You know, I almost didn't go inside Chili's in August," she said suddenly. "I went in for Justin's sake." She shuddered to think what the ramifications of that decision would have been had she driven away.

"I'm glad you came," Jessie said.

"I'm glad we all did," Brenda added.

Nora nodded. "I can't believe how much has happened. But we're only halfway through."

She was right. Who knew what challenges still lay ahead between then and August? The year after would have its own share of difficulties as the wives and their soldiers adjusted and adapted and got to know one another again.

And yet.

Kim didn't worry so much now. Deployment still stunk. But these four women made it bearable. They'd always be close to her. Their husbands were certainly as close as brothers.

She smiled to herself. "You know what we are?"

"Besides sleep-deprived, stressed, and overweight?" Brenda asked with a laugh.

Kim caught the eyes of each wife in turn. Each one had taught her something. Each had learned from someone else. Each had been lifted by another.

"We're a band of sisters."

"A band of sisters," Nora repeated.

"I like the sound of that," Jessie said quietly.

Marianne nodded, her eyes tearing up. "Yeah," was all she said, and they all knew what she meant.

Holding little Brian in the crook of her left arm, Kim put her right hand forward. The four other women did the same, piling their hands one atop the other like a team.

In a chorus, they cheered together.

"Hooah!"

About the Author

Photo by Heather Adams

Annette Lyon, Utah's 2007 Best of State medalist for fiction, has been writing for most of her life. While she's found success in freelance magazine work and editing, her true passion is fiction. In 1995, she graduated cum laude from BYU with a BA in English. Her university focus on 19th-century literature proved beneficial years later while writing historical temple novels. Her fifth novel, *Spires of Stone,* was a 2007 Whitney Award finalist.

When she's not writing, Annette enjoys spending time with her husband and their four children. She also loves reading, knitting, and chocolate—not necessarily in that order.

Readers may contact her via her website, www.annettelyon.com.

Author's Note

Researching and writing *Band of Sisters* was a powerful experience, one that left me with a greater respect and gratitude to the men and women who serve in the military—and to their families who stay behind. Many people want to help a family going through a deployment but don't know what they can do that would make a difference.

You can make a difference. Here's how:

The Flat Daddies program creates life-size, adhesive photographs of deployed parents from the waist up, which a family can attach to cardboard or foam core and then, if they wish, cut into a silhouette.

Families benefit from Flat Daddies (or Flat Mommies) by having a physical presence and image of the deployed parent in the home, which especially benefits small children, who might even forget what Dad or Mom looks like without it.

Many families dress up their Flat Daddy and take "him" trick-or-treating for Halloween and bring him along for daily activities, like soccer games, or play with him—a little girl might include her Flat Daddy in her tea party. They kiss him good night. A child can bring Flat Daddy to kindergarten graduation and take pictures to send to Iraq or Afghanistan so their real dad can see what is happening in their lives and that in a sense, he was a part of the event.

In many small but powerful ways, Flat Daddies help ease the pain of having a parent absent.

You can benefit a family through the Flat Daddies program in these three ways:

(1) Donate a monetary amount of your choice to be used toward the creation of new Flat Daddies.

(2) Buy a Flat Daddy for a military family you know personally. (You'll need to enter their e-mail address. A code will be sent to that address so they can claim their Flat Daddy.)

(3) Buy a Flat Daddy for a deserving family who wants one, even if you don't know them. When a family receives a Flat Daddy from you, they are encouraged to send a thank-you note via e-mail so you know your gift was warmly received and is making a real difference.

For more information or to donate, visit the Flat Daddies page on my website: annettelyon.com/flatdaddies.